P9-DMO-303

SUZANNE BROCKMANN
JILL SORENSON

PASSION
AND PERIL

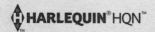
HARLEQUIN® HQN™

ISBN-13: 978-0-373-77820-1

PASSION AND PERIL

Recycling programs for this product may not exist in your area.

Printed in U.S.A.

www.Harlequin.com

· CONTENTS

SCENES OF PASSION

For Melanie and Jason.

CHAPTER ONE

Traffic on Route 95 was in a snarl again.

Maggie Stanton sat in her car, too tired even to flip through radio stations to find a song that annoyed her less than the one that was playing. She was too tired to do much of anything besides breathe.

Or maybe tired wasn't the right word. Maybe discouraged was more accurate. Or downtrodden.

No, downtrodden implied a certain resistance to being trod upon.

Maggie was just plain pathetic. She was a doormat. A wimp without a life of her own.

She was twenty-nine years old and she was living at home. Yes, she'd moved back in with her parents because of the fire in her apartment.

But that was three years ago.

First her mother had asked her to stay to help with Vanessa's wedding.

When 9/11 happened, her father had asked her to keep living at home a little longer, and somehow another year had passed.

Then right after Maggie had found a terrific new place in the city, her grandmother had died, and she couldn't leave while her mother was feeling so blue.

It was now way past time to leave—a quarter past ridiculous—and her mother was making noise about how silly it would be for Maggie to get a place of her own when she was on the verge of getting married.

Uh, Mom? Don't get the invitations engraved just yet. The bride kind of needs to be in love with the groom before that happens, doesn't she?

Although, like most of the major decisions in Maggie's life, it was possible that this one would be made by her parents, too. And she would just stand there, the way she always did, and nod and smile.

God, she was such a loser.

Maggie's cell phone rang, saving her from the additional tedium of self-loathing. "Hello?"

"Hey, pumpkin."

Someone kill her now. She was dating a man who called her *pumpkin.* No, she wasn't just dating him; she was—as her mother called it—preengaged.

Yes, Brock "Hey, Pumpkin" Donovan had actually asked her to marry him. Maggie had managed to stall for the past few weeks—which turned out to be an enormous mistake. She should have said no immediately, right before she ran screaming from the room. Instead, because she was a wimp and rarely screamed about anything, she'd put it off. Her wimp thinking was that she'd find the right time and place to let him down without hurting his feelings. Instead, he'd gone and told Maggie's older sister Vanessa, who was married to Brock's former college roommate, that he'd popped the question. And Van had told their parents, and…

Segue to Mom buying *Bride* magazine and starting negotiations with the Hammonassett Inn.

Maggie's parents had been so excited, they'd wanted to throw a preengagement party, for crying out loud. Fortunately, the only date Mom had had available was this Saturday—the day that Eastfield Community Theater was holding auditions for their summer show.

And they knew not to schedule something on *that* day.

Maggie's involvement in theater was the only thing she had ever put her foot down about. Her parents had wanted her to go to Yale, so she'd gone to Yale instead of Emerson's performing-arts school. Yale had a terrific drama department, but her parents had made so much noise about starving artists needing a career to fall back on, she'd majored instead in business. After college, the noise had continued, so she'd gone to law school instead of moving to New York City and auditioning for a part on a soap opera. Her father had wanted her to work for his lawyer buddies at Andersen and Brenden here in New Haven, and here she was.

Stuck in traffic after putting in a twenty-seven-hour day at A&B. Preengaged, heaven help her, to a man who called her pumpkin.

Living her life vicariously through the roles she played onstage at ECT.

Because God forbid she ever say no and disappoint anyone.

Wimp.

"I'm still at work," Brock told her now, over the phone. "It's crazy here. I'm going to have to cancel, sweetheart. You don't mind, do you?"

Maggie had actually taken her gym bag with her to work despite the fact that she and Brock were supposed to have dinner. More often than not, Brock canceled or arrived at the restaurant very late.

Of course, tonight was the night she'd planned to let

him down. Gently, with no screaming and relatively little pain.

And yes, that *was* relief flooding through her, chicken that she was. There was also annoyance, she realized. This man allegedly loved her. He said he wanted to marry her, for crying out loud.

And yet his idea of wooing her was to repeatedly break dinner dates at the last minute.

She could imagine their wedding day—Brock calling her as she sat dressed in her wedding gown in a sleek white limo being driven to the church.

"Pumpkin!" he'd boom over the cell phone's little speaker. "Something's come up. Compu-dime's systems have gone haywire! They need me in Dallas, pronto. We're going to have to reschedule—you don't mind, do you?"

And there it was—one of the reasons Brock wanted to marry her. She was so completely, idiotically compliant.

Of *course* she didn't mind. She *never* minded. She always did what was asked or expected of her, with a smile on her idiotic face.

She was *such* a loser.

"I'll call you tomorrow," Brock said now. "I've got to run."

And he was gone before she could say anything at all.

With his curly hair and Hollywood-star cleft in his chin, Brock was a good-looking man. And, as Maggie's mother kept pointing out, he got six weeks of vacation each year.

Yeah, *there* was a reason to get married—for a man's extensive vacation time.

Be careful, Angie had said the last time they'd talked

on the phone. Maggie's best friend from high school was convinced that if Mags didn't stay alert, she'd wake up one morning married to the Brockster. Kind of the same way she'd woken up one morning with a law degree, a job at A&B and living at home again at age twenty-nine.

But Angie was Angie. Her goal in life was to make waves. She'd just gotten married herself to a man from England and was living now in London, working as a stage manager in the theater district. She had a dream job and a dream husband. Freddy Chambers, a seemingly straitlaced Brit, was the perfect match for Angie Caratelli's rather violently passionate nature.

Kind of for the same reasons quiet Maggie had gotten along so well with Angie.

It had been more than ten years, but Maggie still missed high school. She and Angie and Angie's boyfriend, Matt Stone—all part of the theater crowd—had been inseparable and life had been one endless, laughter-filled party. Well, except when Angie and Matt were fighting. Which was every other day, because Matt had been as volatile as Angie.

Life had been jammed with anticipation and excitement and possibilities. There was always a new show to put on, a new dance to learn, a new song to sing. The future hung before them, glowing and bright.

Matt would have been as horrified as Angie if he knew Maggie was a corporate lawyer now, and that her office didn't even have a window. But he'd disappeared over ten years ago, after graduation. His and Angie's friendship hadn't survived that one last devastating breakup, and when he'd left town, he hadn't come back.

Not even a few years ago, when his father had died.

No, Maggie was the only one of them still living

here in town. Wimp that she was, she *liked* living in the town she'd lived in most of her life. She just wished she weren't living at home.

"Help," she said to the woman in the car in the next lane over who looked nearly as tired as Maggie felt. But with the windows up and the air-conditioning running, they might as well have been in different rockets in outer space.

Angie repeatedly suggested that Maggie quit her job, dump Brock and run off to live in a recreational vehicle with that really gorgeous, long-haired, muscular Tarzan lookalike Maggie had caught glimpses of while at the health club. The *jungle man,* she and Angie had taken to calling him since he first appeared a week or so ago. She'd first noticed him hanging from his knees from the chin-up bar, doing midair sit-ups.

He had long, straight, honey-brown hair, and as he effortlessly pulled himself up again and again, it came free from the rubber band and whipped in a shimmering curtain around him.

Maggie had never gotten a clear look at his face, but the glimpses she'd seen were filled with angles and cheekbones and a clean-shaven and very strong chin.

She could picture him now, walking toward her, across the tops of the cars that were practically parked on Route 95.

He would move in slow motion—men who looked like that always did, at least in the movies. Muscles rippling, T-shirt hugging his chest, blue jeans tight across his thighs, hair down around his shoulders, a small smile playing about his sensuous mouth, a dangerous light in his golden-green eyes.

Well, Maggie hadn't gotten close enough to him to

see the color of his eyes, but she'd always had a special weakness for eyes that were that exotic, jungle cat color.

Oh, *yeah*.

He'd effortlessly swing himself down from the hood of her car and open the driver's-side door.

"I'll drive," he'd say in a smoky, husky, sexy half whisper.

Maggie would scramble over the parking brake. No. No scrambling allowed in this fantasy. She'd gracefully and somewhat magically find her way into the passenger's side as she surrendered the steering wheel to the jungle man.

"Where are we going?"

He'd shoot her another of those smiles. "Does it matter?"

She wouldn't hesitate. "No."

Heat and satisfaction would flare in his beautiful eyes, and she'd know he was going to take her someplace she'd never been before. "Good."

The car behind her hit its horn.

Whoopsie. The traffic was finally moving.

Maggie stepped on the gas, signaling to move right, heading for the exit that would take her to the health club.

Maybe, if she were really lucky, she'd get another glimpse of the jungle man and her evening wouldn't be a total waste.

God, she was *such* a loser.

CHAPTER TWO

MATT STONE NEEDED help.

He'd been back in Eastfield—he wasn't quite ready to call it "home"—for less than two weeks, and he could no longer pretend that he was capable of pulling this off on his own.

His father had been determined to continue messing with Matt's head even after he was dead. He'd left Matt a fortune—and the fate of two hundred and twenty employees of the Yankee Potato Chip Company—provided he was willing to jump through all the right hoops.

As far as Matt was concerned, his father could take his money straight to hell with him.

But for two hundred and twenty good people to lose their jobs in *this* economy...?

For that, Matt would learn to jump.

Still, he needed a lawyer who was on his side. He needed someone with a head for business. And he needed that person to be someone he trusted.

He needed Maggie Stanton.

He'd seen her a time or two at the health club. But she was always in a hurry, rushing into the locker room. Rushing to an aerobic dance class. Rushing back home.

He'd seen her last night—checking him out. She was very subtle. Maggie would never leer or ogle, but she was definitely watching him in the mirrors as he did curls.

She didn't recognize him. Matt didn't know whether to be insulted or glad. God knows he *had* changed quite a bit.

She, however, looked exactly the same. Blue eyes, brown hair, sweet girl-next-door face with that slightly elfin pointy chin, freckles across her adorable nose…

It was a crime to humanity that she'd gotten a law degree instead of going to New York and working toward a career on Broadway. She had a voice that always blew him away, and an ability to act. And, oh, yeah, she could dance like a dream.

She'd won all the leads in the high school musicals starting when she was a freshman. She was Eliza Doolittle to his Henry Higgins when he was a junior and she was a sophomore.

The following year, they were Tony and Maria in *West Side Story.* It was the spring of Matt's senior year, and the beginning of the end of his friendship with both Angie and Maggie.

Because Angie knew.

As Tony and Maria, he and Maggie had had to kiss onstage. It was different from the polite buss they'd shared as Eliza and Henry the year before. These were soul-sucking, heart-stopping, full-power, no-holds-barred passionate kisses. The first time they went over the first of them, Matt had followed the director's blocking with his usual easy confidence, pulling Maggie into his arms and kissing her with all of his character's pent-up frustration and desire.

Maggie had become Maria, kissing him back so hotly, pressing herself against him and…

And Matt had to stop pretending to himself that he hadn't fallen for his girlfriend's best friend.

And of course, Angie knew. The only person who *didn't* know was Maggie.

It was entirely possible she never knew.

Or maybe she *did* know, and she had been as angry with him as Angie.

In which case she probably wouldn't return his phone call.

Which meant that he'd just have to keep calling.

Because he *needed* Maggie Stanton, and this time he wasn't going to take no for an answer.

LADEN WITH FILES, Maggie staggered back into her office at five o'clock the next afternoon after a six-hour meeting with a client.

She pulled the wad of phone messages off her spiked message holder with a sigh, taking them with her into the former closet that was her office. She closed the door, dumped the files in the only other chair in the room, and, sitting at her desk, spread the message slips on the desk in front of her.

Brock had already called twice. Seven of the messages were from clients she knew, three were names she didn't recognize.

There was a brand-new pile of files on her desk, with a casually scrawled note atop saying, "Deal with these before tomorrow, will you?"

Oh, yeah, sure. No problem—if she stayed here at the office until midnight.

Maggie let her head fall forward onto the desk. "I hate this job," she whispered, wishing she were brave enough to say it loudly enough for either Andersen or Brenden to hear.

There was a knock on her office door.

Maggie lifted her head. This was where he'd make the scene. Her jungle man. She'd say, "Come in," and the door would open and he'd be standing there, just looking at her with those golden-green eyes.

He'd step inside and close the door behind him and say, "Ready to go?"

And she wouldn't hesitate. She'd say, "Yes."

And he'd smile and hold out his hand and she'd stand up and slip her fingers into his and...

The door opened a crack and Janice Greene, the firm's receptionist, peeked in. "You *are* still here."

"Oh, yeah," Maggie said. "I'm still here."

"You missed one," Janice told her, handing her the phone-message slip.

"Thanks," Maggie said as Janice went back out the door. She glanced down at the slip and... "Whoa, wait a minute, please— Didn't he leave a number?"

Matthew Stone, read the slip in Janice's neat handwriting.

"He said you would know it," Janice said. "I'm sorry, I should have—"

"No," Maggie said. "It's all right." The only number she knew for Matt was the one for the big old house he'd once shared with his father, down by the water.

As Janice shut her door, she picked up her phone and started to dial.

But then hung it back up.

She'd always felt a little funny about the fact that she'd taken Angie's side during her and Matt's last big fight—

the one that had broken them up for good and even managed to disrupt Maggie's own friendship with him.

Angie had never gone into detail about what it was that Matt had supposedly done.

All Maggie knew was that Matt and Angie had had the mother of all fights shortly after rehearsals for *West Side Story* had started. And that was saying something because theirs was a very stormy relationship, filled with conflict.

Angie had come running to Maggie's house for comfort. And soon after, Matt had shown up, too.

Maggie could tell he'd been drinking from the aroma of alcohol that surrounded him. It had been whiskey she could smell, which alarmed her. Usually he only drank beer.

"Are you okay?" she'd asked him, coming out onto the front stoop.

He sat down heavily on the steps, and she knew as she sat next to him that something was really wrong. In addition to having too much to drink, he looked anxious and ill at ease.

He couldn't quite meet her eyes. "Mags, there's something I have to tell you," he said.

"Get the hell out of here, you creep!"

Maggie turned to see Angie inside the front door. Her eyes were blazing and her arms were crossed as she glared down at Matt.

He swore softly. "I should have figured you'd be here."

Maggie had looked from Angie to Matt, feeling hopelessly caught in the middle. She stood up. "Look, you guys, why don't I go inside? This doesn't have anything to do with me."

Matt started to laugh, and Angie kicked him, hard, in the back. He fell off the steps, landed in the shrubbery and came up mad.

"Damn it!"

"Stay away from me," Angie shouted back at him. "And stay away from Maggie. I'm warning you, Matt!"

Maggie had never seen such venom in her friend's eyes.

Matt turned deliberately away from her and looked at Maggie. "I would like to talk to you. Alone. Will you come for a ride with me? Please?"

"I wouldn't let her go for a ride with you even if you were sober," Angie shouted. "Get lost, you son of a bitch!"

"I wasn't asking you," Matt shouted back. "Just shut the hell up!" He turned back to Maggie. "Come on, Mags. If you don't want me to drive, we could take a walk."

"I'm sorry," Maggie said as Angie pulled her back into the house.

After that, she'd only seen Matt at rehearsals.

She'd urged him to patch things up with Angie, but he'd simply smiled. "You still don't get it, do you?" he'd asked.

Finally, she *did* get it. Matt and Angie were through, and their three-way friendship was over.

The next year, Matt went off to college. Angie found a new boyfriend and life went on. Maggie had kept track of Matt for a while.

The last address Maggie had had for him was from nearly seven years ago, when he was living in Los Angeles. Since then, she'd heard nothing of him, as if he'd dropped off the face of the earth.

But now he was back.

Maggie picked up the phone and dialed.

It rang four times before a breathless voice answered it. "Hello?"

"Hey, Matt."

"Mags!" he said, genuine pleasure ringing in his voice. "Thanks for calling back so quickly. How are you?"

Awful. "I'm fine. Welcome back to the East Coast."

"Yeah, well." His voice sounded subdued for a moment. "I, uh, actually, I'm back in Eastfield on business and, um, that's partly why I called. I mean, aside from just wanting to see you. God, it's been forever."

"You sound exactly the same," she said.

"Yikes," he said. "Really? That's kind of scary."

Maggie laughed. "So what kind of business are you in these days?"

"The inheritance business," he told her. "Can you meet me tonight for dinner? I'm going to ask you to do me a giant favor and I'd rather not do it over the phone. I need the opportunity to use visuals—you know, so I can properly grovel."

He *did* sound exactly the same. "How giant *is* this favor?"

"It's about twenty-five million dollars giant."

Maggie choked. "What?"

"I really want to wait and talk to you about this in person," Matt said. "How about if I pick you up at six-thirty?"

Maggie looked at that new stack of files on her desk. "Let's make it later. I'm going to be here for a while, and I was hoping to hit the health club tonight. I want to go to a class that ends at eight. Is that too late?"

"That's right. Tonight's that dance class you like to take. I've seen you over there, you know."

"You're kidding. You saw me at the club and you didn't bother to say hello?" Maggie couldn't believe it. "Thanks a million."

"You didn't see me?" he asked.

"If I had, I would've said hi. Jeez, Matt."

He laughed. "It makes sense that you wouldn't recognize me. I've put on some weight."

"Really?" Maggie tried to picture Matt carrying an extra fifty pounds around his waist. Oh, dear. He was probably balding, too. No doubt it was his cosmic punishment for being too gleamingly handsome as a seventeen-year-old.

"Look, why don't we meet at the club?" he asked. "We can get something healthy to eat in the café."

Maggie snorted. "Yeah—since when do *you* eat anything healthy, Mr. Cheese Fries?"

Matt laughed. "I'll see you a little after eight."

THANKS TO THE files on her desk, Maggie missed the dance class. It was eight-fifteen before she pulled into the health club parking lot.

And there he was. Her jungle man. Hanging out right by the door, leaning against the wall. Dressed in jeans and that white T-shirt, just like in her fantasy.

Only this was real.

He was just standing there, as if he were waiting for her. And she was going to have to rush right past him, because she'd already kept Matt waiting.

Boy, she hated being late.

But as she moved toward him, the jungle man pushed himself up and off the wall. His hair was down around his shoulders, shiny and clean. His shoulders and chest were unbelievably broad, and the muscles in his arms actually strained against the sleeves of his T-shirt.

His face was twice as handsome as she'd imagined—although the twilight still made it hard to see him clearly.

He smiled as she drew closer, and she realized that his cheekbones were indeed a work of art. And his chin and his smile with those gracefully shaped lips, and those golden-brown eyes that were—oh, my God!—*Matthew's* eyes...

Maggie couldn't remember the last time she'd been completely speechless. But she sure as hell was speechless now.

Matthew.

Her fantasy jungle man was actually her old buddy *Matthew.*

He'd put on some weight, all right, but it was all solid muscle.

"Hey, Mags," he said—Matt's voice coming out of this stranger's mouth. He was laughing at her. He knew damn well that she'd noticed him in the club but hadn't recognized him.

Come on, Maggie. You're an actor. *Act.*

"Hey, Matt," she said, her voice coming out perfectly matter-of-fact. "I'm sorry I'm running late."

"That's all right," he said. "I'm just glad you're here. You look great, by the way."

"I still look fourteen," she told him. "*You* look great. God, Matt, I've seen you around here for days, but I didn't know it was you."

"Yeah, well, I've changed a lot," he said, his eyes suddenly serious.

Maggie had to look away, suddenly uncomfortable with this new man-size Matthew Stone. Somehow, she'd been expecting the kid she'd known in high school. This man was not only taller and broader, but he'd also lost the nervous energy that had ruled the teen. Young Matt had never sat still for longer than a few minutes, hopping from chair to chair around the room, smoking one cigarette after another.

This man exuded a quiet strength, a steadfast calmness. And that was really why she hadn't recognized him—never mind the long hair and muscular body.

Matt smiled at her, not one of his old devil-may-care grins, but a gentle smile of genuine pleasure.

"I really missed you," he said.

"I missed you, too," she told him. "But right now I have to visit the ladies' room. It's a long drive from New Haven at this time of night."

"No problem. I'll go up to the café. Want me to order you something?"

"Yeah, thanks," she said as he held the door open for her. That was a new one, too. Matt—holding a door? "Will you get me a salad?"

"Italian dressing on the side," they both said at the same time.

Matt grinned. "Some things never change."

CHAPTER THREE

WHEN MAGGIE WALKED into the café, Matthew was standing at the juice bar, talking to three healthy, young college girls. What was it that he'd said? Some things never change.

He turned as if he'd felt her eyes on him and quickly excused himself. Coming toward her, a smile lit his handsome face. "Hey."

Their food had already come out, and he pulled her by the hand to a table. And held her chair for her.

She looked up at him as she sat, half expecting him to pull it out from underneath her, so he could laugh as she hit the floor.

But he just smiled at her, and sat down. Behind a huge salad and a plate of steamed vegetables. The hamburger kid was eating *vegetables*.

"Before we get down to talking about twenty-five-million-dollar favors," Maggie said, "I'm dying to hear what you've been up to this past decade."

And where was the beer? Even at seventeen, Matthew Stone never sat down to eat dinner without a cigarette and a bottle of beer.

"It would take a full ten years to tell you the whole story," he said with a smile, digging into his salad.

Maggie looked around the open, airy café. The ceiling was high; the colors were muted grays and maroons.

A sign on the wall proclaimed that there was absolutely No Smoking.

"Do you still smoke?" she asked.

"Nope. I quit three years ago," he told her. "I also stopped drinking and started eating vegan. See, I, um... Well, I got sick, and I needed to take some kind of action—feel like I was doing something to help myself get better. I don't know if it really helped, but it certainly helped my head, you know?"

"How long were you sick?"

He shook his head. "A long time. Do you mind if we don't talk about that? It's not... I have these superstitions about... Well, I'd rather not—"

"I'm sorry," she said. "Of course, you don't have to... I had an address for you in California."

"Yeah," he said. "Yeah. I was, uh, all over the southwest for a while. Right after dear old dad gave me the boot. He kicked me out—did you know about that?"

She shook her head. "No."

"Yeah, there was trouble at one of the colleges and he wouldn't even hear my side of it. I mean, sure, it was the fourth college I was..." he cleared his throat "...politely asked to leave, but... That time it really wasn't my fault. Still, I got the 'never darken my door again' speech."

"That's terrible," she said.

"It was good, actually. I finally learned to take care of myself. I kind of floated for a while. I actually did some acting—and got paid for it. My most legit job was at this dinner theater in Phoenix. I did two shows with them—*Cat on a Hot Tin Roof* and *Guys and Dolls*."

"That's great—getting paid for acting?" Maggie smiled at him, and he smiled back.

"I guess. It was... It really wasn't that great. They

didn't pay very much. I had to wash dishes, and…" he shrugged "…their leading lady had nothing on you."

Yeah, right. "Thanks."

When he looked at her, something sparked. Maggie felt it deep in the pit of her stomach, and she had to look away. She'd trained herself for so long to feel nothing more than friendship for Matt that this kind of physical attraction seemed odd and unnatural.

His eyes gleamed with humor. "Oh, here's a story you'll really like. When I was in L.A., I managed to get this agent. What a sleazeball. He told me he could get me some work in the movies. Nothing big, you know— bit parts. But still, it was the *movies*…. Anyway, he sent me on an audition, right?"

Maggie nodded, watching Matt's face as he talked, the corners of his mouth quivering with restrained laughter. It was hard to believe that it had been ten years since she'd seen him. It just seemed so natural, sitting here together.

"So I go into this place," he said, "and I realize that it's not a cattle call. You know, there're not four hundred other guys that look sort of like me lining up to audition for the part of the store owner who says 'A dollar fifty,' to Keifer Sutherland when he comes into the convenience store to buy a pack of cigarettes. The director actually comes out and shakes my hand—if you can believe that—and he takes me into the studio. I was so jazzed. They had cameras set up on a sound-stage, along with this living room set. It looked like a stock American-home set—something out of a sitcom, you know?"

He paused, taking a sip of water. "Well, imagine my

surprise when the director told me to go ahead and take off my clothes."

"What?"

"Yeah." Matt grinned. "It didn't take me long to figure it out. I asked to see the script and it was called—I'll never forget this—*Sleazy Does It*. It was a porno flick, Mags. It wasn't an audition—they were just going to shoot the film that same day. Is that too scary or what?"

Maggie had to laugh. Poor Matt. Thinking he was going to get a part in a major motion picture... "Did you do it?"

He choked on his water and glared at her, mock outrage on his face. "Thanks a lot. No, I did *not* do it."

She was still laughing. "Your past ten years have been much more exciting than mine."

"You graduated from Yale, went to law school and managed to get an M.B.A. at the same time. You had a fire, moved back in with your folks. You dated someone named Tom for four years, and now you're seeing a guy named Brock Donovan. You've had the lead in *Oklahoma!, Carousel, Paint Your Wagon, Showboat, The Boyfriend, Superman, Anything Goes, Guys and Dolls, Li'l Abner* and one more.... What was it?"

"Annie, Get Your Gun." Maggie couldn't believe it. "How do you know all that?"

He closed his eyes, placing his fingertips on his forehead. "Matthieu senses all," he said with a heavy Eastern European accent. "I also know that Angie's married now," he added in his regular voice.

There was something in his face, in his tone, that Maggie couldn't read.

"Yeah," she said. "Freddy's great. You'd like him. But it's kind of a drag—they live in London."

"That must be tough," he sympathized. "You and Angie stayed close, didn't you?"

Maggie nodded. "I miss her."

"Did she ever tell you…"

"What?"

He shook his head. "Why we broke up. I don't know. It all seems so silly now."

He was looking at her, and she felt herself blush under his scrutiny.

"Why did you break up?" she asked.

"Maybe I'll tell you some other time," he said. His eyes were warm. Hot, almost….

Where are we going?

Does it matter?

No.

Maggie cleared her throat. "Are you going to audition for the summer musical? I mean, are you going to be in town for a while?"

"Yeah, I'll be here at least three months," he said. "I don't know about the show, though. I saw the audition notice in the paper. It's tomorrow, right? But the show was one I didn't recognize."

"It's called *Day Dreamer.* It was written by this local team of writers. It's not… It's really funny. And the music's good, too…." Maggie felt herself babbling in an effort to keep the conversation pointed securely away from the physical attraction that seemed to simmer between them.

But she lapsed into silence as he sat back in his chair, his eyes still glued to her face. As he moved, the muscles in his arms and chest moved, too. It was hypnotizing. With a motion that was clearly well practiced, he tossed his hair out of his face, back behind his shoulders.

"I guess I'll audition," he said. "If you're going to…"

"Matt, why do you wear your hair like that?" she asked. "I mean, it's beautiful, but you always had short hair. In school, you used to make fun of the boys who wore their hair long…."

"It's a complicated story," he said evasively. He sat forward, pointing at her salad. "Are you going to eat that?"

She wasn't very hungry. "Do you want it?"

"No, I want to get out of here," he told her. "I want to take you to see something."

He stood up, tugging down on the thighs of his jeans in a movement that was all Matthew. How many thousands of times had she seem him do that?

But going vegan and quitting drinking and smoking, and the new superhealthy body…

As they left the café and walked down the stairs to the lobby, he caught her puzzled look and said, "What?"

It was remarkable, really. With his dazzling white T-shirt tucked into the top of his blue jeans, his long hair cascading halfway down his broad back, he was an odd mixture of her friend Matt and her fantasy jungle man. He looked sort of like Matt and he moved and talked sort of like Matt, but there was so much more that was different about him now. She could see so many changes in him, the most startling being his confidence—his solid, quiet strength.

Again, she found herself attracted to him, and that felt strange.

"I'm trying to figure out exactly who you are," she said bluntly, "just who it is you've become."

He looked startled for a moment, and then he laughed. "You know, Mags," he said, "I really did miss you. You and your honesty."

He opened the door leading out of the club. With a grand gesture, he motioned for her to go through.

Outside, the night air was cool, and Maggie shivered slightly. Matt casually draped an arm around her shoulders.

His touch was warm, and Maggie felt the urge to lean against him, to rest her head on his shoulder, wrap her own arm around his waist.

But he was just being friendly old Matt. Wasn't he?

She pulled away. "Your car or mine?"

Matt turned around and gave her such a look that she had to laugh. "I assume that means you still *have* to be the driver, right?" she said.

He grinned. "I've got the old man's Maserati. He never drove it anywhere. What's the point in having a car like that if you never use it?"

"Do you remember when you stole it and used it to drive Angie to the junior prom?" That was one of the best times they'd had together and one of the worst.

He unlocked the front passenger-side door of the gleaming black sports car and opened it for Maggie. "How could I ever forget? I spent four days in jail for that one. God, my father was such a bastard."

Matt got into the driver's seat and closed the door. He looked over at Maggie, real sadness in his eyes. "I was such a disappointment to him. Right up to the end."

She didn't know what to say, and then there was no reason to say anything because he put the key into the ignition and started the engine with a roar. "Oh, yeah," he said, flashing her a smile. "This is a very nice car."

Maggie wanted to ask about his father, but she held her tongue. Mr. Stone had died over a year ago, and even though he and Matt had never gotten along, she'd been surprised when Matt hadn't shown up for the funeral.

She shook free of the thought, fastened her seat belt and got ready to hang on for dear life as he pulled out of the parking lot. But he drove almost slowly.

"Where are we going?" she asked.

Does it matter?

She loosened her fingers from her grip on the hand strap as she realized he was going to stay under the speed limit.

"Out to my father's office," Matt told her. "*My* office," he corrected himself with a laugh. He shot her a look. "Can you believe I have an office?"

Maggie was confused. "You mean, over at the factory?"

"No," he said. "The main office was in our house."

Matt glanced at her.

Maggie's face was lit in regular intervals by the streetlights. The pale yellow glow made her seem unearthly.

She was prettier than ever. She still had the biggest, bluest eyes he'd ever seen. They were surrounded by thick, dark lashes. Her complexion was fair—a fascinating contrast to the dark brown of her soft, wavy hair. Her nose was small and almost impossibly perfect, her lips soft and full and always quick to curve into a smile.

For the first time since he'd hit town, he was honestly glad to be back.

Very glad.

"I want to offer you a job," he told her as they neared the house. "I'd like to hire you as my corporate attorney and business advisor—for three hundred thousand dollars a year."

She stared at him.

She didn't say a word as he pulled into the driveway of his father's huge white Victorian house. All the outside lights were on, spotlighting it against the darkness of the night.

He'd grown up in this house, playing on the vast lawns that overlooked the Long Island Sound, scrambling on the rocks at the edge of the shore. It was a wonderful old place, full of nooks and crannies. It had rooms that weren't perfectly square, windows that opened oddly and closets that turned out to be secret staircases.

"What's the catch?" Maggie finally found her voice.

After Matt's mother died, his father had had the house renovated and restored. And although he knew his father hadn't intended for it to happen, the renovations had removed every last trace of her, every homey, motherly touch, leaving the house as impersonal and empty as a museum.

Matt pulled around to the back, where the office was, and parked the Maserati under another bright spotlight.

"The catch," he said, turning toward her in the sudden silence after the car's powerful engine had been shut off. "Yeah, there's definitely a catch. You know my father had money. Big money."

Maggie nodded. The Yankee Potato Chip Company, the mansion, the twelve-car garage with the twelve cars to go in it.

"Dear old dad decided to leave it all to me, all twenty-five million, if—" Matt took a deep breath "—I can show that I can run the business within a three-month time period, which started last week. If I can't—adios to everything. The executor of the estate will shut down the business, auction off the factory and all the money will go to charity. If that happens, I'll get nothing. And if I get nothing, your job—and everyone else who works for YPCC—will be terminated." He looked at her. "How's that for a catch?"

Maggie nodded again, her eyes serious. "That's some catch. What exactly does the will stipulate?"

Matt opened the car door. "I've got a copy inside. I'll let you take a look at it."

She got out of the car, too, staring up at the house. "You know, Matt, all those years we were friends, I never went inside your house."

"That's because my father hated Angie," Matt told her. Angie had taken Mr. Stone's crap and handed it straight back to him. "He would've really liked you, though."

"Is that a compliment or an insult?" she asked with a laugh.

"Oh, it's a compliment," he told her. And wasn't that strange? He and the old man would've finally agreed on something.

Maggie followed him up the path to the office door and into the house.

The outer office was large and spacious, with rows of file cabinets along one wall. There was a huge oak conference table in front of enormous bay windows that looked out over the water. The hardwood floors glistened, as did the intricate wood molding that surrounded the windows and door. It was a modern office with computers, copy machine and fax, but the feel of the room was Victorian. It was gorgeous. And in the daytime, with the view of the sun sparkling on the water, it would be even more beautiful.

Matt led the way to a dark wooden door and, pushing it open, he turned on the light.

Maggie had to laugh, looking around at the late Mr. Stone's private office—Matt's office now. "Oh, Matt," she said. "It's *you*."

He grinned.

Thick red carpeting was underfoot. The walls were paneled with the same dark wood as the built-in bookcases. Row upon row of books lined the wall, and Maggie glanced at the varying titles and subjects. Mr. Stone had a few books on astronomy, several on geology, an entire shelf of medical books on cancer, many titles on the Second World War, but the vast majority of the books in the room were fiction—mysteries.

Matt's father had been into whodunits. He had always seemed so practical and down-to-earth, with no time for nonsense of any kind. She just couldn't picture him biting his fingernails in suspense as he read faster and faster to find out who was the killer.

The inner office had big windows, but they were shuttered with elaborately carved wood. The centerpiece of the room was a massive cherry desk with what looked like a black leather Barcalounger behind it.

Maggie slowly circled the desk. It was quite possibly as large as a queen-size bed, its rich, dark wood buffed to a lustrous shine. She picked up the single item that rested on its clean surface—a photo of Matt at about age six, clinging possessively to his smiling young mother's neck.

"Why didn't you come to his funeral?" she wondered.

He turned away.

"I'm sorry," she said swiftly, putting the picture down. "I shouldn't have asked—"

"I saw him about two weeks before he died. I was in the hospital—it was back when I was sick. Somehow he'd managed to track me down, and he came to see me."

He was leaning against the door frame now, arms crossed. His pose was relaxed, but Maggie could see tension in his jaw. And she could hear it in his voice.

He laughed, but it didn't have anything to do with humor. "I don't know how he did it, but he managed to pick a fight. I mean, I'm lying there, dying for all he knows, and he's telling me I never did anything worthwhile with my life."

Maggie didn't hesitate. She crossed toward him and put her arms around him. "I'm so sorry."

"I told him to go to hell." Matt rested his cheek on the top of her head. "I told him to stay out of *my* life, because no matter how short it was going to be, it was my life. So he got up to leave, and I thought he was just going to walk out, but he turned and he told me that he loved me, and that he didn't want me to die. I told him—"

His voice broke, and Maggie held him even more tightly. She felt him take a deep breath, then exhale loud and hard. "I told him that I hated him," Matt said, "and that I couldn't wait for him to die." He made another noise that wasn't quite laughter. "God. *Why* did I *say* that? Of course, two weeks later the son of a bitch went and had a massive coronary. It was his ultimate revenge—he couldn't have planned it better if he'd tried."

She looked up at him. "Matt, he loved you. He knew you didn't mean what you said."

He sighed. "I hope so."

In this light, from this angle, flecks of color made his eyes look more green than gold. Green, and very warm. As he looked down at her, his face held something—a sadness, a sweetness and also a tenderness—that she hadn't ever seen there in all the years she'd known him. At least not when he wasn't acting.

It was entirely possible that back then, he simply hadn't let it show.

His arms were still around her, and she was still holding him. They'd stood like this, leaning against each other, so many times—Matt had always been very casual with affectionate embraces. But everything felt different now, and as she looked into his eyes, she knew he felt it, too.

Attraction. Desire.

It seemed inappropriate. It had been years, but it was still hard not to think of Matt as Angie's boyfriend.

Except Angie was married now to someone else. And this new, fantasy-jungle-man version of Matt was here, looking at Maggie as if he were thinking about kissing her. Not just a Matt kiss—he'd always been generous with friendly kisses on the cheek, too—but a real, on-the-mouth, tongues-in-action kind of kiss.

Like the way Tony had kissed Maria. Maggie's stomach did a flip as she remembered kissing Matt onstage. Except that hadn't been them—it was the characters they were playing who had kissed so passionately.

Still…

She pulled away from him and went to stare once again at the books on the shelf. This was just too weird.

"I'm sorry," he said quietly. "I shouldn't have laid all that on you."

Maggie shook her head. "Oh, no, I'm glad you told

me," she said as she turned to face him. "That's what friends are for, right?"

Their eyes met. And Maggie felt it again, that spark of sexual energy that seemed to flow between them. Friends.

"You were going to give me a copy of that will," she reminded him breathlessly, reminded herself, as well.

He took a step toward her, and another, and she knew he was going to kiss her.

But the kiss he gave her was only a Matt kiss, on the cheek. He stepped past her, going into the outer office. She followed, feeling oddly disappointed—was she insane?—as she watched him switch on the copy machine.

"You can take this home and look it over," he told her as he opened one of the file cabinets and took out a manila folder. "Let me know what you think by Monday. I know it's short notice, but I need you to decide by then because if you aren't interested in the job, I'll have to start looking for someone else to help me right away."

Maggie watched as he copied the document.

A three-hundred-thousand-dollars-per-year job, guaranteed to blow up in three months if she didn't help Matt become a businessman.

Was it exciting? Absolutely. Was it crazy? More than absolutely. What would her mother, her father, God, even *Brock* think?

They'd think she was irresponsible, silly, reckless, wild.

But what did *she* think? How about answering *that* question for once?

Sure, there was a chance this decision would backfire, leaving her without a job and laughed at by her friends and family. But there was a chance that something special was going on here—that she finally had an opportunity to take control of her life, to get out of her cell and make a difference in some way, even if only in her life and Matt's and the people who supported their families from the Yankee Potato Chip Company.

To do something she wanted to do, something *she* would be proud of…

But the risk…

There were butterflies in her stomach—just like when she was little and in line for the Ferris wheel at the firemen's carnival. As the line got shorter and the moment of truth approached, she would nearly sweat with anxiety. Would she do it or would she chicken out?

She would look up at the seemingly shaky structure that would take her on a ride fraught with danger, up to terrifying heights. Then she'd remember the exhilaration of the wind in her hair as she looked way, way down at the little people below and out at the horizon that seemed to stretch on forever.

It had been worth it. It always had been worth it.

She looked at Matt as he shut off the copy machine, as he stapled together the copies he'd made, as he put the original back in the folder, back in the file cabinet.

Where are we going?

Does it matter?

No.

"I'll take the job," she told him.

He turned and stared at her. "But you haven't even read the—"

"I don't care," she said. "You offered, I'm taking it."

Matt laughed. "Since when do *you* make a decision without forty-eight hours of soul searching?"

"Since right now," she said.

"Are you sure?" He looked worried.

She felt a twinge of uncertainty. "Are you sure you want me?"

"Absolutely!"

"Then I'm sure."

Matt just looked at her. With that same disconcerting heat in his eyes. She had to turn away, look out the window at the night.

"I've been thinking for some time now about making some changes," she confessed. "It occurred to me that if I took your offer I wouldn't have to go back to that horrible office without a window."

"You don't have a *window?*"

She glanced at him. "You've got to earn a window at Andersen and Brenden."

"God."

"I wouldn't have to make that awful commute, I wouldn't have to wear uncomfortable shoes— Would I?"

"No way." He was grinning at her. "If you work for me, you don't have to wear shoes at all. Of course, if in three months you won't be able to afford to *buy* shoes…"

"Not if I can help it," she said. "This is a beautiful office. It's ten minutes from home, inches from the ocean…" She made a face. "Although, telling my dad that I'm leaving A&B isn't going to be fun…."

His smile had faded. "Maggie," he said seriously. "I don't want to pressure you." He paused. "Don't get me wrong. I want you to say yes. I *really* want you to say yes. But this isn't going to be easy. Your job will be to help me figure out how to run this business. At this point, I can barely remember how to add or subtract. It'll mean really long hours. I've only got three months, and right now, quite frankly, I couldn't run a business if my life depended on it. So if you aren't absolutely sure or if you're doing this just to help me out of a tough spot or if you're going to regret this tomorrow…" He looked searchingly into her eyes. "I want you to be really sure."

She looked back at this man who was half Matt, half her fantasy man and didn't hesitate. "I'm sure."

A flood of emotions crossed his face. "Well, all right," he said and handed her the copy of the will. "Let's have dinner tomorrow after the auditions. We can start work then."

Maggie glanced through the will—it was fourteen pages long. "We should forget about the auditions. If we only have three months—"

"No," Matt said. "I'm not giving up a chance to be in another show with you. And rehearsals are only, what? A couple evenings a week?"

"Except for the last week before it opens," she chided him. "Then it's every day. We really can't—"

"Yes, we can," he said. "The show won't open until the end of my fiscal quarter. If we haven't succeeded by then…" He shrugged. "It'll be too late."

"I just don't think we should take on too much at once," Maggie told him.

The smile he gave her was beautiful. "You worry too much."

"You don't worry enough," she countered.

"This is going to work out just perfectly."

CHAPTER FOUR

THE AIR IN the community-theater auditorium was cool compared to the outside warmth of the sunny spring morning. It smelled like sawdust and paint, musty curtains, a little bit of sweat and a whole lot of excitement.

It smelled like a show.

Maggie smiled and waved to friends from past productions as she put her gym bag down on one of the seats in the first row.

There was an audition sign-up sheet posted on the apron of the stage, and she signed in.

"Sign me in, too."

She looked up to see Matt leaning over her shoulder to look at the list. His hands were on the stage, on either side of her, effectively pinning her in.

His teeth flashed white and perfect as he grinned at her. He was standing so close, Maggie caught a whiff of the spearmint toothpaste he'd used, probably right before leaving his house. He was wearing all black—a snugly fitting T-shirt, sweats and a pair of jazz shoes that had clearly seen a lot of use. Howard Osford, the slightly balding, slightly overweight tenor who usually won the romantic leads out of lack of competition didn't stand a chance today.

"What are you singing?" she asked as he watched her add his name to the list.

Matt shrugged, straightening up and freeing her. He followed her back to her gym bag, throwing himself casually into the seat next to it. "Want to do a duet?" He stretched his long legs out in front of him, and looked up at her, a glint in his eyes.

Maggie stopped taking off her street shoes to glare at him. "That always really pissed me off."

"What?" He grinned, knowing darn well what she was talking about.

"The way you could come into an audition totally unprepared and walk away with the lead."

Matt tried not to be obvious about watching her as she pulled off her T-shirt and adjusted her sports bra. She was wearing tight black pants that flared and a colorful dance top that left her midriff bare.

"You should get a belly-button ring," he said.

She rolled her eyes. "Ouch. No thanks."

"You know, it's been more than three years since I've gone on an audition," he said. The room was filled with dozens of hopeful singers and dancers. It didn't matter the town or the state—the hope that hung in the air at an audition was always the same.

"Are you scared?" she asked.

Matt tried to look frightened. "I won't be if you sing a duet with me."

She just laughed. "Not a chance. I, for one, worked hard to prepare a song."

"Then let me use you as a prop."

Maggie crossed her arms. "Come again?"

Ooh, he loved it when she put on a little attitude. Sweet Maggie had a backbone beneath that soft outer layer. "A prop," he repeated, working hard not to smile.

"You know, a warm body to sing to. I always do much better when I'm not up onstage all alone."

She laughed in his face. "Tough luck. That's what an audition is all about—being onstage all by your little old self. You can sing to me all you want, but I'm going to be right down here." She shook her head in disgust. *"Prop."*

"Okay," Matt said.

"That's it? No fussing? No begging? No whining? Just, okay?"

He tipped his head back and smiled up at her. "It's only an audition."

"I hate you," she said, and walked away.

Ten minutes later, the first trembling victim stepped onto the stage, and Matt joined Maggie at the back of the room.

"I'm up twentieth," she whispered. "You're twenty-first. Have you decided what to sing?"

He nodded yes. "I'm doing something from my favorite show."

"What is your favorite show?"

"West Side Story. It was the most fun I've had onstage in my entire life."

Maggie looked at him, perplexed. "You mean, back in high school?"

"Yup."

He looked up at the stage, watching as the director cut the singer off midsong. Maggie studied his profile, remembering the turmoil of his senior year.

Another singer mounted the stage and made it through about sixteen bars before being stopped and thanked for coming.

"Sheesh." Matt glanced at her. "This director is bru-

tal. They're dropping like flies. He doesn't give anyone time to warm up. At this rate, you're going to be
up there in less than a minute."

"He is pretty harsh," Maggie agreed, then asked,
"How could *West Side Story* be your favorite show?
You were miserable the entire time. You had that big
fight with Angie...."

"As Matthew I was miserable," he told her. "But I
sure loved being Tony."

He had a funny little half smile on his face and a look
in his eyes that made her heart beat faster.

He looked back at the stage, and Maggie watched
him watch the auditions.

"Maria was a great part," she told him softly. "But it
was very hard each night to watch you die."

He glanced at her, and the look on his face was one
she absolutely couldn't read.

"Maggie Stanton," a stout woman with cat-eyed
glasses and a clipboard finally called. "You're next."

Yikes.

Matt caught her arm as she started for the stage, pulling her into his arms for a hug. "Break a leg, Mags."

She looked up at him and the realization hit her hard,
leaving her feeling weak. She wanted him to kiss her.

He was handsome and vibrant and so very alive and
she wanted him to kiss her.

He wasn't Angie's boyfriend anymore and *she wanted
him to kiss her*.

And he did.

On the cheek.

She swallowed her disappointment as she walked
down the theater aisle toward the stage. Those sparks

she'd thought were flying all over the place must've been only in her mind.

Or else he would have really kissed her, wouldn't he?

He saw her as a friend, a buddy to hang with.

Which was a good thing. Matt had never been cut out for anything but short-term, intensely passionate flings. True, they wouldn't leave his bedroom for a week, but after that week, it would probably be over. Any kind of romance with him would definitely be a mistake—particularly since she was going to be working with him.

She *was* going to work with him.

She'd called her boss at A&B this morning and he'd accepted her resignation gracefully. In fact, he'd told her he didn't even need the usual two-weeks' notice. Times were tough all over, Maggie knew, and business had been off lately, even at the big law firms.

She just had to go in some time next week, clean out her desk and drop off the company cell phone.

She handed her music to the accompanist with a smile, moved center stage and nodded to the director. He was someone she'd never worked with before, someone who didn't know her from Eve. She could see him glancing through her resume, and she turned back to the piano player and nodded.

As the first strains of music surrounded her, Maggie closed her eyes and took a deep breath, letting herself become the character—a thirtysomething dancer pleading for a second chance on the stage.

As Maggie started to sing, Matt looked up from his search through the piles of sheet music that had been tossed on a table in the back of the auditorium. God, she

was good. He'd forgotten how good. He'd never understood why she hadn't studied acting, gone professional.

He had to laugh. Yeah, he'd met her parents many
times. He did understand. And it was a shame.

She sang the first part of the song standing absolutely
still, but with tension in every part of her body. When
she reached the refrain, she exploded, both in volume
and movement. She was fantastic, her voice clear and
true, her body graceful.

Matt moved closer to the stage and sat on the arm
of a chair. He could see the back of the director's head,
and the man hadn't moved once since Maggie started
singing. He grinned as the director let her sing the entire song, right down to the very last note.

The entire room burst into applause, and Maggie—
typically—actually looked surprised. She blushed—
also typical—and bowed.

"Very nice," the director called, his usually bored
voice actually showing interest. "Don't go anywhere. I
want you to read for me."

She collected her music from the piano player and
went down the stairs as Matt went up. He gave her a
high five.

"Your turn to break a leg," she said.

"You're a hard act to follow."

Maggie sat down in the front row, feeling the last
surges of adrenaline leaving her system. Matt came
center stage and looked down at her and smiled, and
somehow the adrenaline was back, making her heart
flip-flop.

The music started and Maggie recognized the song
instantly. "Something's Coming." Of course. Matt had
always loved that song. It was all about hope and ex-

citement and limitless possibilities. She had to smile. It was practically his theme song.

"Hold it," the director called, and the accompanist stopped. "Matthew Stone?"

"That's me," Matt said.

"From Los Angeles?"

"Yeah, I lived there for a while." Matt squinted slightly, looking past the bright lights at the director. "Dan Fowler? Is that you?"

"Yes. Thank you. Next," the director said in a bored voice.

Matt's eyes flashed. "What, you're not even going to hear me sing?"

"I don't want you on my stage," Fowler said.

The room was dead silent. No one so much as moved.

Maggie stared up at Matt, holding her breath, waiting for him to explode. But he merely crossed his arms.

"Mind telling me why not?" he asked, his voice almost too calm.

"Because the last time I cast you in a show, you disappeared off the face of the earth halfway through rehearsals. That screwed me up pretty badly."

"I called," Matt countered. "I apologized. But I had to go into the hospital."

"A detox center, wasn't it?" Fowler challenged.

"Detox?" Matt laughed. "Yeah, I guess it kind of was." He looked out at the director. "That was three years ago, Dan."

Detox. God. Maggie had always known that in the past Matt had lived recklessly, always pushing the edge. It wasn't hard to believe that somewhere down the line he'd become addicted to either alcohol or drugs.

"It's still fresh in *my* memory, Stone."

"I'm not leaving this stage until you let me audition." Matt said the words easily, evenly, but in such a way that left no doubt in anyone's mind that he would not give in.

Fowler scowled. "You can audition until your face is blue. I'm not going to cast you. You're wasting everyone's time."

Maggie stood up, grabbing her gym bag. "Matt, let's go. There'll be other shows—"

"Hold it," Fowler said. "Maggie Stanton?"

There were a few moments of whispering as Fowler leaned over and spoke with his producers and assistants.

"Come here for a sec," he finally called.

Maggie looked uncertainly at Matt, who nodded to her, telling her to go ahead. He then sat as if unconcerned, on the apron of the stage.

She left her bag on the seat and made her way to the director. She was outraged at the way he was handling this situation. To publicly humiliate someone like this was unprofessional. It was rude, inexcusable…

Dan Fowler was about thirty-five years old, but he had streaks of gray in his full, thick beard that made him seem at least fifteen years older. His eyebrows were large and bushy, making him look as if he had a permanent scowl. He didn't speak until Maggie stood directly in front of him.

"You with him?" he asked quietly, motioning up to the stage and Matt.

"Yes," she said tightly. "I don't know what happened three years ago, but right now he's clean."

Fowler tapped his fingers on the table in front of him, looking from Maggie to Matt and back again. "Will he agree to urine testing?"

"For *drugs?*" Maggie asked in amazement.

Fowler nodded.

"You can ask him," she said, "but I doubt he'll go for that."

"Hey, Stone," the director called. "I'm willing to audition you if you consent to drug testing."

"I meant, ask him *privately,*" Maggie hissed, throwing up her hands in despair. She risked a look at the stage, fearful of Matt's reaction.

But he pushed himself to his feet and looked out at them serenely.

Only Matt knew how difficult it was to appear that calm. Inside, his blood boiled. He may have played hard and fast at one time with drugs and alcohol, but that had nothing to do with his admission into the hospital. But he wasn't about to go into those details here. Not in front of a crowd, and especially not in front of Maggie.

He looked out at her. He could tell from the tightness of her shoulders that she was mad as hell. But he knew that she really wanted this part—she *deserved* this part—and he didn't want her to lose it on account of him. And if he walked out of there, she'd go with him. He knew that. On top of that was the fact that he desperately wanted to play opposite her again....

"Okay," he said, keeping his voice light.

"Good," Fowler said. "Sing your damn song and get your ass off my stage."

Matt snapped out a count and the accompanist played the introduction. He started to sing, his eyes following Maggie as she moved down the aisle, back to her seat. He could see the shine of unshed tears in her eyes, and he knew she'd realized that he'd let Dan Fowler push him around because of her. And she would, no doubt, chalk it all up to friendship. He was just her good old pal Matt, doing something nice for his buddy Maggie.

And yet there was attraction simmering between them. Although if it scared her even a third as much as it terrified him, was it any wonder she kept trying to ignore it, to push it aside?

But, God, imagine if she could let herself love him....

She looked up at him, and he channeled everything he was feeling into the music. Like most actors, he could be supercritical of his own performance, but this time... Well, even he would have cast himself.

He stopped the song halfway through, looking out at the director. "That's enough, don't you think, Dan?"

"Thank you," came the standard reply. Then, "Stick around to read."

Victory. He was going to get a chance to read lines. Whoopee.

Matt swung himself gracefully off the stage to find Maggie waiting for him. She silently took his hand and pulled him down the aisle to the back of the auditorium, ignoring all the curious eyes that were on them. She led him out the closed double doors into the lobby and started for the door to the street.

"Whoa," he said. "Where are we going?"

"We're leaving."

He planted himself. "No way."

"*Yes* way. That man is a creep." She was seriously angry.

"He's a good director, though. Wait and see."

Now she was angry with *him*. "You're only doing this for me, aren't you?"

Yes. And he'd do far more for her, too, if she'd only let him. "Nope," Matt told her. "I'm doing it for myself."

Maggie didn't buy it. "Matthew, you've had enough crap dumped on you from your father—with the will and everything. You don't need to deal with this, too."

"Hey!" He grabbed her by the shoulders and shook her gently. "It's okay. Really. It's just my lurid past catching up with me. It happens. I don't mind drug testing—"

"Liar."

Matt laughed at the look of intense indignation on her face. God, she was wonderful.

"Well, okay," he admitted. "It sucks. But life's not always fair, and it's no big deal." She started to react, and he put one finger on her lips. "Really. If there's one thing I've learned over the past few years, it's to know the difference between big problems and little problems. And Dan Fowler is definitely a little problem."

The woman with the clipboard and the cat glasses poked her head out of the door. "Stone and Stanton?" she said. "He's looking for you. Onstage, to read."

"I want to do this," Matt said, looking into Maggie's eyes. "Let's do this, okay?"

Maggie nodded, letting him drag her back into the auditorium. He took the bag from her shoulder, put it onto a seat and pushed her up the stairs to the stage.

"Take a few minutes to read it over," Fowler called out from his throne behind the bright lights, a benevolent monarch lazily granting the peasants some crumbs from his table.

Maggie quickly skimmed the scene. And oh, God. She could feel herself start to blush. Of course. It had to be *this* scene. She glanced up to meet Matt's eyes. He raised an eyebrow at her, then looked back at his script.

Oh, God.

"Whenever you're ready, boys and girls," Fowler's indolent voice commanded.

"I read the entire play last week," Maggie quickly told Matt. "This scene is part of a fantasy that my character is having. She's just imagining that you're there in her bedroom, okay?"

"Got it," Matt said. He looked out toward the director. "We're ready, Dan."

"Quiet," Fowler roared, and suddenly the room was still.

Sieg heil. Maggie couldn't believe they were still here, auditioning for this tyrant. But then Matt read his first line, and she thought of nothing but the script.

"Lucy, are you still awake?" he read.

"Go away," Maggie read, with weariness and annoyance in her voice.

"Hey," Matt read, throwing up his free hand. "I don't really want to be here. I'm just part of your overactive imagination. You want me to leave, you have to imagine me gone."

"All right. I will." As the script directed, she squeezed her eyes shut, concentrating for a moment. When she opened her eyes, he was still standing there, of course. "Oh, damn," Maggie read.

"Cody Brown, at your service," Matt read.

"What kind of name is Cody, anyway? It's a ridiculous name for a man born in Manhattan. You sound like a cowboy or a rodeo rider. What were your parents thinking?"

"Aha," Matt read. "So that's why I'm here. You want to insult both me and my parents. Well, go for it, Luce."

"I'm much too tired to be properly insulting," Maggie sulked.

"Why else would you have imagined me here in your bedroom at one o'clock in the morning?"

Maggie looked up at Matt, her alarm not entirely feigned. He smiled, a smile that started very small and grew across his handsome face. "I know why I'm here," he said as he advanced across the stage toward her.

Maggie stared at him, frozen in place. Was he really going to…? "No…"

"You're wondering what it would be like to kiss me," he read, moving closer to her. "Aren't you?"

"No!"

As Maggie stared up at him, he came closer, until they were less than an inch apart. But he still wasn't touching her.

Matt had the next line, but he waited a moment before reading it. The look in his eyes was remarkable as he gazed down at her, the perfect mix of nervousness and desire on his face. Oh, he was such a good actor. "You're wondering what it would be like if I put my arms around you, like this," he read, then tossed the script onto the floor as he did just that.

"And you're wondering what it would be like to put your arms up around my neck." Matt was going on memory now, but the lines were easy from here on in.

Maggie let her own script slide to the floor as she, as if almost in a trance, put the palms of both hands on Matt's chest and slowly slid them upward. She felt him inhale, as if he found her touch exciting. It was a nice addition to what was already fabulous acting.

Her hands met behind Matt's neck and she could feel his long, soft hair against her bare arms. She was Lucy. And this was make-believe. They were acting. *Acting.*

"And you're wondering what it would feel like," Matt

said slowly, "if you brought your lips up, like this—" and he gently pulled her chin up, then tenderly pushed the hair back from her face "—and if I brought my lips down, like *this*..."

Maggie was expecting a gentle kiss, but the moment his mouth found hers, something exploded. She felt his arms tighten around her as he kissed her, and she kissed him, as she opened her mouth to him and...

Oh, God. She was lost.

But just as suddenly as that kiss began, it ended. Matt pushed her away from him and took several large steps to the other side of the stage.

"Well, forget it," Matt said, his voice perfectly hoarse with emotion as he turned to look at her. "Because I'm not going to kiss you."

They stared at each other, both breathing hard.

"*Very* nice," Dan Fowler's voice cut in. "Stick around for the dance audition."

Maggie's hands were shaking as she bent down to pick up her script. Matt took it from her.

"You okay?" he asked, concern in his eyes.

"Sure," she lied, looking up at the man who seemed intent on turning her world inside out. "I'm...just fine."

CHAPTER FIVE

MAGGIE DRAGGED HERSELF up the stairs to her bedroom. The dance audition had been grueling. A sane person would take a hot shower and curl up in bed with a good book. But somehow she'd let Matt talk her into having dinner with him, as they'd planned the day before.

"Nothing fancy," he'd insisted, with that little smile that could turn her to jelly.

Did he know? Could he tell that she'd finally succumbed to Matthew Fever? That was what Angie had scornfully called it back in high school when one after another pretty young girl had fallen prey to Matt's charms and followed him around adoringly, sighing soulfully.

"Everyone gets it," Angie had insisted.

"Not me," Maggie had said.

Now she wondered if it were like other childhood diseases—much more dangerous if contracted when an adult.

She closed the door to her room and undressed quickly, slipping into her bathrobe.

There was a soft knock on her door, and she opened it cautiously, not wanting to get into another discussion with her mother about the pros and cons of an October wedding.

But it was her little brother, Stevie, who stood there, yawning as if he had just gotten out of bed.

"Morning," he said, scratching his head, making his short dark hair stand up straight.

"It's five in the evening. Don't tell me you slept all day."

"I cannot tell a lie," Stevie said, a weak smile on his still-boyish face. "Your evening is my morning."

"That's pathetic." She softened her words with a smile.

"I didn't get home last night until noon," he told her. "That is noon, as in this morning."

"Are you kidding? Are you grounded for the rest of your life?"

"It was prom night." Her brother grinned. "It was very wholesome. I went to two different after-prom parties, and there was absolutely no alcohol served at either one. I felt like one of *My Three Sons*. Believe it or not, it was fun. And I'm not hungover. What a bonus."

"How'd it go with Danielle?"

Stevie rolled his eyes. "Great—if my goal was for her to still not realize that I'm alive."

"It must run in the family," Maggie said. "I know what you mean."

He narrowed his eyes at her. "You can't accuse the Brockster of not knowing you're alive. He wants to marry you. What's doing, Mag-oid? You got a boy toy on the side?"

Maggie smacked him on the rear with her towel. "None of your business, Dr. Love. Outta my way. I need to take a shower."

"Be nice to me," Stevie said. "I came here to warn you. I overheard the 'rents talking, and it sounds like

Her Royal Highness, Queen Vanessa, is coming over for dinner tonight."

"Oh, thank God," Maggie said. "I've already got an excuse. I'm having dinner out with a friend."

"Lucky you, you'll miss *that* magic. Give a shout when you're out of the shower."

As MAGGIE WAS putting the finishing touches on her makeup, the doorbell rang. It was only 6:18 p.m. She'd never known Matt to be early, but he was doing an awful lot of things differently these days.

She stood back and looked at herself one last time in the mirror. Jeans and a red tank top, sandals on her feet. Who'd've thought she'd ever wear something this casual to a dinner meeting with her new boss?

A boss she happened to have the screaming hots for. And *that* was something she couldn't let happen. Talk about ways to destroy a friendship. And what would *Angie* say?

The doorbell rang again, and she clattered down the stairs, throwing the door open.

"Hi." She smiled, expecting Matt.

Brock looked back at her, his arms filled with suitcases. Vanessa stood behind him, also laden with luggage.

Uh-oh.

Maggie's sister never traveled light, but seven suitcases for a two-hour dinner...?

"My arms are breaking here," Vanessa said, and Maggie stepped back, holding the door open for them.

Brock piled the suitcases near the stairs, smiling at Maggie. "Hey, kiddo." His deep voice boomed in the small foyer. "Bet you didn't expect to see *me* tonight."

"No," Maggie said faintly. "I didn't."

Stevie came down the stairs, his hair still wet from his shower. He stared from Van to Brock to the large pile of suitcases to Maggie. *Uh-oh.* He was thinking the same thing she was.

Maggie's dad came out of the den and shook hands warmly with Brock. "Glad you could join us," he said, then turned to Maggie. "Van told us Brock was giving her a ride over tonight, so we invited him to stay for dinner."

"Oh." Maggie looked back at Stevie.

He shrugged. "I didn't overhear *that* part," he mouthed to her. "Yo, Van," he said out loud. "You planning to change your clothes between every bite of your roast beef?"

"I'm staying for a while." Van's voice sounded brittle.

"Oh, wow." Stevie looked at Maggie again. They both loved their sister, but it was much easier to love her when she lived under a different roof. "What, is Mitch away on business or something?"

"Or something."

Uh-oh.

The phone rang.

"I'll get it!" Maggie and Stevie said in unison.

But their mother picked it up in the kitchen. "It's for you, hon," she called to their father.

"I'll take it in the den." He disappeared down the hall.

"Help me get this stuff upstairs," Vanessa commanded.

"Yes, sir!" Stevie fired off a salute as Vanessa and Brock led the way. "She's staying for *a while,*" he muttered out of the side of his mouth to Maggie.

"Matt's going to be here any minute," Maggie muttered back.

"Matt?" Stevie was delighted. "The friend you're having dinner with is a *Matt.* Oh, boy."

"Dinner's almost ready," their mother called from the kitchen.

"I'm going out. I've got a business dinner," Maggie called back, loudly enough for Brock to hear. Except he was leaning close to Vanessa, listening intently to whatever she was saying.

"I can't hear you with the water running!" her mother called back.

"What are you going to do?" Stevie whispered to Maggie. "I know—you could invite him to stay for dinner, too."

"Bite your tongue!"

Stevie was laughing. "It's the only solution. You know, this evening is turning out to be much more interesting than I thought."

Maggie rammed Vanessa's suitcase into the back of his leg.

"Ouch!" he yelped.

"Margaret!" their father shouted from the bottom of the stairs. "I want to talk to you. Now."

Maggie froze, looking at Stevie. Uh-oh.

"God, what'dya do?" he asked, sotto voce.

"I'm almost thirty years old," she whispered back. "Why do I feel as if I'm thirteen and I've left the basketball out in the driveway?"

The doorbell rang.

Uh-oh. "I'll get it," Maggie called, desperately trying to sound normal as she hurried down the stairs.

"I'll help!" Stevie dropped Van's suitcase and scrambled after her.

They both nearly crashed headlong into their father, who seemed to materialize out of thin air. He had on his fighting face.

"Maggie, that was just Bob Andersen on the phone," he said. "He just happened to mention that you *quit* your *job* this morning!"

"Yo, Mags! Finally makin' that rockin' career move?" Stevie said approvingly.

"You did what?" Vanessa came down the stairs, followed closely by Brock.

The doorbell rang again.

"She quit her job at Andersen and Brenden." Her father shook his head in disbelief.

"Will someone please answer the door?" Maggie's mom came out of the kitchen, wiping her hands on a dish towel.

"I'll get it," Maggie said again, hurrying to reach the door before her mother got there. She took a deep breath and pulled it open.

Matt was standing there, wearing his usual jeans and white T-shirt, his hair loose, looking like a dream date from a music video. "Hey," he said with that smile that lit his entire face.

She reached for his hand and pulled him into the foyer. His smile turned to surprise as he saw her entire family staring at him.

"Everyone," Maggie said in her best stage voice. "I'd like you to meet my new boss, Matthew Stone."

"Oh, my *God,*" Vanessa said.

"Your new *what?*" Brock asked as he sized Matt up.

"Intense." Stevie was impressed.

"Close the door, dear," Maggie's mother said, her voice faint with shock, "or bugs will come inside."

MAGGIE SAT AT the dinner table, buzzing with nervous energy. How did this happen? She'd thought she'd been in control. She'd intended to stick to her plans and go out with Matt. After all, it *was* business, right? Instead, they'd ended up here, in one great big, hostile room.

She looked across the table and met Matt's tranquil gaze.

Well, the *entire* room wasn't hostile.

"You have *how* long to do *what?*" her father was saying as her mother passed Matt a plate heaped with mashed potatoes, vegetables…and a large slice of roast beef.

And he was a vegetarian. She opened her mouth to protest, but Matt caught her eye and shook his head very slightly, taking the plate with a graciously murmured thanks.

"We have a fiscal quarter," he told her father. He seemed entirely at ease with the fact that everyone was staring at him. "And I'm not really sure *what* I have to do in order to inherit the business." He smiled at Maggie. "That's one of the things we're meeting to discuss later this evening."

"Let me get this straight," Vanessa said. "You've actually hired Maggie to do…what?"

"She's going to be both my lawyer and my business advisor," he said.

Maggie glanced down the table at Stevie, who was looking at Matt in something akin to shock. Her brother looked at her, realization in his eyes and a rapidly growing grin on his lips.

Oh, damn. Stevie had figured out that Matt was the man who had come up in their earlier conversation. What was that phrase Stevie had used? *Boy toy.*

She looked down the table at her brother, promising him with her eyes that the wrath of Satan and the winds of hell would be nothing compared to her if he let this one slip. He smiled at her and made a zipping motion across his mouth.

Yeah, you'd better keep it zipped, junior....

"Maggie, aren't you hungry? You haven't touched your plate," her mother said.

She stared down at her dinner, her appetite gone. Her stomach churned nervously at the sight of roast beef congealing in a puddle of gravy. "Um," she said.

Brock slipped his arm around her shoulders and he gave her a squeeze. "You know how girls are," he said. "Always dieting."

Matt sent Maggie a disbelieving, amused look. She knew what he was thinking. *Girls.* Brock's feminist awareness quotient was a shade lower than a Neanderthal's.

And she really wished he wouldn't touch her.

"I'm curious as to why you didn't discuss Matt's job offer with Brock before you took it," Vanessa asked. "I mean, you *are* planning to get married, aren't you?"

And now everyone was looking at Maggie.

But oh, my God, she was *not* going to turn Brock down in front of her entire family.

"Um," she said.

Steve had his glass of milk in his hand, and Matt, who was sitting right next to him, elbowed him.

No one else saw it. Just Maggie.

But the milk went everywhere. "Whoops," Stevie said as Vanessa jumped up to avoid getting drenched.

"Clumsy me," Stevie said as Maggie's mom ran for the kitchen towel.

Matt threw his napkin down to start soaking up the spill. He looked up at Maggie and smiled as Stevie kept on making noise. "Wow, how did *that* happen?"

No one was looking at her anymore. *Thank you,* she mouthed silently to Matt.

He blew her a kiss.

Which Vanessa, unfortunately, saw.

"Didn't you date Maggie back in high school?" she asked Matt after the worst of the spill was cleaned up and they were all sitting back down.

He shook his head. "No. I went out with Angie. You know, Caratelli, off and on for a couple of years."

"But you *wanted* to date Maggie," Vanessa persisted. She laughed. "Date being the euphemism that it is in high school." She looked at her brother. "Right, Steven?"

"Has anyone seen the new James Bond movie?" Stevie asked brightly.

"Am I right or am I right?" Van asked Matt.

"Van," Maggie said. What was her sister doing? As if Brock weren't already prickly enough just at the sight of Matt. "Don't."

"Matthew's not denying it," she pointed out. She'd had far too much to drink tonight and Maggie's heart broke for her. Her mother had pulled her aside to report that Van was home because Mitch had made it official. He was filing for divorce.

Maggie met Matt's eyes again across the table, and the look on his face was…

God, was it actually true? Matt had wanted to go out with…

But…

"I was seventeen," Matt said to Vanessa. "I wanted to *date* everyone."

Maggie stood up. Enough already. "We have to get to work."

"For the record," her father said. "I'm not happy about this job change."

"For the record," Maggie said, "I am."

MATT LEANED AGAINST the Maserati, watching Maggie say good-night to Brock, who was going to stay and keep Vanessa company for a little while longer.

He clenched his teeth as he watched the other man kiss Maggie. True, she turned her face away so that first kiss landed on her cheek. But Brock was a persistent bastard, and…Matt had to look away.

He jumped slightly, surprised to see Stevie leaning next to him. He hadn't heard the kid approach.

"So. You're a millionaire."

"Not quite." Matt glanced at Maggie. She'd pulled away from Brock, but he still held her hand.

"Answer me honestly," Stevie said. "Are your intentions toward my sister honorable?"

Matt looked at Stevie in surprise. The kid was already as tall as he was, but he was lanky with that big-boned pony look that teenage boys so often had. He wore his dark hair buzzed at the back and sides, with a long lock of curls in the front that flopped down over his eyes. His face was just starting to lose its boyish prettiness as he began to fill out.

"I guess that's not really my business, is it?" Stevie

continued with a shrug. "You know, she's as much as told me that she's not going to marry the Blockhead."

"She did?"

Stevie smiled. "Yeah, well." He imitated Brock's deep voice. "You never know with girls. They're always changing their minds."

Matt laughed. "God, he's a jerk."

"Who's a jerk?" Maggie said, joining them.

"No one," Matt and Stevie said in unison.

"Oh, great," Maggie said, looking at their matching Cheshire cat grins. "That's all I need. You two as cohorts. As if I didn't know who you were talking about. Come on, Matt. Let me grab my briefcase from my car, then we can go."

"Have fun," Stevie said. With his back carefully to Matt, he dropped her a wink that was loaded with meaning.

Maggie let her own smile drip saccharine. "You have fun, too, Stevie-poo. Maybe if you're lucky you can get Vanessa and Brock to play Monopoly with you."

"Sounds real neat, but no," Stevie said. "I've got plans. I'm going to go drive past Danielle's house, oh, twenty-eight, twenty-nine times." He glanced at Matt. "Unrequited love."

Maggie got into Matt's car as Stevie leaned over to look in the window. "Maybe you can offer me some advice," he said to Matt, "you know, with the wisdom of your great age and all. There's this girl, see?"

"Danielle," Matt clarified, looking up at Stevie.

"Check. She's the most fabulous, beautiful, wonderful... Well, you know. But she doesn't think of me as a *guy*. We're friends, that's all."

Maggie leaned forward to look out Matt's window

at her brother. "Just go knock on her front door and tell her that you love her, for crying out loud!"

"Oh, no way," Matt said.

"God!" Stevie reeled back in shock. "That's very uncool."

"Yeah, and potentially humiliating," Matt said. "If I were you, I'd take my time. Go slowly. You know, don't scare her away."

"Meanwhile the captain of the football team takes the more direct approach and ends up taking her to the prom," Maggie said.

"Oh, no." Matt cringed.

"Oh, yes." Stevie nodded. "Pathetic, but true. And on that cheerful note, I'll bid you good night." He vanished into the shadows.

Matt glanced at Maggie. "Your little brother isn't so little anymore."

"Scary, huh?"

He started the car, shaking his head. "Sometimes I wish I could be eighteen again. Man, what I'd give to be able to go back and do it over."

Maggie groaned. "Not me. Once was enough, thanks."

He pulled out of the driveway. "There are definitely some things I'd do differently."

"Like what?"

"Like, I wouldn't start smoking. I wouldn't drink or do drugs. I would've taken better care of myself." He glanced at her. "I would've asked you out."

Maggie looked back at him, but now his eyes were firmly on the road. Vanessa had been right. Matt *had* wanted to date her in high school. *Date.* Right. Wow, she'd never known. "Why didn't you?" she asked.

He glanced at her with a smile. "Would you have gone out with me if I had?"

"No." Her loyalty to Angie had been too strong. She never would have risked that friendship. Even for… "Matt, to be honest, I never thought of you as anything but a friend."

Ten years ago. Now she was aware of him to the point of distraction.

He smiled at her again. "That's why I never asked you out. I wasn't a big fan of rejection."

They rode in silence for a few miles, then Maggie said, "I'm sorry about dinner. Are you sure you still want me to work for you? It's obvious that insanity runs rampant in my family."

He just laughed. "And it doesn't in mine?"

He was pulling into the parking lot of Sparky's, the town watering hole. "What are you doing? Why are we…? You don't drink anymore. Do you?" she asked.

"No, I don't," he said. "But *you* do. And after that dinner you definitely need something with a kick."

"Roast beef," Maggie shook her head. "I can't believe my mother served roast beef to a vegetarian. Why didn't you let me say something?"

He pulled her out of the car. "Because people tend to feel embarrassed and rejected when you don't take what they offer for dinner. I took the plate and didn't hurt your mom's feelings." Still holding her hand, he led her across the parking lot and into the dimly lit bar. "But I didn't eat the meat. It's an old trick I learned in California. Cut it up and move it around the plate and no one notices that you didn't eat it. Everyone's happy."

Maggie hadn't been inside Sparky's in close to seven

years, but the place hadn't changed. It was dark and it smelled like a frat-house basement.

Matt pulled two stools out from the bar, then stepped back so Maggie could climb up. He sat next to her, pulling his stool so close that his thigh brushed hers. He caught the bartender's eye. "Coupla drafts."

The touch of his leg against hers was making her crazy. Matt had never been careful with her personal space, constantly draping an arm around her, often coming up behind her to massage her shoulders or braid her hair.

His casual, friendly touch had always been part of the package. True, Maggie had heard tell that a friendly backrub had at times led to far more friendly activities, but she had never been subject to his amorous advances.

Or had she? Maybe she'd been too naive to realize....

He leaned against the bar and his shoulder grazed hers and she nearly jumped off the stool.

The bartender slid two foaming mugs of beer in front of them, and she gratefully took a long swallow. And risked a look at Matt.

His elbows rested on the bar and his T-shirt was pulled tight across his strong back. He was watching her, his face shadowy in the weak light, his eyes reflecting the yellow of a neon sign. It made him look otherworldly and alien, reminding her that he was in some ways a stranger, after all that time away.

Ten years ago, she never would've dreamed of kissing Matthew Stone. Tonight, she was having trouble thinking about anything else.

Maggie remembered her own words, spoken only minutes before to Stevie, realizing how impossible her advice had been. There was simply no way on earth *she'd* ever be able to turn to Matt and tell him that she was falling in love with him.

But she was.

But she couldn't. What would Angie say if she knew? What would *Matt* say?

She stared morosely into her beer, taking another sip and feeling its coolness and accompanying warmth course through her.

Matt drew lines in the frost on the outside of his glass of beer. *His* glass of beer? What was a guy who'd been in a detox center three years ago doing with a glass of beer?

"You're not going to drink that, are you?" she asked.

"No." Matt laughed. "I'm not an alcoholic, despite what you heard from Dan Fowler today. I don't drink because I *choose* not to, not because I can't."

He met her gaze steadily, and she felt herself blush. "I'm sorry."

What had happened to him three years ago? She wished he would talk about it, but he didn't. And she was afraid to push.

He reached over and pushed her empty glass toward the bartender, then slid the full glass in front of her. "I ordered this for you. Let's go play pool."

"I thought we were going to talk business."

"I'd rather play pool. We can talk business tomorrow."

"Tomorrow's Sunday," she said. "I'm having dinner with Brock."

Matt let his opinion of Brock show on his face. "Why do you waste your time with him?"

"I'm not," she said. "I mean, I won't be anymore."

There was a flare of something in his eyes. Satisfaction. And something else. "Good. Because he's…" Matt laughed. "Don't get me started. I can't believe you've been dating him for, what is it? Six *months?*"

"Five months," she corrected him. "And we've never actually…*dated*." At least not according to Van's definition.

Matt knew what she was saying. "Wow," he said. "That's… Wow." He laughed. "So okay. If his being fabulous in bed *wasn't* the reason you were with him… Why the hell did you go out with him more than once?"

Maggie closed her eyes. "Because he wanted to be with me," she told him. "Because nice men don't exactly fall out of the sky. Because I hoped he'd grow on me. Because I want a family. I want babies. Did I tell you that Angie is pregnant?"

She looked at him, expecting to see disbelief on Matt's face. Angie. Pregnant. Instead, he was looking at the floor, real sadness in his eyes.

Was it possible he still loved her?

Maggie touched his arm. "Are you okay? I mean, I know it must be a shock. Angie always swore that she'd never have kids, but…"

Now he looked perplexed. "What did you say about Angie? I think I missed something."

"She and Freddy are going to have a baby," Maggie repeated.

"No kidding? That's great."

Okay, now *she* was the one who was confused. If it hadn't been the news about Angie, what *had* made him look so unhappy?

"Angie's going to be a really cool mom," Matt said. "Although I can't picture her changing a diaper."

She finished her second beer and, almost magically,

another appeared. She narrowed her eyes at Matt. "Are you trying to get me too drunk to talk business? Another beer and we'll *have* to play pool. I won't be coherent."

"I'm trying to get you relaxed," he admitted. "You're wound pretty tight."

He slid off his seat and, standing behind her, he slipped his hands under her hair and began massaging the muscles in her neck and shoulders.

God, it felt good. Too good. Maggie felt herself get even more tense.

"Man, you have to loosen up. Is this what being a high-powered attorney does to you?"

No, it was what *he* did to her. She closed her eyes, letting his fingers work their magic, letting herself pretend that they were in an alternate time line—one where Matt was more than just a friend.

Matt could see Maggie's face in the bar mirror. Under his hands, her shoulders were starting to relax. Her eyes were closed, her lips parted slightly.

Oh, brother. That was just too inviting. He was dying to kiss her the way he'd kissed her that morning at the audition. She'd actually commended him on his fine acting job, unaware that he hadn't been acting at all.

He was praying that they'd both get the leads so that he'd be able to kiss her that way again and again. And again.

It was an odd blend of torment and delight. Delight that she could kiss him and make his heart pound and his blood rush. Torment that she could seem so unaffected by it herself.

And, oh, my God, she'd never slept with Brock.

"We should talk about work. What time do you want

to start tomorrow?" Maggie murmured, her eyes still closed.

"What time is your dinner with Brock?" he countered.

"We made plans to meet at six," she said.

"Then let's start early," he leaned close to her ear to say. "Eight o'clock. Let's have breakfast together, okay?"

It was an innocent enough suggestion, but somehow with his hands on her shoulders, his fingers caressing the bare skin of her neck, it seemed like a different sort of invitation. Maggie's heart nearly stopped when she felt him lean forward and kiss her just below her ear.

He spun her bar stool so that she faced him.

He was going to kiss her. Wasn't he? As Maggie looked up into his eyes, she only saw uncertainty. Oh, boy, she was probably looking at him as if she wanted to gobble him up, which would freak him out if he'd only intended that kiss on the neck—as sensual as it had felt—to be friendly.

"As your lawyer," she said, half to fill in the sudden odd silence, "I recommend that we gain access to any other papers that might be in the court's files."

Matt backed off. "Other papers?" He was puzzled.

"Your father's will states only that you must, and I quote, 'improve the business,' within a three-month time period. It's much too vague. What exactly did your father mean by 'improve the business'?"

"Make more money," Matt said. "That was always the bottom line for him."

Maggie frowned. "I'm going to need to look at the company's yearly financial statement, as well as the last few years' quarterly reports. As far as we both know,

Yankee Potato Chip is thriving despite the recession. I'd bet that gross profits aren't going to vary from quarter to quarter."

And it wouldn't be easy to improve a healthy business in only three months. Any action made by an increased, aggressive advertising campaign wouldn't bring about increased sales within three months. Maggie put her chin in her hand and stared into space.

"What are you thinking?" Matt asked.

She looked at him. "I was just wondering what could possibly be in that codicil."

"What's a codicil?"

"It's an addendum to a document. There was a note at the bottom of your father's will, with your father's signature, saying that his will has a codicil. It was dated only a few weeks before he died, but it wasn't included in the other pages you gave me. The court has a copy. We'll need to see it," Maggie told him.

"You think it's going to be any help?" Matt asked.

"I don't know. There's probably a copy of it somewhere in your office. We should go back and start looking for it." She slid off the stool and nearly landed on the floor.

"I'll look for it later," Matt told her as he caught her. "I think you're ready for a game of pool. You want to break or should I?"

CHAPTER SIX

MAGGIE UNLOCKED THE kitchen door and went into the house without turning on the light. She was feeling wobbly from all that beer she'd had. She normally didn't have a single beer, let alone *four*. Or was it five?

It was after midnight, and her parents had gone to bed. The house was dark, so she locked the door behind her and crept into the living room and...

And there, on the stairs, in the glow from the street-light, was Vanessa.

Kissing Brock.

She was in her nightgown.

His jacket was off and his shirt was unbuttoned.

And it was pretty damn obvious that he'd been with her, up in her bedroom.

"Wow," Maggie said. "*That* was fast."

Her sister and the man who'd asked her to marry him just a few weeks ago—never mind the fact that she was intending to tell him no tomorrow—leaped apart.

"God," Vanessa said. "Maggie, you scared me to death."

Maggie turned on the light. Brock, at least, had the decency to look embarrassed.

Vanessa, from the looks of things, was even more drunk than she was.

Maggie sat down on the couch. "Your car's not out front," she said to Brock.

"I, uh, parked it down the street," he admitted. "Look, Maggie, I'm sorry—"

"I thought you were Mitch's friend," she said.

"I am."

"Some friend."

Vanessa took offense at her tone. "Mitch is a son of a bitch who should rot in hell," she said, sitting down on the step between the entryway and the living room.

"Who filed for divorce because *you* were cheating on *him,*" Maggie said. She looked at Brock. "Did you know that?"

"Because *he* was cheating on me!" Vanessa started to cry. "You're so self-righteous."

"Hey," Maggie said. "I think I'm allowed a little self-righteousness when I come home to find out that you slept with my boyfriend."

"I didn't think you'd be coming home," Vanessa countered. "Out with Matthew Stone? No woman in her right mind would make him drive her home. Except you. You're so perfect, Margaret. So perfect and proper and *cold.*"

"This probably isn't a good time to be having this conversation," Brock said.

"Shut up," Vanessa said, just as Maggie said, "Zip it, Brockster."

"Maybe I should go…"

"How could you sleep with her?" Maggie asked him. The answer was right there on his face. All along, he'd wanted Vanessa. Even drunk, with her makeup faded and her hair a mess, Maggie's sister was hot. All along, Brock had just wanted to get close to Maggie's hotter sister. She looked up at him in amazement. "Maybe the question I should ask is how could you ask me to marry you, when you're in love with *her?*"

"I'm sorry," he said. "I thought…" He shook his head. "I'm sorry."

This was why he didn't push when she'd said she wanted to wait before they spent the night together. She'd thought he was just nice. But oh, my God… "Have you been sleeping with her all this time?"

"No," Brock said. "Absolutely not."

"No," Maggie echoed. "You just *wanted* to sleep with her." God, she'd almost spent her life married to a man who really wanted her sister. She stood up and looked at Vanessa. "And you knew it. You *bitch.*"

"Fine," Vanessa said. "I'm a bitch. I'd rather be a bitch than little miss no-no-no we've only been going out for four months, we can't possibly have sex yet."

"Oh, my God," Maggie looked at Brock. "You discussed our sex life with my *sister?*"

"What sex life?" Vanessa laughed. "You don't *have* a sex life."

"Not like yours," Maggie said hotly. "No. I don't have sex with strangers in the parking lot of a bar."

"Yeah," Vanessa shot back. "Miss Goody-Goody. You just don't have sex, period. I can't imagine why Matthew Stone even bothers to look at you. Sure, he'll sleep with anything female, but the way you dress it's hard to tell you're actually a woman. If you *did* sleep with him, I'd give it one week. Although I'd bet big money that Matt would be bored to tears after only one *hour* in bed with *you.*"

Maggie gasped. "That's an awful thing to say!"

"Van," Brock said.

"It's true." Van started to cry. "You're so perfect. I *hate* you."

"And I won't live in this house with you," Maggie told her sister. "I know you say things like that because *you're* the one who's messed up, and because you can't deal with Mitch's leaving you, but I am *so* out of here. Tell Mom and Dad I've moved out. For good," she added, the words making her feel remarkably light, despite her anger and hurt, despite the growing nausea from her churning stomach.

"Maybe this conversation should wait for the morning," Brock said again.

"Maybe you should go to hell," Maggie told him, and, grabbing her briefcase, she went into the kitchen and out the door.

She got into her car, but her head was spinning and her stomach definitely felt sick.

She was going to throw up.

She stared down at her car keys. How many mugs of beer did she drink?

Too many to drive.

Savagely, she opened the car door and got out.

As if on cue, the skies opened and it started to rain.

Maggie squared her shoulders and, still carrying her briefcase, started the long walk into town.

STEVIE CRANKED UP the volume of the radio and switched on the windshield wipers as the rain came down harder. He flipped his bright lights lower as he saw someone walking along Route One.

Poor wet son of a bitch. Didn't need to be blinded, too.

But then Stevie hit the brakes and did a one-eighty,

tires squealing. That was no ordinary son of a bitch. That was his *sister!* He pulled up alongside her and rolled down the window.

She didn't stop walking.

"Yo, Mags." He slipped the car into first to keep up with her.

She didn't look at him.

She was soaked to the skin and dripping wet, hair plastered to her head. And she was carrying her brief-case like some deranged zombie commuter.

"So where you going?" Steve dared to ask.

"Into town," she said, as if it were a perfectly normal answer.

"You, uh, want a ride?"

"No, thank you."

Stevie pulled his car to the side of the road and got out, trotting to catch up to his sister. "Maggie, are you okay?" He stood in front of her.

She stopped. "Stevie, if you don't move, I'm going to throw up on you."

He moved, fast, and Maggie kept walking.

"Maggie, come on," he called, but she didn't look back.

MAGGIE WAS WALKING to the Sachem's Inn Motel, one step at a time. She didn't feel good, but she felt a whole lot better since she'd stopped at the corner of Lily Pond Road to throw up behind the O'Connors' shrubs.

It was another few miles into town, another mile after that past the harbor to where the motel overlooked the water.... She couldn't handle the thought of walking three more miles. But she could walk one step. One step and one step and one step. Eventually, they'd all add up to three miles.

She stopped short.

Matthew.

Steam rose from the cooling hood of his car, creating a wall of mist behind him. He was wearing only a very small khaki-colored pair of running shorts. Light from a streetlamp glinted off the moisture on his bare skin. It was cold enough so that his breath hung in the air, but he stood still, just watching her.

"Hey, jungle man," Maggie said. "I've run away from home."

"So I've heard," Matt said. "Steve called me. It's about time you moved out of there. Can I give you a lift?"

Maggie looked at him, at his bare feet and athletic legs. Bare skin started again on the other side of his shorts. His stomach was a six-pack and his chest was... Fantasy material, indeed.

Vanessa was right. This was not a man who would ever want to be anything more than friends with Maggie. "Will you take me where I want to go?" she finally asked.

"Depends."

"Then forget it," she said. "I'll walk."

She stepped around him, but he caught her arm. "If you're walking, Mags, I'm walking with you." It was not an idle threat.

It was freezing. "You're not exactly dressed for a stroll in the rain."

"Neither are you. Come on, get into the car."

Maggie looked at him for several long moments.

"Please," he said.

"I look like I've really lost it, don't I?" she asked.

He smiled. "Kind of. But I figure you must have a good explanation. Why don't we get into the car and you can give it to me."

"Will you take me where I want to go?" she asked again.

"Yes," he said this time.

Maggie got into the car.

Matt turned the key and cranked up the heat.

"I'm ruining your leather seats," she realized with dismay, reaching for the door handle.

He hit the lock button and slipped the car into gear. "That's okay. In a few months I'm going to be a millionaire. I'll buy new ones."

"I want to go to the Sachem's Inn Motel," she said.

"Really?" He gave her a sidelong glance. "With me?"

"Very funny. Just take me there."

Matt sighed. "I'm not going to take you there and simply drop you off."

"You *promised.*"

"Did not."

"You *said* you'd take me where I wanted to go."

"Yeah, but I didn't *promise.* I'm taking you home with me."

"You *jerk.*" Maggie started to cry. She'd finally left home, and damn it, she'd left it under her own power, despite the fact that she'd had too much to drink to drive safely.

But now she'd gone and gotten rescued. Well, she didn't want to be rescued, not even by Matthew Stone, jungle man.

Matt stopped at a red light and turned to look at her.

"I want to do it my way, Matt." Her blue eyes were swimming in tears. "Let me. Please?"

The traffic light turned green, but he ignored it. He took a deep breath, hardening himself against her tears. "I don't think it's a good idea for you to be alone tonight," he told her. "If you insist on going to the motel, I am coming with you."

"I insist," Maggie said, wiping her eyes and sticking out her chin. "And I don't need a babysitter."

"Too bad, because I've made up my mind."

"Well, *I've* made up my mind, too, and I'm staying there alone."

Their eyes locked and held. And the traffic light turned red again.

"Let's compromise," Matt told her. "First come home with me. We can get warmed up, maybe get something to eat and talk—"

"I don't want to talk." She crossed her arms, staring straight ahead.

"Fine," he said. "We can sit in silence in the hot tub. After that, I'll take you over to the motel. If you still want to go there."

Maggie looked at him. "Hot tub?" she said.

"You already turned it on," Maggie said, wonder in her voice. "It's already hot."

She stood shivering in the bathroom in Matt's house, staring at the steam rising from the hot tub.

"I was sitting in it when Steve called." Matt tugged impatiently at the zipper on her jacket. It stuck slightly, but he finally got it down, and peeled the wet sleeves off her arms. Her skin was icy.

He reached for the button on her jeans, but she pushed his hands away. "I can do that."

Yeah, but it had always been one of his fantasies. Not a good time to tell her that. "Then do it," he countered. "Come on, let's get you in there before you die of hypothermia."

She hesitated. "I don't have a bathing suit."

Matt laughed. "You don't need a bathing suit for a hot tub. For God's sake, Maggie, I'll turn around. Just get in, will you?"

He pointedly did just that and she peeled off her clothes. Yeah, she was definitely tanked—otherwise she surely would have noticed that the room was filled with mirrors and his turning his back was useless. He could see her from all angles, and, oh, mighty God... A more chivalrous man might've closed his eyes, but life was just too short.

Matt watched as she slipped into the water, and... Wasn't that just perfect? Now it was his turn to get naked. But maybe that was good. Let her see what she did to him.

But, "Eek," she said, as he started to pull off his shorts right in front of her. She closed her eyes until he was sitting across the tub from her. "Doesn't this strike you as weird?"

Matt stretched out his legs to get more comfortable and brushed against her. All right. Don't do that. He was purposely sitting over here so there'd be no contact. "What's weird about it?"

Her eyes were so blue and her face was pale and she was still shivering slightly. The last thing he should do was go over there and put his arm around her. He drew an imaginary line around her. Whatever happened, he was *not* going to cross that line. Not tonight, anyway.

"Well, to start with, we don't have any clothes on," she told him.

He shrugged as the water bubbled around them. "Personally, I'd find it much weirder if we did."

She narrowed her eyes at him. "It's weird and you know it."

Matt nodded. "Yeah, it's weird. That doesn't mean it's not nice, though."

"I have this fantasy," she told him, "where this perfect stranger just kind of holds out his hand to me, and takes me away from my life."

Oh, man. "That's, uh… That's probably one a lot of people have."

"It's pretty wimpy," she said. "Like, I just want to lie back and be rescued."

"Nothing wrong with that," Matt said.

"No," she said. "Because who's to say that his choices would be any better for me? My fantasy should be that I go up to the jungle man and say come with me—let's escape, but let's do it *my* way."

Jungle man. That wasn't the first time she'd mentioned this jungle man. "That's a good fantasy, too." He laughed. "Mags, I get the feeling that you're telling me something, but I'm not sure if I understand exactly what it is. Can we stop talking in code? I really want to talk about what happened tonight after I dropped you off."

She sank down so that the water covered her mouth. Okay.

"Steve said he thought you and Vanessa got into a fight or something?"

Her eyes filled with tears.

"Talk to me," he said.

She lifted her mouth above the water line. "If we made love, would you be bored with me after only an hour?"

Matt choked on the air he was breathing. *"What?"*

Great, now he'd embarrassed her. She closed her eyes. "Nothing. Never mind."

"No," he said, moving across the tub to her. Mistake, mistake, *mistake.* He moved back, just not as far as he had been, but still safely on the other side of his line. *"Not* never mind. You just asked me if I thought you'd be boring in bed, didn't you?" *Damn.* "Did Vanessa say that to you? Mags, she already had too much wine at dinner. And she's nuts on top of that...."

But Maggie was just sitting there, eyes closed, looking like she actually thought...

"To answer your question," he told her, "no. No, I certainly don't."

She opened her eyes and looked at him, looked away. "It was stupid to ask. I mean, what are you really going to say? 'Yes, sorry, I think making love to you would be dull?'"

Okay. Game over. Matt crossed his line, moving so that he was sitting right next to her. "For the record," he said, pulling her chin up so that she was forced to meet his gaze, "I don't think making love to you would be even remotely dull. I would not be bored after even a hundred hours. And this is something that would *not* be difficult to prove."

"What would you do if I said, okay, prove it?" She was looking into his eyes, no longer needing his hand under her chin to meet his gaze, but he didn't move. Her skin was so soft, and she was finally warm. Her lips were slightly parted, her cheeks charmingly flushed, her eyes bright.

Too bright.

No, no, no. No. He wanted to cry. Instead, he shook his head. "I can't," he said. "Not tonight, anyway. You're drunk. It wouldn't be fair."

"I'm *not* drunk," she said with the kind of indignation that only someone who'd had too much to drink could pull off.

"I think you are," Matt countered. "But okay. Let's take that off the table. Even if you're not drunk, you're upset. I don't want to sleep with you because you're mad at your sister."

"There." Maggie pulled away from him. "You don't want to sleep with me. You just said it."

"No way! Misquote! Sound-bite attack! Take it back, or you're going to get dunked!"

She'd moved all the way to the other side of the hot tub, but as he advanced on her, she actually came toward him.

"Matt, kiss me."

That he could do.

He leaned forward, moving slowly now, until his mouth met hers in the sweetest of caresses. Her lips were soft and warm, and oh, Lord, so willing.

Matt carefully kept himself from touching her, aware once again that they were both naked, knowing that if he felt the softness of her body against his, he'd be lost.

And oh, although it was careful and gentle, it was the kiss he'd been waiting for, for a lifetime.

Maggie was kissing him. She wasn't pretending to be someone else who was kissing the person he was pretending to be.

It took his breath away.

It was hard as hell to pull back, to stop kissing her, and he had to turn away to keep her from seeing the tears that had jumped into his eyes.

He forced a smile.

Maggie didn't know whether to laugh or cry. Matt was treating her the way everyone always treated her— as if she might break. And if she were going to feel embarrassed about this in the morning—and she knew she was—then damn it, she wanted the kind of kiss Matt had been legendary for in high school, the kind of kiss that would knock her socks off.

Provided she had socks on.

"I think we should try that again," she said.

"I think I need to get out of this tub," he countered.

"I think there's suddenly some doubt as to who would bore whom in bed," she told him, amazed at the words coming out of her mouth.

"Oh, really?" he said. There was an odd light in his eyes as he looked at her. He didn't move, he just sat there, very, very still.

She shifted slightly, so that the water barely covered her breasts. Matt's gaze flickered down and then back to her face.

"I'm not going to take advantage of you," he said, but he still didn't move.

"It's not taking advantage if it's what I want," she countered. She stood up, water sheeting off her.

Matt stood, too, and scrambled out of the tub, grabbing a towel and wrapping it around his waist. "You're too angry and drunk to know what you want."

"I am not!"

"Please, just—"

"For the first time in ages, I'm actually making my own decisions—"

"This is no decision. It's a knee-jerk reaction." He raised his voice to interrupt her. "If we make love tonight, everything changes between us. Maybe it would be great. Maybe you'd wake up in the morning and still want me. Maybe we'd be lovers until the day I die. But maybe not."

He handed her a towel. "Maybe it wouldn't be anything more than a one-night stand," he continued, the lateness of the hour suddenly evident in his voice. "I really don't mind if you use me, Mags, but I'm not going to let you use me up. I value your friendship too much to throw it away for just one night."

"I'm sorry," she whispered.

He headed for the door. "Dry off. I'll go find you some clothes. Then we can duke it out over whether or not I'm going to drive you to the motel."

MATT CAME BACK into the bathroom with his smallest pair of shorts, a T-shirt and a sweatshirt.

Maggie was gone.

He'd walked right past her—she was curled up in the middle of the bed. It wasn't his bed, but she probably didn't know that.

He sighed, moving closer, but then realized she was fast asleep.

She clutched the sheet to her chest, and her dark hair fanned out against the white pillow. He stood looking down at her, at her long, dark eyelashes that lay against her fair skin, at the smattering of freckles that ran across her cheeks and nose. She looked like the teenage girl he'd first met so many years ago.

As a seventeen-year-old boy, he wouldn't have been able to resist shedding his own clothes and climbing into that big bed with her.

As a thirty-year-old man, he swore softly, then picked up the towel she'd dropped on the floor. He carried it into the bathroom and hung it up to dry, tossing the clothes he'd brought with him on the back of a chair. He covered the tub and turned off the light.

Okay. Leave. Walk away. Go upstairs.

Instead, he came back to look at her in the light from the hallway.

Instead, he sat on the edge of the bed. He'd leave in a minute.

God, he was a fool. He could have had her, made love to her. He could have been lying next to her right now, basking in the afterglow.

But tomorrow was coming with a vengeance. And tomorrow they both would've had to live with the consequences.

Maybe he could make her fall in love with him. Maybe. And wouldn't that be nice. Then she'd be in love with someone who could make her no promises. Maggie wanted a family—babies and a husband who was going to stick around. Matt could give her no guarantees.

But he knew what he wanted. For the first time in years, he was certain. He wanted *her.* After all this time, he still wanted her.

He remembered the day more than a decade ago that he'd realized he was in love with Maggie Stanton. He'd been shocked, horrified, disbelieving. The great Matt Stone, slayer of hearts, did not fall in love. Then, as time passed and he realized that he had, indeed, succumbed, he'd had to face the fact that she didn't see him as anything more than a friend.

When he'd left for college, he'd partied hard, sure that now that he was away, he'd forget about Maggie. It was only a high school crush, right?

He'd dated a long line of long-legged blondes, he'd drunk hard and had been horribly unhappy.

Somewhere down the line, he'd stopped missing her.

At least he thought he had.

Matt reached out to touch her. Her skin was so smooth, so soft. He wanted to kiss her, taste her, inhale her...

He'd leave in a minute. Really.

But he swung his legs up onto the bed, leaning back, resting his head on his hand, propped up by his elbow. He leaned forward to kiss her shoulder, and she smiled in her sleep and snuggled against him.

He knew then that he wasn't going anywhere, and he put his arms around her.

Tomorrow Maggie would wake up and find him there. And if she still wanted him in the light of morning, there'd be no holding him back, regardless of the consequences.

CHAPTER SEVEN

MAGGIE AWOKE TO the sound of the window shade rubbing against the sill in the gentle ocean breeze.

The room was dim, but bright sunlight seeped in around the edges of the shade. She could tell from the brightness that it was late morning, possibly even past noon.

She stretched and her leg bumped something very solid and memories from the night before came roaring back to her.

It was indeed Matt, lying beside her, fast asleep. His long hair was tangled around his face. He was on his side, one arm tucked under his head, his legs kicked free from the sheet. He was wearing a pair of shorts—what a relief. Maggie was hyperaware of her own lack of clothing.

She'd tried to seduce him last night, but he'd refused.

Her face heated. She'd thrown herself at him, but he'd made it clear he didn't want to be anything more than friends.

So what was he doing in bed with her?

The phone rang, suddenly, shrilly, and Matt stirred. His eyes opened and focused on her for one brief moment before he turned and picked it up from the bedside table. "Hello?" His voice was husky from sleep. He sat up, pushing his hair out of his face, swearing softly. He listened for a moment longer, than handed the phone to Maggie. "It's your brother."

"Stevie?" she said, clutching the sheet to her. Her own voice was rusty sounding, and, God, her head was throbbing.

"Yo, Mags," he said, wonder in his voice. "Are you guys still in *bed*?"

"Well, sort of," she told him. "But it's not what—"

"I'm very impressed. I'm also very glad I called. Mom and Dad are on their way over."

"Oh, God!" Her eyes met Matt's and from the look on his face, she knew he'd heard what Stevie had said.

"I'm going to shower," Matt told her. "I left some clothes for you in the bathroom."

"They're coming out to have a little chat, if you know what I mean," her brother said. "Hang tough. And don't let 'em get close enough to throw the straitjacket around you."

"Very funny," Maggie said. "Stevie, thanks for calling."

"Anytime. Good luck. And don't forget to practice safe sex."

She and Matt had had the safest kind of sex there was—none. But if he wanted to keep their relationship limited to friendship as he'd claimed last night, why was he sleeping in her bed?

Maggie hung up the phone and went into the bathroom. She drank directly from the sink faucet, trying to rehydrate and make her head feel a little less like it was about to explode.

She dressed quickly—her underwear was mostly dry, but everything else was still damp. She put on Matt's clothes—which made her look like a kid playing dress-up. And her hair...

Nothing like falling asleep with a wet head to create a noteworthy style. Her only chance at looking semi-normal was to put it into a ponytail.

She went in search of Matt, who surely had a vast collection of ponytail holders.

Following the sound of running water, she went up a huge curved staircase to the third and then the fourth floor.

The fourth story of this old house wasn't a full floor. There was a very small landing at the top of the stairs and a single door. Maggie knocked, but there was no answer. She tried the knob and the door swung open.

Another door was off to the immediate right. The bathroom—she could hear the sound of the shower. More stairs led up, and she climbed them.

This was Matt's room—Maggie knew it without a doubt.

It was the tower room, large and airy. Its octagonal walls were all windows. There were no curtains, only miniblinds, and they'd all been pulled up.

Sunlight streamed in from all angles, and the hardwood floor gleamed. The woodwork around the windows was white, as was the ceiling and all the furniture and the spread on Matt's double bed. There wasn't much color in the entire room. There didn't need to be. Nature provided all the color anyone could possibly want.

The view was breathtaking. The sky—and there was so much of it—was a brilliant blue. She could see the deep blue-green water if she looked in one direction. When she turned she could see the gentle hills that led into town, covered with the new green leaves of early summer. The white steeple of the Congregational Church peeked up over the treetops.

A wind chime of fragile white shells hung in front of an open window, and it moved in the breeze, creating a delicate and soothing cascade of music.

The bathroom door opened, and Matt came into the room. Maggie blushed—he was wearing only a white pair of briefs.

"Nice room, huh?" he said, unfazed at the sight of her, as he rubbed his hair with a towel. He made no attempt to cover himself, as if it were entirely normal for her to be there in his room while he was in his underwear.

"It's beautiful," she said. "I'm actually looking for a ponytail holder."

"In the bathroom drawer," he told her.

She went down the stairs. The bathroom air was still heavy with moisture, the mirror steamed up despite the fresh air from an open window. It was a modest little room, nothing like the bathroom with the hot tub, downstairs.

She fished through a drawer jammed with combs and razors.

"I think you should tell your parents that you're going to live here for a while," Matt told her, coming to stand in the doorway.

"I don't think that's a good idea." She used his brush to attempt to tame her hair. "And I don't think my parents will, either."

"I've got eight empty bedrooms," he pointed out. "They don't have to fear for your virtue."

And neither did she, obviously. Maggie put his brush back on the edge of the sink.

"Mags, we have to talk about what happened last night," he said as if he could read her mind.

"What's to say?" She pushed past him and headed down the stairs to the main part of the house. "Except I guess I should probably apologize. And thank you. I would have been *really* embarrassed this morning if we'd actually, you know…"

She would have been *beyond* embarrassed and well into mortified. If he'd made love to her, it would've been as a favor.

Matt followed her down the stairs.

She turned to face him. "You *are* a good friend," she said. "And you were right. Our friendship is too valuable to risk losing."

His expression was unreadable.

The doorbell rang.

"We should talk more about this later," he said. "Right now it's showtime."

He brushed past her as he went down the stairs, and Maggie had to cling to the thick oak banister, shocked at the way her body responded to even such casual contact. It was a symptom of Matthew Fever.

Could she really live in a house with him? Without embarrassing herself further? On the other hand, could she pass up the opportunity to be near him?

And she wanted to be near him—desperately. Maybe it would pass. Maybe this illness would leave as quickly as it had struck.

Her parents were dressed in their church clothes. They peered at Matt and Maggie through the screen.

"Mr. and Mrs. Stanton," Matt said graciously. "Please come in."

"Maggie, are you all right?" her father asked.

Her mother came and hugged her. "My poor baby. Get your things. We'll take you home."

"I don't want to go home," Maggie told her.

Her father glanced at Matt. "Honey, we want to talk to you, and it'll be much easier at home."

"Anyone thirsty?" Matt asked. "I'll go get some lemonade."

"No," Maggie said sharply. "I'm not thirsty and neither are my parents."

"Mags, I was trying to be polite—give you some privacy."

"We don't need privacy." She turned back to her parents. "I'm going to stay here for a while."

Her parents both started talking at once.

"Margaret, I understand how unhappy you must feel about Brock and Vanessa—"

"Vanessa's gone to Brock's," her father told her. "What's she's done is inexcusable. It's not fair that you should be the one to leave. And moving here seems rather sudden and—"

"Wait a minute," Maggie said. "Don't get the wrong idea. Matt has lots of room here, and he offered me a place to stay. We're friends, Dad. It's like me moving in with Angie."

Her father glanced at Matt again, this time sizing him up. "You don't really expect us to believe that, do you?" He turned to Matt. "Maybe you should get that lemonade, son."

But Matt, thank God, knew that she desperately didn't want to be alone with her parents. "Sure," he said easily, but then turned to Maggie. "Want to give me a hand?"

She nearly bolted toward the kitchen.

"Go on into the living room," she heard Matt say, before he followed her and shut the kitchen door behind him.

"What's this with Vanessa and Brock?" he asked, as he crossed to the cabinets and took out four tall glasses.

"I got home last night just in time to see Brock kissing Vanessa good night," she told him, sitting at the kitchen table and putting her head in her hands. "She actually slept with him."

Matt swore. And then he put a couple of aspirin on the table in front of her, along with a glass of water.

"Thank you. Apparently Brock's been interested in Van all along," Maggie told him. "She and I had a little confrontation."

"What a jackass," he said. "So that's what last night was about, huh?"

Maggie nodded, unable to meet his eyes. "I can't believe I was too stupid to notice that I wasn't the one he really wanted."

Matt took a pitcher of lemonade out of the refrigerator and stirred it with a long spoon. "Maggie, the man wanted to marry you."

"Until Vanessa became available. Then it was no contest."

"But you didn't want to marry him—"

"That's not the point," she nearly shouted at him. "God, how many times back in high school did boys ask me out because they wanted to get closer to Van?"

"Too often," Matt said quietly. "It sucked. I remember how hurt you used to be."

"I thought that was over with," she admitted. "I thought people were finally interested in me, for who I

am, not for whose sister I am. But I was wrong. I feel…
insignificant and…worthless and *stupid*."

And when she'd come to him, he'd rejected her, too.
Matt's heart sank. Damn, he'd thought he was doing
the right thing last night, and it had been exactly, perfectly wrong.

"Maggie—" he started, but she cut him off.

"I'll get over it," she said. "I always did before. But
I've got to confess, I'm seriously considering moving
someplace where no one's ever heard of Vanessa Stanton."

"Maybe that's not a bad idea," Matt said. "I'll make
a deal with you. In three months, if I don't win my inheritance, we'll get one of those big camper things and
cruise the United States."

Maggie looked up at him with the most peculiar expression. "You mean a…recreational vehicle?"

"Yeah." He grinned at her. "It'll be a blast. What
do you say?" It was always good to have a plan B. Especially since he really didn't expect plan A to work.

She put her face in her hands. It was hard to tell
whether she was laughing or groaning.

"As for right now, I know what to tell your parents."
He handed her the pitcher of lemonade. "Carry this
out, will you?"

"What?" asked Maggie. "What are you going to tell
them?"

Matt picked up the tray with the glasses. "They're
not going to believe that there's nothing going on between us. We can deny it until the end of time, but
they're going to think you're living here with me. You
know, *with* me."

"But it's not true."

"I know that and you know that, but I'm telling you that denying it will only make them crazy. Just follow my lead," he said with a smile. "Think of this as an improvisational skit."

"I *hate* improv," Maggie muttered, following him out of the kitchen.

The Stantons looked up as Maggie and Matt came into the living room. They were sitting stiffly on those chairs his father had bought—the uncomfortable ones with wooden legs that were curved into bird's claws. Matt put the tray down on top of the coffee table.

"Just set the lemonade over here, then come sit next to me, babe," he said to Maggie.

Babe? She didn't say it, but the look she was giving him nearly made him laugh out loud.

He poured the lemonade, handed glasses to Mr. and Mrs. Stanton and then patted the couch next to him.

Slowly, she approached. Slowly, she sat down. And he draped an arm around her shoulders. "Mags and I discussed it in the kitchen," he told her parents, "and we decided that you should know the truth."

Mr. Stanton nodded. "That would be appreciated."

"Last night I asked Maggie to marry me," Matt told them. He could feel disbelief radiating out of Maggie, and it was all he could do not to laugh.

"What?" said Mrs. Stanton.

"What?" said Mr. Stanton.

"Matt!" said Maggie.

He shut her up with a quick kiss. "It's no secret that I've been crazy about her for years," he told them, then looked at Maggie. "Right, babe?"

The Stantons—all three of them—wore identical

looks of shock. Matt knew not to kiss Maggie again. If he did, they'd all fall out of their chairs.

Mrs. Stanton looked at Maggie. "But…"

"She said yes," Matt said, squeezing her shoulder.

"I said no," she countered, elbowing him in the ribs.

"Obviously, we're still working it out," he said quickly, putting his hand on her knee and sliding it up her smooth, bare thigh. His shorts looked good on her. "You can understand her hesitation. She's not sure if this is the real thing or if she's just on the rebound."

"I see." Mr. Stanton was staring at Matt's hand, still moving north on Maggie's thigh.

Out of desperation, Maggie grabbed Matt's hand and held it tightly. But that was, of course, exactly what he'd wanted her to do, since it looked as if she'd taken his hand intentionally, instead of in self-defense.

"We've decided the best thing to do is to live together, see how it goes," Matt said.

Her parents, of course, were appalled.

"You must know that we don't approve."

"I realize that, sir," Matt said solemnly. "But I want Maggie and I'm afraid if she goes back home with you, she'll never make up her mind."

Hey. Maggie shot him a look, but he refused to look at her. The muscle in the side of his jaw was jumping, though. Matt was clenching his teeth to keep from laughing. He actually thought this was funny! She squeezed his fingers, wishing she actually had nails to dig into him.

Her father shook his head. "Well, decision making's never been her strong suit," he said ruefully.

They were talking about her as if she were a horse being sold or a child or a…a…houseplant.

"I can make up my mind quite easily," she said hotly. "In fact, there's absolutely no decision here. This is ridiculous and…"

And she stopped, suddenly realizing that if she said no, she'd end up going back home with her parents.

They were all watching her, her parents with anticipation, Matt with one eyebrow lazily lifted, his expression carefully bland. But his eyes were sharp and he was watching her as if he were trying to read her mind.

What would he do if she said yes? Wouldn't *that* scare him to death? She smiled, imagining his frantic backpedaling as he tried to keep her mother from pulling out her Polaroid camera to snap an engagement photo to send to the society page of the *Shore Line Times*.

Matt watched Maggie smile and realized that she was actually considering saying yes. The shock value would be tremendous—it would blow her parents right out of the water. *Come on, Mags, say it.*

Except, God, he'd have to tell her the truth about where he'd been, what he'd been doing these past three years. If they were going to get married, he'd *have* to tell her all that, and more— Whoa, Stone, slow it down. This was fiction. This was acting. This was not real life.

Still, he leaned toward her. "Say it," he whispered. She stared at him.

"Say it," he repeated. "Come on, Maggie. Marry me." He slid off the couch onto his knees on the floor in front of her and brought her hand to his lips as the audience— her parents—watched in undisguised shock. "Please?"

Maggie couldn't believe him. *Oh, overacting!* she wanted to shout. God, she *hated* improv because she was never really sure how the other actors wanted her to respond. Now, did Matt really want her to say yes, or did he want her to say no? Or was he too caught up in the drama of the scene even to think rationally?

Didn't it occur to him what would happen if she actually said yes?

She looked down at Matt, still waiting on bended knee like some kind of fantasy husband-to-be. Damn him for making her wish this wasn't just a game. She almost smacked him.

"This is silly," she said. "Matt, get up off the floor. We have to tell them the real truth."

Whatever he was expecting her to say, it wasn't that. Matt covered a laugh with a cough. "The real truth." He pulled himself back onto the couch. "Oh, you mean the *real* truth."

She looked at him expectantly, innocently, waiting for him to take the lead. Which of course he couldn't take since he had no idea what she had in mind.

She threw him a bone. "The internet thing," she said, "www.VegasWedding.com?"

He almost completely lost it, and he covered by kissing her. In front of her parents.

"God, I love you," he said, with so much emotion in his voice she almost believed him, too.

Her father cleared his throat. "What internet thing?"

"You don't have to go to Las Vegas anymore for a quickie wedding," Matt explained to her parents, taking her cue and running with it. Were they actually going to believe this? "You just go online and visit the website, and you can actually get married in a virtual ceremony." He kissed Maggie's hand. "We did that last night."

"Is it legal?" her mother asked.

"Absolutely," Matt said. "They send the marriage

certificate in the mail. It takes a couple weeks, though, because they, you know, laminate it first."

Her father looked as if he was going to protest, and Maggie cut him off. "Dad, I'm twenty-nine years old."

He nodded. "You are. I think your living here is a mistake, and I think rushing into marriage with someone you haven't seen in ten years is also a mistake. We would like it if you came home. That's what we came here to say. That, and we love you." He looked at Matt. "And if you hurt her, I'll make you wish you were never born."

He stood up, held out his hand for Matt to shake then gave Maggie a hug. "This is the biggest barrel of crap I've ever heard," he whispered to her. "But your mother believes you. You just decide whether or not you're going to marry this guy, and you do it fast, you hear me?"

Maggie nodded, and he kissed her cheek. Her mother hugged her, too, and then they were out the door.

Matt put his arm around her as they watched her parents drive away. "How about another kiss for show?" he asked, nuzzling her neck.

She elbowed him hard in the ribs. "You had your chance last night, babe," she said. "Matt, how could you tell my parents that we were going to live together? Didn't it occur to you that my mother might have a heart attack right there on the living room rug?"

"And I'm telling you they weren't going to believe that we could live here in platonic harmony," Matt said, rubbing his side. "I can't believe you came up with www.VegasWedding.com. It was beautiful—I wish I'd thought of that. You know, this was the best improv I've been in in a long time. Did you see their faces?"

Maggie glared at him. "That was no improv, Matt, that was my *life*. Now my mother thinks we're *married!*"

"But it worked," he pointed out. "You didn't get pressured to go back home."

"She's going to want a look at our laminated wedding certificate," she said. "Jeez! Laminated. Very classy, Matt!"

"I was thinking on my feet," he said as she pushed past him into the house. "Give me a break!"

She turned back to him. "Give me the keys to your car."

He went into the kitchen and came back with the keys to the Maserati. "Where are you going?" he asked as he handed them over. "Can I come along? After all, it *is* our honeymoon."

"Shopping," she said. "No. And stuff it."

CHAPTER EIGHT

THE SUN WAS sinking in the sky by the time Maggie returned from the mall.

Matt was out on the front porch swing. He watched as she unloaded one huge shopping bag after another from the car.

"Honey, I'm home," she singsonged.

"Well, if it isn't the little wife," he said, coming to help her. "Thank God you've got your sense of humor back."

"Nothing like a little shopping to ease the soul."

"A little?" His arms were piled high with packages. "You're going to be paying off your credit cards until you're eighty years old."

"*Your* credit cards," she said smoothly. "We're married now, remember?"

"Oh, good, I'll keep that in mind later, when it's time to go to bed," Matt said in his best Groucho Marx imitation.

"I was kidding," Maggie said darkly.

Matt wasn't.

"I paid cash for this stuff," Maggie told him. "I worked at A&B for three years. Remember me? I used to live at home. I saved all my money all that time. I can afford to splurge. I wanted to splurge. So I bought myself clothes that I like." She hadn't bought one single corporate clone suit.

Matt pulled a sundress out of one of the bags. "Put this on," he said, draping it over her shoulder. "I'm taking you out to dinner. We're celebrating."

She shot him a look. "Celebrating what? And if you say 'our recent marriage,' I'm going to smack you."

"How about celebrating our getting the leads in the summer musical?"

"No kidding?" Maggie's face completely lit up.

"Nope." He smiled back at her. "Dan Fowler called while you were out. You got Lucy. And I'm 'Cody Brown, at your service.' First rehearsal's tomorrow night."

"This is great!" Maggie did a victory dance around the entry hall. "I'm so jazzed—I really, *really* wanted this part."

Matt grinned, watching her. But then she stopped and stared at him accusingly. "Why didn't you tell me right when I got home?" she asked.

"I did. I mean, I am. I mean, this *is* right when you got home. So you want to go out and celebrate?" Dinner—and then maybe another, less public celebration…

"Definitely." She beamed at him.

"Get dressed," he ordered her. "I'll meet you on the porch in twenty minutes."

MAGGIE PUSHED OPEN the screen door and stepped out onto the porch. The last traces of the sunset were facing from the sky. Matt had lit a citronella candle and was sitting back in one of the rocking chairs, his cowboy boots up on the rail.

"You look great," he said simply, getting to his feet.

"You do, too." Maggie laughed. "I thought you only wore T-shirts and jeans."

He had on a pair of brown pants and a soft, white poet's shirt with full, billowy sleeves. With his hair down, he looked like a time traveler from the past.

"This is about as dressed up as I get," he said. "I mean, aside from a tux."

It was plenty. Matthew Stone in a tux would create riots. Women would faint in the street.

In fact, more than one female head turned as they walked into the little harborside restaurant that was only a few miles from Matt's house.

Maggie was much too aware of his fingers on her back as the hostess brought them to a table overlooking the water. *He's just a friend. He's just a friend. He's just a friend.* Maybe if she chanted it silently, she wouldn't do anything stupid.

Dinner was lovely, and Matt carefully kept the conversation on safe topics—movies they'd seen, books they'd read, and since they had ten years of catching up to do, they never ran out of things to say.

As they were finishing dessert, the waitress brought over a florist's box and handed it to Maggie with a smile—and an appreciative glance at Matt.

Maggie gave him a quizzical look, but he just smiled.

She untied the ribbon and lifted the lid.

A dozen roses—deep red and gorgeous. "They're beautiful."

"Only eleven," he said quietly. "You make it a dozen."

There was a card among the flowers, and she opened the tiny envelope.

Make Love To Me Tonight was printed in plain block letters on the card.

She looked up at Matt. His face looked mysterious in the candlelight. Shadows accentuated his cheekbones, giving him an exotic look. His eyes glittered slightly, looking more golden than usual in the dim light.

Maggie felt like crying, because she knew exactly why he was doing this.

But she must have hidden what she was feeling, because he reached across the table and took her hand, raising it to his lips and kissing her softly on the palm.

It was the perfect thing for him to do. He was perfect. Everything was perfect. Except none of this was real. He was only doing this out of pity.

"Matt," she started, but he shook his head.

"Don't say anything now," he said. "Let's take a walk."

He tossed a small wad of bills onto the table and held out his hand for her. She let him lead her out of the restaurant and onto the sidewalk that led to the marina.

The sky was clear and the moon was up.

Maggie shivered in the cool air, and Matt moved to put his arm around her shoulders, but she sidestepped him.

He caught her arm. "I made a mistake last night," he said, breaking their silence.

"Matt, I know—"

"Wait. Just hear me out, okay?"

She nodded, moving over to the railed fence that lined the edge of the seawall. She couldn't meet his eyes, instead looked at the moonlight reflecting off the surface of the water.

"I was trying to be noble," he told her. "I thought I

was protecting you. But I was wrong, and I want to re-wind and take it from the hot tub, okay?"

She closed her eyes.

"Come on, Maggie, look at me."

Slowly, she turned.

"I want to make love to you." He pulled her toward him. She didn't know how he did it, but he actually managed to make his eyes hot with desire.

"Matt—"

"I've wanted to make love to you since we were in high school," he said as he pulled her close, as he kissed her neck, her throat, her jaw.

"Please stop," she said weakly. If he kissed her on the lips, she wasn't sure if *she'd* be able to stop.

And then he did. His lips found hers, and he kissed her slowly, languidly, his tongue exploring her mouth and...

Maggie smacked him on the butt with the cardboard flower box. He let go of her, staring as if she were in-sane.

Maybe she was. Anyone who would willingly stop a man from kissing her like that had to be more than a touch crazy.

"I know what you're doing." She backed away so that there was distance between them. "I thought you'd try something like this. When you found out today about Vanessa and Brock... You feel sorry for me and you're trying to make me feel better."

He laughed. "Yeah, I don't think so—"

"It's not working," she told him. "You can turn off the act."

"This isn't an act." He reached for her, but she brandished the flower box again. He laughed. "Maggie, I swear—"

"And I've kissed you often enough onstage to know that you can play the part of the passionate lover with your eyes closed and both hands tied behind your back."

"Oh, come *on*—"

"Please, Matt," Maggie begged. "I'm exhausted. I don't want to fight with you right now. Don't make this worse than it already is."

He shook his head and started to speak but stopped himself. Without another word, he led her back to his car.

They drove home in silence, but as he pulled into the garage, he looked at her. "It's not an act."

"Good night," she told him, and nearly ran into the house, into the room she'd claimed as her bedroom.

She locked the door behind her. But she wasn't sure if she was locking him out—or herself in.

CHAPTER NINE

MATT'S EYES OPENED as the sun streamed into his tower bedroom.

He glanced at his clock: 6:19 a.m. Four hours of sleep. Not bad. Not great, but not bad, considering...

Maggie was only one floor beneath him, but after last night, she might as well be a million miles away.

He'd spent most of the night tossing and turning, trying to ignore how much he wanted her, trying to figure out how he'd be able to return to his status of *friend* after tasting her lips. But he'd done it before. He'd fallen desperately in love with her more than ten years ago and he'd survived.

Or had he?

Matt had spent the night alternately praying that it would simply be a matter of time before she came to him and praying that he would have the strength to keep his distance from her.

It was probably a good thing that she'd told him no last night.

It was ten days and counting until he was scheduled to go back to the hospital for a checkup. He'd all but decided not to go, thinking it was little more than a visit to a high-tech fortune-teller. Whether he was going to live for one year, ten years or a hundred years certainly mattered to him, but knowing wouldn't change the way he lived his life.

Except now everything had turned upside down, and now he desperately wanted to know.

He pulled himself out of bed.

He had work to do.

MAGGIE GRABBED AN apple from the refrigerator, still humming the melody from the summer musical's closing number.

The first rehearsal—a read through of the script—had gone well, except for the fact that she'd counted seven different times she was going to have to kiss Matt onstage. Each kiss would have to be set up, blocked and rehearsed. Over and over again. She wasn't sure whether to laugh or cry.

As she took a bite of the apple, she opened up the connecting door to the office and turned on the lights.

"Whoa," Matt said. "What are you doing?"

"I want to look over those numbers some more," she said.

She held her apple in her teeth as she used both hands to clear a stack of file folders from one of the chairs. The conference table itself was stacked high with files and bound reports and computer printouts. They had worked hard all day, right up to the rehearsal.

"It's nearly midnight." Matt cleared off another chair so he could sit, too. "This will still be here tomorrow."

"These numbers are bad," Maggie said. "I've looked at the quarterly reports for the past four years, and the gross profits have remained pretty darn constant, even after your dad died. There's not a lot of room for increased profits here, Matt."

"So what do we do?"

She stretched her arms over her head. "I guess we have to start thinking creatively."

"Oh, good."

"Good?" She looked at him in disbelief.

He grinned. "Quarterly reports and gross profits make my head spin. But creative thinking is something I can handle."

It was true. Even back in school, Matt had never had the patience for math. He hadn't been very good at following rules. But in terms of creativity, he was a pro. Put him in an empty room with a canvas and paints and you'd get a masterpiece. Most likely the canvas would remain blank and the masterpiece would be painted on the wall, but it would be truly magnificent.

"Tomorrow we should go down and take a look at the plant," she said. "Maybe that will trigger your creative process."

"Okay," he said easily, idly picking up a thick file folder and leafing through it. "God, can you believe a temporary secretary costs more than forty dollars an hour from some of these agencies? *That's* not within our budget, is it?"

Maggie searched through the piles of reports for the current year's annual budget. "Actually, it is. But we can cut costs. I mean, jeez, we could hire Stevie to be our slave for fifteen dollars an hour."

Matt smiled. "That's a great idea. Let's hire Steve."

She looked at him in exasperation. "I was kidding."

"Can he type?"

"Probably. He's always online."

"I'll call him tomorrow."

"Matt, sometimes I think you're totally nuts." She

rubbed the back of her neck, twisting her head to stretch the muscles. She'd have to make time tomorrow to get in a workout at the club.

With a start, she felt Matt's hands touching her shoulders. She stood up quickly, breaking free. "Don't," she told him.

"Mags, lighten up. I was trying to help you relax."

"Well, just don't, okay?"

He didn't say anything then. He stood there, looking at her, his eyes guarded, his face nearly expressionless.

"I'm sorry," she said. "I don't know what's wrong with me. I know it must have confused you when I… did what I did the other night. I was upset and angry and I wasn't thinking clearly. Sometimes I wonder if I'm still not thinking clearly. But I do know that you were right. Our friendship is far too valuable to throw away for a little sex."

She risked a glance at him, and found he'd turned to stare out the window. Part of the lawn was lit by spotlights aimed at the house, and the semicircles of bright green grass stood out as islands in the surrounding sea of darkness.

"I'm still feeling really vulnerable," she said softly. "Every time you touch me, I question your motivation. And damn it, I don't want your pity, Matt."

He just shook his head. "You know, if I'm feeling sorry for anyone here, it's myself."

She rolled her eyes. "I need you to give me some space so we can get things back to normal." Sooner or later she'd start feeling human again. Sooner or later she'd be able to accept a back rub from him without wanting his hands to caress her entire body.

"All right." He glanced at her and forced a smile. "I'm going up to bed. I'll see you in the morning."

He made a wide circuit around Maggie, careful not to get too close, and went out of the office without looking back.

Wait, she wanted to say, but she kept her mouth tightly shut.

"You did *what?*" Angie's voice sounded remarkably clear over the international connection.

Maggie smiled, imagining the look on her friend's face. "I moved out. It was right after I had a fight with Van, who moved back home because she and Mitch are getting a divorce, and now she wants to go out with Brock, so he dumped me, but that's okay because he was a jerk, and this all happened on the same day I quit my job because I'm working full-time for Matthew now."

Angie's stunned silence was extremely impressive because she was Angie and rarely stunned or silent.

"So what else is new?" she finally asked.

"I got the lead in the summer musical," Maggie said.

"I was kidding," Angie exploded. "Damn, Mags, is that all?"

"That about covers it."

She sat in her nightgown, with her feet up on the late Mr. Stone's big desk, talking on his private line. She'd gotten up very early to give Angie a call. It was already lunchtime in London, and she knew her friend was rarely home in the afternoon.

"Let me get this straight. You're working for Matthew?"

"Yep."

"He's paying you?"

"What, do you think I'd do it for free?"

"You? Yes."

Maggie laughed. "Yeah, you're probably right."

"How is he?" Angie asked.

"He's fine," Maggie told her friend. "He's great, actually. He's changed an awful lot, Ange."

She snorted. "Don't count on it. With Matt, you never know what's reality and what's just an elaborate song and dance. My guess is right now he's taken on the role of the prodigal son. He's probably imitating his dear departed father, dressing like a businessman and saying things like, 'Let's do lunch.'"

"No," Maggie said. "He's not. I don't know exactly what happened, but he went through some very tough times over the past few years. He's different now. You'd probably have trouble recognizing him."

"Now *that* I refuse to believe," Angie said. "Hey, tell me what happened with that jungle guy from the club. You meet him yet?"

"Um," Maggie said cautiously. "Yes, I did."

"And…?"

"And…I don't know." She couldn't tell Angie that her fantasy man and Matt were one and the same. She just couldn't.

"Is he human?"

"Extremely human," Maggie said. "Totally, absolutely human. Incredibly human."

"Uh-oh." Angie laughed. "You've got it bad, haven't you?"

"It's terrible," Maggie admitted, pulling her feet off the desk. "I may never recover."

"That's the way I felt when I first met Fred. Obviously you don't have a choice. You've got to marry the guy."

Maggie closed her eyes. "I don't think so. Angie, look, I've got to go. I've got to go down to the courthouse this morning, and there's a ton and a half of paper sitting in the office waiting to be read. I'll call you again soon, okay?"

"Mags, where are you staying?" Angie said. "You told me you moved out, but you didn't say where you're living now."

"I'm staying with a friend," Maggie told her, feeling doubly dishonest. "I've got to run. See you, okay? 'Bye!"

She hung up the phone and put her head down on the desk.

She should have told Angie the whole truth, but she couldn't deal with the thirty-minute lecture on the evil of Matthew Stone that would have been sure to follow.

Maybe she wouldn't ever have to tell Angie. Maybe her feelings for Matt would conveniently vanish. But her own words came back to her. *I may never recover.*

She had to smile, thinking of Angie's solution. Marry the guy. Ange would be horrified to know that she'd even inadvertently advised her best friend to aim for marriage with Matthew Stone.

Angie would be even more horrified to find out that Mrs. Stanton thought Maggie and Matt were already married.

Married. To Matt.

She'd have a better chance of winning the lottery. Matt simply wasn't the marrying kind.

He *was* however, the hot sex in the hot tub kind.

She had to stop thinking about that.

The clock on the wall said six forty-five. She was too wired to go back to sleep. She might as well get to work.

On her way through the kitchen, she put on the teakettle and searched the cabinets for the tin of tea bags. Hoping against hope, she opened the refrigerator, looking for a lemon.

There were five in the lower drawer.

That was odd. Fresh fruit and vegetables filled the refrigerator. She'd been here for two days now and she hadn't noticed anyone delivering groceries. And Lord knows she hadn't had time to pick anything up. Yet the refrigerator was packed with food—

"Hey, you're up early." Matt came into the kitchen. His skin was slick with perspiration and his shorts and T-shirt were soaked through. He was still breathing hard, as if he'd just finished some strenuous exercise.

"So are you," she managed to say.

Matt wiped a bead of sweat that trickled down his face as he looked at her. She was backlit by the light from the refrigerator, and her nightgown had become diaphanous. Her hair was still messy from sleep, and without makeup, her face looked fresh and young. But her body was all woman.

She had no idea of the show she was putting on for him. And wasn't that a shame. At first glance, he'd dared to hope that she was purposely trying to drive him crazy, that maybe she wanted him to pick her up and carry her into the nearest bedroom and make love to her.

God knows that was what he wanted to do.

"I didn't expect you to be up so early," she said, clutching a lemon to her chest.

Yeah, no kidding. She didn't move, so he reached past her into the open fridge for the orange juice. He drank directly from the plastic container. "I was out running," he told her. "I try to do five miles a day, but sometimes I miss."

"You've *already* run five miles this morning?" The teakettle began to howl, and she closed the refrigerator door—too bad—and carried her lemon to the stove. She took the kettle off the burner, then turned to look at Matt skeptically. "Sometimes I think aliens have invaded your body. The Matt I know had to be dragged out of bed every morning to make it to school on time. I remember when noon on a Saturday was unbearably early for you."

"It's not a Saturday," Matt pointed out, finishing off the juice.

Maggie shook her head as she filled her mug with steaming water. "What time *did* you get up?"

"Four-thirty," Matt told her. "Usually I don't wake up till six o'clock, but for some reason I've been having more trouble than usual sleeping."

And guess what—or rather who—that reason is?

She didn't meet his eyes, because she knew.

"So far this morning," he told her, "I've memorized the first ten pages of my dialogue for the show and I've gone grocery shopping."

"Grocery shopping this early?"

"The Stop and Shop is open twenty-four hours." He shrugged. "Sometimes if I can't sleep, I'll go over at 3:00 a.m." He smiled. "No crowds, you know."

"If you write out a list, I'll get the groceries next time we need them," Maggie volunteered.

But Matt shook his head. "No, that's okay. I like to do it."

She took her mug of tea and headed for the door. "Aliens have *definitely* invaded your body."

THE YANKEE POTATO Chip factory was a huge brick building on the other side of town, surrounded by a parking area that was almost entirely filled with the employees' cars.

Maggie flipped through her file as Matt pulled up in front of a parking spot marked President near the main door.

"I don't know if I can do this," he said.

"Of course you can." She glanced up from the papers. "You own this company. You're perfectly within your rights to inspect—"

"No, I mean, I don't know if I can park here."

Maggie looked at the parking spot, then at Matt.

"I mean, that word *president*," he said. "It implies a certain dignity, a certain knowledge. Maybe I should have them paint over it with Ignorant Son."

Maggie laughed. "I can think of better ways to use the money."

"So can I."

Inside the plant, the manager gave them a complete tour, explaining as they went what he saw as the strengths and weaknesses of the operation. Matt grasped each issue quickly, asking probing and intelligent questions. He stopped frequently as they walked, speaking to the employees, listening intently as they talked. By the time they were through, five hours later, Maggie was exhausted.

And Matt was silent in the car on the way home. It wasn't until an hour later that he turned from staring out the office window to say, "Have you come across blueprints and specs for the construction of the plant?"

"I just saw them." Maggie dug through the piles of papers and files, and found the thick three-ringed binder. She hefted the blueprints onto the table. "What do we need these for?"

"Hmm," Matt said. He punched the speaker phone and dialed. "Hey, Steve, it's Matthew Stone."

Steve? As in Stevie? As in her brother? She hadn't thought Matt was serious about...

"Yo, Matthew Stone." It was indeed Stevie. "'Sup, my man?"

"How are you at internet research?"

"I think I once surfed around looking for historical information on the Ramones," Stevie said. "Why?"

Maggie rolled her eyes. "He got 1520 on his SATs."

"Hush there, Mags," Stevie said. "If you say that too loudly, you'll ruin my rep. Chicks don't dig the brainiacs."

"You want to bet?" Maggie countered.

"Steve, you want to earn twenty bucks an hour?" Matt asked.

"Tell me who to kill," her brother said. "I'll ask no questions."

"Consider yourself hired," Matt said.

"When do I start?"

"Now. I need you to get me all the information you can find about... Got a pencil?"

"No," Stevie said, "but for twenty bucks an hour, I'll open a vein and write with my own blood."

"Get a pencil," Matt said. He looked up at Maggie and smiled. "I think I can improve this company."

"OKAY, BOYS AND girls." Dan Fowler raised his voice and the actors immediately fell silent. "Break's over. We've got mucho work to do tonight, so don't turn off your brains yet. Let's walk through the blocking for the opening number. Places onstage!"

The cast scrambled for their spots.

Maggie moved center stage. So far Dan's storm-trooper attitude was working. He was among the most efficient directors she'd ever worked with.

"Okay," Dan called. "Lucy is center. Spot comes up on her. The stage is dark and misty. Creepy-crawly things start moving behind her...."

As he spoke, the cast walked through their onstage movements.

"Lucy says, 'Stop,' and the creepy things scramble away. Lights come up. Out from the wings come my men in top hats and tails. They pick her up and carry her around...."

Maggie looked nervously at the eight men who would be hoisting her onto their shoulders in this part of the opening number. They didn't lift her now, since it was only a walk-through, but they were going to spend a great deal of time rehearsing this particular move to make it look effortless.

"On comes the full chorus, including all four secondary leads. We talk, talk, talk, sing, sing, sing. The stage is packed but the crowd parts as Cody enters upstage center."

This was as far as they'd got before the break.

"Okay, Cody," Dan ordered Matt. "You come directly downstage to Lucy. You sing your bit of the song and then you talk. Lucy, don't back away, I want you directly center stage for the kiss that's coming."

Maggie nodded, glancing up at Matt, who was making notes on his script.

"This kiss has to be very 1940s Hollywood," Dan continued. "Very big-screen passionate. The music underneath swells, so you've got to time it just right. I think you've got eight bars of music to fill. Rhonda, dear, play it for them, would you?"

The accompanist played as Maggie and Matt listened. God, eight bars was an awfully long time.

"Try it with the music," Dan ordered. "Whenever you're ready."

Matt tossed down his script and positioned himself next to Maggie. "Your last line is what? *So go away,*" he remembered. "You should turn your back to me, as if you're going to walk away, stage left. I'm going to grab you by the arm and swing you back around toward me, okay?"

Maggie nodded, suddenly frightfully nervous.

"Give us about four measures before the kiss," Matt called to Rhonda, who began to play.

Maggie listened for the musical cue, then turned away from Matt. He pulled her hard toward him, and she slammed into his chest. As Matt's lips met hers, she couldn't keep from giggling.

"Wrong!" Dan's nasal voice interrupted. "Stanton, you're as stiff as a board. Get into character! Think about your motivation! This is one of Lucy's fantasies, and she's as hot as hell for Cody, even though she won't admit it. Come on, people, what happened to that chemistry I saw at your audition? I want steam! I want pheromones! Try it again."

Once again the music started. Matt pulled her toward him, more gently this time, but she knew she was still too tense.

"I'm sorry," she said, pulling away before he kissed her.

"Can we take a few minutes?" Matt called to Dan.

"Not right now," Dan's bored voice intoned. "Work on it at home. We've got to move on."

"I COULDN'T GET into character tonight," Maggie said in the car on the way home from rehearsal. "What's wrong with me?"

Matt glanced at her. Her expression in the dim reflection from the dashboard light was woeful. She was stuck inside of her own head, that was what was wrong.

He spun the steering wheel hard to the right, pulling into a side street. Maneuvering the car to the side of the road, he cut the engines and the lights, and they were plunged into total darkness.

"Matt—"

He grabbed her and kissed her.

"There," he said as he let her go. God, he didn't want to let her go. But that was probably why she was freaking out about kissing him in the first place. "*That's* how long those eight bars of music are. That wasn't so terrible, was it?"

"No," she said faintly.

"Good," he said as matter-of-factly as he could manage. He started the car and did a one-eighty to get them back to the main road, glad that the car was too dark for her to see his face, because his eyes surely would have betrayed him.

CHAPTER TEN

MAGGIE READ ANOTHER selection from the endless pile of business reports as she ate a bowl of oatmeal. Matt sat across from her with a giant bowl of fruit.

She glanced up at him and he smiled.

"Don't you ever eat anything but fruit for breakfast?" she asked.

Matt laughed. "Wow, we wouldn't do too well on the *Newlywed Game,* would we? No. The only thing I eat before noon is fruit."

"Why?"

"Because it makes me feel healthier."

Maggie gazed across the table at him, wishing he'd tell her why he'd been in the hospital three years ago. But whenever she brought the topic of conversation even vaguely in that direction, he changed the subject. Like right now.

"Speaking of newlyweds, your mother left a message on the answering machine. She wants us to come for Sunday dinner sometime next month. Talk about advance notice—I guess she figures this way we can't make up an excuse."

Maggie sighed.

"Also, we've got a rehearsal tonight," he added.

She nodded. Great.

"We're doing a run-through of the first four scenes," he reminded her.

She nodded again, focusing her attention on her oatmeal.

He didn't get the message. "You know that means we've got to go in there and do that kiss from the opening scene."

The kiss. Oh, God.

"We should practice it," Matt said. "Don't you think?"

Maggie took a deep breath. "Yeah. We should. How about after lunch?"

"How about now?"

She looked at him, looked at the clock. Stevie was due to arrive in about fifteen minutes. "Okay." Somehow that made her feel safe.

Safer.

She stood up and headed toward the stairs.

Matt followed. "Where are you going?"

"To brush my teeth."

He caught her arm, pulled her in to him and kissed her. His mouth tasted sweet, like watermelon and bananas with a hint of peaches thrown in.

"Yum," he said. "Brown sugar is definitely better than mint at this time of day."

Maggie's insides were doing flip-flops. He hadn't touched her since that kiss in his car after last week's disastrous rehearsal. She'd thought she was getting over him—or at least *used* to him. But if all it took was one little nothing kiss to make her knees feel weak, she was in big trouble.

"Here's what I'm going to do," Matt told her. He maneuvered her around as he spoke, going through it in slow motion, putting her into the right position for the best angle for the kiss. She tried to pay attention, but couldn't. "Lucy is really nuts about this guy, despite everything she says. We should show that right from the start."

As Maggie looked up into Matt's golden-greenish eyes, she realized that she understood Lucy's motivation perfectly. Because damn it, she wanted Matt, no matter how hard she tried to deny it. Maybe that was her problem. This role was hitting too close to home. But maybe if she kissed him not as Lucy, but as *Maggie*— Maggie kissing Matt. He'd never know the difference, and she'd bring a certain authenticity to the role.

"Ready?" Matt asked.

"Yeah." She smiled. She was ready.

She stepped away from him as per the stage directions, and he pulled her toward him. This time, her movement was fluid, and she seemed to flow into his arms. Her lips went up to meet his and she kissed him with all the fire in her soul. Unable to remember any of the blocking he'd just explained, she put her arms around his neck and pressed herself against him.

She heard him groan, and felt his hands move down her back to the curve of her derriere, as he kissed her harder, more deeply. His thigh pushed against her, and she opened herself to him, wrapping one of her legs around his. The sensation of her bare skin against his made her ignite, and she pulled him even closer.

And still she kissed him. The eight bars of background music could have played over and over and over again.

He slipped his hand up underneath her T-shirt and she shivered at the touch of his fingers against her skin.

But then his hand cupped her breast and her heart nearly stopped beating.

"Yo, dudes— Oops, looks like I've come at a bad time."

Maggie and Matt jumped apart to see Stevie backing out of the room.

"We were just rehearsing," Maggie said breathlessly, her cheeks heating.

Matt sat down at the kitchen table and put his face in his hands. When he glanced up at Stevie, his expression was black, with only a hint of amusement in his eyes to offset it.

"Oh, gee, I just remembered, uh," Stevie said, "I've got to run some errands—"

"Oh, knock it off." Maggie was annoyed. "It wasn't what it looked like." She turned to Matt, blushing again as she remembered the feel of his hand on her breast, but determined to be professional. "I think we sort of overshot the mark, but at least I wasn't stiff."

Matt fought the urge to laugh at her word choice. *She* may not have been stiff...

"Do you want to try it again?" she asked.

"No," Matt said. He couldn't. He couldn't even stand up right now. "Maybe later."

Stevie followed Maggie into the office, turning back to give Matt one last apologetic look. Matt made a face at him, shaking his head and rolling his eyes in frustration.

Stevie glanced in the direction Maggie had disappeared, then came back into the kitchen. "Maybe this is none of my business," he said quietly to Matt, "but she's in love with you."

"I wish."

"I'm telling you, it's true." Steve was serious. "I know her. She's... Just don't hurt her, okay?"

Matt was silent as he met the kid's gaze, uncertain how to respond. He couldn't decide himself which was worse torture—thinking she didn't love him or thinking maybe she did.

As usual, Maggie and Matt rolled into rehearsal several minutes early.

The assistant director, the stocky woman with the cat eyeglasses and the clipboard—her name was Dolores, but Dan Fowler called her Hey!—approached Matt immediately, holding out a plastic-wrapped cup with a screw-on lid.

Maggie's stomach took a downward plunge.

"Time for you-know-what," Dolores said, tossing the cup to him. "The rules are I've got to walk you into the little boys' room."

Matt was serene. He just laughed. But when he glanced at Maggie, she knew this bothered him more than he was letting on.

She watched him walk away, wondering how it would feel to be haunted by a bad reputation. It didn't seem fair that people didn't notice how much he'd changed.

"Stanton!" Maggie turned to see Dan Fowler waving to her from up on the stage. "Come here for a sec."

"What's up?"

He was sitting on one of the chairs that served as makeshift scenery, and he motioned for her to sit, too. When she did, he crossed his arms and looked at her.

And she panicked. He was having second thoughts about casting her. He didn't think she was going to be able to do those kisses, and he was figuring out the best way to break the news....

"How long have you been seeing Stone?" he finally asked.

She blinked. Stone. Matt. "I'm not... I mean, we're not dating or anything, if that's what you mean."

"You always show up with him. And leave with him."

What was this leading up to? Maggie didn't have a clue. "We're housemates," she told him.

"You live together."

"Yeah, but as friends," she clarified. "We went to high school together."

"And you're not involved with him?"

"No." Why was he asking this?

Dan smiled, his beard parting to expose white, even teeth. His eyes were warm, the dark brown flecked with gold. When he wasn't frowning, he was actually quite handsome.

"I was wondering if you'd have dinner with me tomorrow night," he said.

THEY RAN THROUGH the opening number, even daring to hoist Maggie onto the shoulders of the men's chorus. It was awkward and she giggled, but they were on their way.

Then the dreaded kiss approached. Matt gave her hand a reassuring squeeze as they began the sequence.

He pulled her to him, and instead of kissing her immediately, he gazed down into her eyes for several beats. When his lips finally met hers, Maggie melted. She forced herself to keep the embrace open, only putting her arms around his neck at the very end of the musical phrase.

When he pulled back, he didn't immediately move away. He looked into her eyes again and smiled.

"Perfect!" Dan shouted. "That was *exactly* what I wanted."

Maggie finished up the song on a cloud of relief and desire.

AL, THE CHOREOGRAPHER, was nearly as much of a slave driver as Dan Fowler. Sweat dripped off Maggie's face as they stopped for a break.

"One of these days," she swore as she threw herself onto the stage next to Matt, "I'm going to be in a show that rehearses in a theater that has air-conditioning."

The dance they were doing was a blend of athletic street dancing and graceful jazz, with several steps reminiscent of the old dirty-dancing craze thrown in. Most of the steps had no body contact—instead they had to maintain eye contact. Maggie found that almost more dizzying than when Matt actually touched her.

Almost.

She rolled onto her stomach and put her chin in her hand. "Matt? How well do you know Dan Fowler?"

He turned his head to look at her. "I don't know. Well enough. I know he's a good director—he gets the job done, and his end result is better than average. Why?"

She shrugged.

"Why?" Matt asked again, his eyes narrowing. "What aren't you telling me?"

God, he knew her too well. "Nothing," she said.

"*Tell* me."

She laughed. "No."

"Tell me." He rolled onto his side, head propped up

on one hand. She could tell from looking at him that he wasn't going to let this slide.

And okay. Maybe she could actually get a rise out of him. She glanced around to make sure no one else was in earshot and Matt leaned in closer as she said, "Dan asked me out."

He laughed. "You're kidding."

Was that jealousy in his eyes, or just amusement? "No," she said. "He asked me to have dinner with him."

"Dinner with Dan," Matt mused. "Do you think he takes the time to eat anything but fast food?"

No, it definitely wasn't jealousy. Was it possible he really didn't care if she had dinner with Dan…? "I'll let you know," she said, even though she'd turned down the director.

Matt froze. "You're *going?*"

Okay. *That* was a slightly better reaction.

"Actually—" she said, but he cut her off.

"I'm sorry," he said. "I didn't mean to… He's great. He's perfect for you, Mags. He's honest and solid and…"

"Oh," Maggie said.

"Break's over," Dan announced.

Matt gave her a smile as he pulled himself to his feet.

She'd been hoping for jealousy—not for Matt to give her and Dan his blessing.

CHAPTER ELEVEN

AT 1:00 A.M., Matt rose stiffly from his seat at the conference table.

He'd worked muscles in that dance rehearsal tonight that he'd forgotten he had.

The evening had been an emotional workout, too.

The more he thought about it, the more he was convinced that Dan Fowler was perfect for Maggie. The guy was honest and dependable and basically decent. Not too tactful, but that was mostly by choice, since being tactful took too much time.

Matt also knew that Dan had a strict personal policy of never, *ever* dating the women from his shows. His feelings for Maggie had to be pretty intense if he was willing to break his rules to ask her out. Of course that didn't surprise Matt at all. The surprise would have been if Dan *hadn't* fallen instantly in love with her.

If he had to handpick a guy for Maggie to become involved with, Dan would be at the top of his list. It couldn't have turned out better if Matt had planned it.

So here he sat, sick with jealousy, knowing without a doubt that no one, not even Dan Fowler, could love Maggie more than he did.

But he also knew that his love for her would do her absolutely no good if he wasn't around.

Matt stretched, knowing that he wasn't going to sleep

tonight. Instead of lying awake in bed, he might as well make himself as comfortable as possible. He went into his father's master bedroom—the room Maggie had fallen asleep in, that first night she spent here—and into the bath, where he uncovered the hot tub.

He tried to be quiet as he took the stairs up to his room. There was a paperback book up there he'd started reading several nights ago. He'd finish it long before dawn, but at least he'd fill a few hours.

He paused as he reached the landing on the third floor, looking at Maggie's closed door. Slowly, he moved toward her room, stopping outside, staring at the doorknob, wishing for the first time in years for a beer.

If he had a beer or two or four, he could use the alcohol as an excuse for reaching out and opening that door. Without the beer, the responsibility was all his.

Maggie sat up in bed, her heart racing. As she listened, Matt's footsteps faded back down the hallway and up the stairs to his bedroom.

With a sigh of frustration, she sank back in the bed. She couldn't take much more of this.

Then she heard him coming back down the stairs, and again, she held her breath. But he went past her door without stopping this time.

Don't think. Just do it.

But even as she threw back the covers and opened her door, she couldn't help but think.

If she went to him and threw herself at him again, they would probably make love.

Still, she went down the stairs, down the hall past the dining room, past the living room, to the master bedroom. The connecting bathroom door was ajar.

Quietly she went to the door and peeked in. Matt

crouched next to the tub, dipping his fingers in to test the temperature.

She closed her eyes and pushed the door open. "Hi," she said, and he jumped to his feet.

He didn't say a word. He simply looked at her.

Now that she was actually here, her confidence faded. She crossed her arms in front of her, suddenly aware that she was wearing only her nightgown. "I heard you going up and down the stairs," she said. "I know you can't sleep. I can't, either."

And still he didn't say a word, didn't move.

"Do you want to talk?" she asked.

Matt shook his head no. Jeez, she always knew just where to stand to be perfectly backlit. He could see her body through her gown, and he wanted her. Man, he wanted her. He had to get her out of here. This was just too difficult.

"I wanted to tell you that I'm not going out with Dan," she said, pushing her hair back behind her ear and sitting on the very edge of the wicker chair. "It would just be...too weird."

No, Matt knew he should say, *it's okay. Dan's a good man. You should go.* But he couldn't make himself say it.

Maggie rolled her eyes. "I started thinking, what if my mother calls when I'm out? If you answer the phone, what are you going to tell her? Maggie's out on a *date?* She thinks we're married."

"But we're not," Matt said tightly. He forced himself to turn away from her and instead stared sightlessly out the window.

"The truth is, I told you I was going to have dinner with him because I was hoping you'd be jealous."

Oh, God. It had worked. However, it had also worked to convince him that Maggie deserved someone more like Dan—and less like Matt.

"You should go back to bed," he said, his back to her, praying that she wouldn't say anything else. "Please? I really don't want to talk right now."

We don't have to talk, Maggie wanted to say, but the words stuck in her throat.

"Please," he said again. It was little more than a breath, an exhale, but it held all the emotion of a cry of pain. "Go."

And there she went. Running away. Too scared to speak out, to speak up.

Matt didn't turn around as she left the room.

MAGGIE LAY IN the darkness, looking up at the shadowy canopy that was draped above her bed, calling herself names.

Chicken. Coward. Scaredy-cat. Baby. Wimp. Only a wimp would have run away like that.

The digital numbers of her alarm clock switched from 1:59 to 2:00.

Maggie swore softly. Sleeplessness had never been a problem for her before. Of course, she'd never loved anyone the way she loved Matthew.

And she did love him.

So why was she lying up here all alone?

Because she didn't want to ruin their friendship? It was no longer a good excuse, because, face it, their friendship was already affected. She wasn't going to pretend to herself that she didn't feel anything for him, because damn it, she did. And she wasn't going to hang back anymore, careful to stay his buddy. She wouldn't be able to bear watching him find some other woman to spend time with.

So where did that leave her?

She knew that if she went to him and openly asked him to spend the night with her, he wouldn't refuse her.

But how would she feel in the morning?

That was a question that only the morning light could bring the answer to. The question facing her right now was, how did she feel tonight?

Maggie shivered, remembering the sensation of his lips on hers, of his body against hers. She wanted him, and she knew he wanted her. She'd seen the way he'd looked at her when she'd walked into the bathroom. She'd seen hunger in his eyes.

She stood up and crossed to the door. Taking a deep breath, she put her hand on the knob and turned it, swinging the door open.

And oh, dear Lord, Matt stood there, his hair down around his shoulders, his handsome face unsmiling. Even though the night had turned cool, he wore only his running shorts, and she could see the taut muscles in his chest rise and fall with each breath he took.

Gazing up into his beautiful eyes, Maggie knew that the desire she saw there mirrored that in her own eyes. She wondered if he could hear her heart pounding from where he stood.

She wasn't sure who moved first, but he reached for her as she fell into his arms.

Matt kissed her, desperately, ferociously. And she clung to him, her mouth demanding, her arms wound tightly around his neck as he pulled her closer to him. Her tongue was in his mouth, and his hands swept the length of her body, and he knew that he shouldn't be doing this, but he couldn't make himself stop.

Their legs intertwined and she rubbed herself against him. And still he couldn't stop himself from reaching down to lift her up so that her legs encircled him.

He pulled back then to look into her face.

She gazed back at him, her cheeks flushed from the heat they'd created, and he felt giddy. He buried his face in her neck, breathing in her scent. She smelled like Maggie—clean and sweet. How many times in his life had he stood close enough to inhale her fragrance, close enough to drive himself mad with wanting her?

She pulled his face up and kissed him.

But again he pulled back. "It's not too late to stop," he said, his voice sounding breathless to his own ears. He prayed that she wouldn't agree.

"Says who?" she countered, tightening the grip of her legs around him, then laughing at the expression on his face.

Another kiss propelled them across the room and they tumbled together onto Maggie's bed, Matt kissing her again and again in an explosion of need and desire.

"I came up here to talk," he tried to tell her.

"I can't talk right now," she said, kissing his cheeks, his eyes, his lips. "I'm busy."

He laughed. She kissed his neck, and he closed his eyes, his laughter turning to a sigh of pleasure as he touched her, as he filled his hands with her breasts, as he stroked the smoothness of her soft skin.

"It's important," he breathed.

"I'm listening." She trailed kisses down his chest to his stomach.

Matt felt her tugging at the waistband of his shorts

and he grabbed her wrist. He spun her over and pinned her to the bed with his body, his hands holding her arms above her head.

"Now I'm really listening." She smiled up at him.

Unable to resist, he brought his mouth down to hers and kissed her slowly, sweetly, deeply. When he pulled back, she was trembling.

And he was, too.

"I really tried to stay away from you," he confessed. "I know this is selfish, but I couldn't help myself because…" He took a deep breath and said it. "I love you, Mags."

"You don't have to say that," Maggie said quietly.

"But I do," he told her. "I'm crazy in love with you. I have been for years. It's important to me that you know that."

She looked searchingly into his eyes, her expression dubious. "Matt, I'm not one of those women who have to think that you're in love with them before they'll—"

"No. Mags, I know that," Matt said. "This isn't a line. I love you. You have to believe me. God, I've never been more sincere in my entire life."

She shook her head. "It doesn't matter—"

"It does to me. Damn it, I love you! You'd *better* believe me."

Maggie stared up at Matt. His eyes held a glint of determination she'd only seen since he'd begun improving the business, and suddenly she realized that he was serious.

He was serious.

He *loved* her.

It was a good thing she was lying down or she'd have fallen over. "I believe you," she whispered.

Relief and satisfaction flared in his eyes before he leaned forward to kiss her again. His mouth caressed hers, gently at first, then with greater need. He was on top of her, and she wrapped her legs around him, pulling him even closer to her.

She was on fire. Everywhere he touched her, she burned. He stopped kissing her, and she pulled her arms free, reaching up around his neck to bring his mouth back to hers.

But he resisted. "Maggie..." His face was so serious.

She pressed one finger to his lips. "Matt, I love you, too," she told him with a tremulous smile. "Make love to me."

But he didn't smile back. In fact, he looked even more troubled. "There's more I have to tell you."

Maggie pushed him off her. "No."

Well, *that* surprised him.

"Not now." She crossed to the dresser and dug through her purse. Matt sat up slightly, leaning back on one elbow, watching her. "You just told me that you love me." She found what she was searching for and crossed back to him, picking up his free hand and slapping the little package into it. "Use this and prove it."

He looked at her in amazement. "You carry condoms in your purse?"

Maggie crossed her arms. "Oh, great," she said in mock anger. "Now you want to talk about that, too?"

He pulled her down onto the bed with him and kissed her. Maggie wasn't sure exactly how it happened, but when she came up for air, she was no longer wearing her nightgown.

He ran his hands and his eyes over her body and Maggie felt the familiar rush of heat to her face as she blushed. Then a deeper, more powerful heat infused her as his mouth found her breast.

She ran her fingers though Matt's long, shiny hair, arching her hips up toward him. She could feel him through his shorts, but that wasn't good enough.

He clearly thought the same thing, rolling over and, in one quick motion, he yanked them down and kicked his legs free.

Matt had dropped the condom on the bed, and now he reached for it and put it on. He really didn't need it—there was no way he could get her pregnant, and he hadn't been with anyone else in—God, it was years. But it would take too long to explain, and Maggie *had* been adamant about this not being the right time for conversation.

He lay beside her and kissed her, intending to take his time. He'd waited so long for this moment. Every minute, every second was going to count.

But when she opened her mouth to him, when she threw one leg over his hips, he knew he couldn't wait. And she was just as eager. He was surprised by her strength as she pulled him on top of her.

She reached for him, guiding him and then...

Oh, *yes.*

She moved with him, breathing his name, kissing him, touching him, surrounding him.

Time stood still and there was only Maggie, only these incredible sensations she was making him feel. His desire for her blazed through him, his heart pumping fire through his veins. His need consumed him and he heard himself call out her name as she exploded around him, as the rush of his own release nearly stopped his heart.

She kissed him so sweetly, so completely, and he knew without a doubt that he would love her until the day that he died.

Please, God, don't let it be too soon.

Matt rolled over, pulling her with him so that her head rested on his shoulder. He kissed her again and again, kisses for the sake of kissing, delighting in the softness of her lips, the sweetness of her mouth.

Her eyes were so filled with love, he nearly wept.

"I love you," he whispered.

She smiled. "I believe you. You're a good actor, but you're not *that* good."

Matt laughed, but it faded away as he realized what he had to do now. There was no putting it off any longer. "We have to talk."

Maggie sighed, running her fingers across his chest and arms, already starting to make him crazy again.

He couldn't do this here. Not like this. "Why don't we go into the kitchen?" he suggested. "Make a cup of tea?"

Something in his voice must've telegraphed his anxiety, because she sat up. "I'm listening," she said. "Really."

"Can we go downstairs?" he asked.

She nodded and reached for her nightgown.

CHAPTER TWELVE

AFTER PUTTING THE kettle on the stove, Matt pushed the kitchen windows closed. The night air had gone from cool to cold, with the wind blowing off the sound. Maggie had a sweatshirt on over her nightgown, but she still shivered slightly.

He sat down at the table across from her, fiddling with the napkin holder as he tried to figure out how to start.

"Now that we're down here," he said with a laugh, "I'm not sure how to say this."

She reached across the table, putting her hands on his. "Whatever you have to say, it can't be *that* terrible, can it?"

He met her eyes. "Mags, it's about when I went into the hospital. And yes, it's terrible."

She looked down at their hands for a moment, and when she looked back up into his eyes again, there was so much love on her face it nearly took his breath away. "You know there's nothing you can say that will make me stop loving you. *Nothing.*"

"I had cancer," he told her. There. He said it.

Maggie couldn't breathe. She stared across the table at him, waiting, hoping, *praying* for it to be a joke. Any minute now he'd tell her the punch line.

"I was diagnosed," Matt said softly, "with Hodgkin's disease."

"Oh, my God," she whispered. It was indeed a joke, a cruel, horrible joke of fate. "Was? Past tense?"

"Well, yeah," he said. Then he shook his head. "No, I don't want to lie to you." He looked up at her, his face apologetic, his eyes dark with unhappiness. "The truth is, I hope it's gone, but I don't know for sure. It's been almost a year since I had my last treatment of chemo. The odds of a recurrence are pretty high for the first year—"

"How high?" Tears were slipping down her cheeks.

"Fifty percent," he said. "Sixty percent, maybe more. I'm on the high end, because my cancer's already recurred."

How could he sit there so calmly and tell her that the odds of his cancer returning were so terribly high?

"But you know, instead of saying I've got a sixty percent chance of dying, I say there's a forty percent chance I'm going to live to be an old man. And that's great. That's... There was a time during my second round of chemo that my chances of surviving barely broke double digits," he said quietly.

"You had chemotherapy," Maggie said, pulling her hands away to wipe her eyes and cheeks. "For how long?"

"Two six-month courses. The second was intensive and kind of experimental."

"God, Matt, why didn't you tell me?"

"Before we made love? I tried to—"

"No, damn it!" Maggie hit the table with the palm of her hand and the flower vase came perilously close to toppling. "When you were in the hospital!"

The teakettle began to whistle, and they both stood up. Maggie reached the stove first, switching off the gas. She turned back to Matt and glared at him. "Why didn't you call me?"

He shook his head. "I couldn't. Besides, what was I supposed to say? 'Hi, how are you, it's been ten years, and oh, by the way, I have cancer?'"

"Why not? God, do you know how it makes me feel that you were in that hospital and I didn't even know? I was living my stupid, mundane life, completely unaware that any minute you were maybe going to *die?*"

She began to cry again, and Matt wrapped his arms around her, holding her close.

"I didn't die," he told her. "I'm not going to die. Not now. Especially not now."

She glared at him. "Cancer isn't something you can wish away."

He shrugged, pushing her hair back from her face. "Hey, why not? I'm willing to try anything. And wishing is relatively inexpensive and pain-free." He kissed her gently. "Tonight was so perfect. I'm sorry I had to ruin it."

"What, now you're apologizing for having had *cancer?*" With her arms wrapped around his waist, he felt so solid, so vital. She could hear his heart beating, steady and strong. It didn't seem possible that cancer was growing inside of Matt's perfect body. "I'm so glad you finally told me."

"I had to," he said.

"No, you didn't." She tilted her head back to look at him.

"Yeah, I did. If you love me, you deserve to know. I just... Don't be scared, okay?"

"I'm not scared," Maggie told him. No, she was terrified. She reached up to touch his hair. "When you had chemo..."

His smile turned rueful. "Yup. I was balder than Yul Brenner. Except I didn't look as good as he did."

"You probably haven't cut it since..."

"Only to even it out." Matt sat down, pulling Maggie onto his lap. "Or to trim the ends. I kind of have this superstition. It's silly..."

"Tell me."

"It's dumb," he admitted, "but after my hair started growing back in, I kind of saw it as a symbol of life. And I got this crazy idea that if I didn't cut my hair, the cancer wouldn't come back. I know it's ridiculous, but it's gotten to the point where it's become like a superstition or a good-luck charm. It's kind of like lifting your feet and touching the roof of the car when you cross railroad tracks, so you'll have good luck. Deep down you know it's not going to matter one damn bit, but you still do it—just in case."

She fingered his hair again. "Gee, if you're never going to cut it, it's going to get pretty long. In about five years, you're going to have to hire someone to carry your hair around behind you."

"I hope so," Matt said.

His eyes were sober as Maggie gazed into them, and she realized with a jolt of fear that there was a very good chance Matt wouldn't be alive in five years. "When will you know?" she asked.

He knew what she meant. "I'm flying out to California at the end of next week."

"California?"

"Yeah, I suppose I could go into Yale New Haven

Hospital, but I'd rather go back to the doctor who treated me," Matt told her. "We know each other pretty well. They'll do a series of tests to find out if I'm still clean."

"And if you are?" she asked. "What then?"

"Then I get happy." He traced her lips with his thumb. "Then I come back and we make love for the rest of our long, happy lives."

Maggie started to cry.

"Whoa," Matt said. "Mags, that was the *good* part."

"I love you," she said. "Don't you dare die!"

Matt held her close, his heart squeezing with pain, knowing that he couldn't make her any promises.

MAGGIE TURNED ON the light in the late Mr. Stone's ostentatious office and went straight to the bookshelf. It didn't take her long to find what she wanted—she'd seen the books before, even though she hadn't realized their significance. She pulled the big *American Cancer Society's Cancer Handbook* off the shelf, along with several others.

As she looked through the books, she realized that her suspicions were true. Mr. Stone had these books because he knew about Matt's cancer. He had used a pink highlighter to mark the sections on Hodgkin's, and she silently thanked him as she leafed through, reading the marked pages.

She was still sitting there an hour later, books spread out in front of her on the huge desk, when Matt came in. His breezy steps slowed as he saw what she was reading.

"Sometimes it's scarier to read about it," Matt said. "The books tell you only so much and make you realize how many unanswered questions you have. And if they go into any kind of detail, you need a medical degree to understand—"

"There's a lot you didn't tell me." Maggie tried hard to keep her voice from shaking. "You didn't tell me that even if there's no sign of a recurrence, that doesn't mean the cancer's gone. All it means is that you have a better chance of living five more years. And if you live the five years without a recurrence, all *that* means is you have a better chance of living *another* five years. And it just keeps on going. Forever."

"Mags, people who live for five years without their cancer returning are virtually cured."

She was silent, just watching him. He stared down at the red carpeting for a moment, then back up at her. His expression was unreadable, his eyes guarded. "Look, I know how tough it is to come to grips with this. If you don't want to deal with it, with *me,* I understand—"

"No!" Maggie stood up fast and the big leather chair rocked wildly behind her. "I just need to know *everything.* Don't hide stuff from me, okay?"

He nodded, watching her pace. "Okay. Then there is something else I should tell you."

Maggie froze, gripped with a sudden rush of fear. "What?"

"The chemo and radiation made me sterile," he said. "I'll never be able to have children." He laughed without humor. "At least not the regular way."

Relief flooded through her. She'd thought he was going to tell her that he felt sick again, that he thought the cancer was coming back.

"I've got some deposits in a sperm bank," he said, "but that's not very romantic—"

"I read something in here that scared me," she interrupted him. "I read that one of the symptoms of this kind of cancer is sleep problems. Night sweats and—"

"No," he said. "The problem I'm having sleeping now is different. It's in my head, Mags. I don't sleep much because it's important to me not to waste any time." He stood up, crossed behind the desk and threw open the heavy shutters. Sunlight streamed in, and then cool fresh air, as he opened the big window. He turned to face her. "I don't kid myself. I know I might not be here this time next year."

"How do you live with that?" she asked softly. "Tell me, so I can learn how to live with it, too."

He smiled at her. "You start by believing in miracles. You know, when I was diagnosed, they gave me seven months, tops. But here I am, three years later." He put his arms around her, kissed her sweetly. "Every day I wake up, Mags, I think of as a gift. I've been given one more day to live, and I'm not going to waste it."

"But don't you feel it's not fair? Don't you feel cheated?"

"Cheated?" He laughed. "No way. I've been given a second chance. I won big, Maggie. They told me I was going to die. I was dead, it was a given. But miracles happen." He kissed her again. "I'm more convinced of that than ever after last night. Not only am I not dead, but I'm living my dream. How incredibly great is that?"

He kissed her again, and she clung to him.

"Let's go back to bed," he breathed into her ear.

She made herself laugh instead of crying. "Taking a nap in the middle of the day," she teased. "Doesn't that fall into the 'waste of time' category?"

He laughed, a glint in his eyes. "Absolutely not."

Matt took her hand and pulled her out of the office,

into the main part of the house, all the way up the stairs to his tower room. The blinds were up and the windows were open wide, letting in the sun and the ocean breeze. The sky was a brilliant blue. It was like being on top of the world.

He undressed her slowly, taking his time to touch and kiss her, as she did the same to him.

And there they were. Naked in the sunlight.

They took their sweet time, falling together back on his bed, touching, tasting, exploring.

He would have spent hours in foreplay, but it was Maggie who grew impatient.

She pushed him back on the bed, straddling him, plunging him deeply inside of her.

She laughed at his gasp of pleasure, smiling down at him as she moved on top of him, setting him on fire.

"Hey." He tried to slow her down. "If you keep doing that, I'm going to lose control."

"I know," she said. "I like it when you lose control."

Oh, dear God, what she was doing to him… But… "Mags, I'm serious—"

"Hey," she said, pretending to frown at him. "Who's on top?"

He had to laugh. "You are. Mistress."

She laughed at that. "Damn straight." God, she was so incredibly sexy. "Tell me when," she ordered him.

Matt could see her love for him in her eyes, in her smile, on her face, radiating from her, and he knew that all the hell he'd been through had been worth it—if only to live for this one moment. And there would be other moments like this one, he knew, not just making love, but sharing their love.

She loved him. Maggie *loved* him. And it was all over for him.

"When," he gasped, and just like that, she dropped out of warp speed. She didn't stop moving, she just made each stroke last an eternity, and he crashed into her in slow motion. And then she was coming, too, and he couldn't believe how incredible it felt.

She collapsed on top of him, and he held her tightly, their two hearts pounding.

"I like it when you lose control," she whispered again.

Matt laughed. "Yeah, that kind of worked for me, too. Where did you, um, learn to…?"

She lifted her head to look down at him, her eyes sparkling with restrained laughter. "I'm extremely well read." Her smile was devilish. "I liked the *mistress* thing."

Oh, dear Lord, it was possible he was the luckiest man in the world. "I love you so much," he told her.

And just like that, she started to cry.

"Oh, Mags," he said, his heart breaking. "God, please don't cry." He kissed her. "Don't be sad—"

"I'm not," she told him, kissing him, too. "I'm crying because I'm so *happy*. Oh, Matt, I'm so glad you didn't die."

He held her close. "Me, too, Maggie," he whispered. "Me, too."

CHAPTER THIRTEEN

MAGGIE SAT IN the theater, looking up at the stage.

Matt was rehearsing a song that his character sang with a vocal quartet. The soprano, a woman named Charlene, was flirting with him, standing too close, her hand lingering far too long on his arm.

He glanced over at Maggie, caught her eye and made a face.

"Some things never change," she mouthed to him, and he laughed. "Behave," she added, with a mock frown.

"Yes, mistress," he mouthed back, heat in his eyes.

Oh, dear Lord, it was hot in here. And when would this rehearsal end?

The soprano was watching them, and Maggie smiled sweetly up at her. Tough luck, Charlene. Matt was taken.

"Time to take ten, no *fifteen*," Dan Fowler shouted, and the cast scattered, knowing that the director was serious about the small amounts of time he allotted for breaks. "Stone! It's time to deal with your hair."

"Yeah, sorry, Dan." Matt dug into this pocket for a ponytail holder and pulled his hair back from his face. "I'll keep it pulled back if you want."

"I want it cut." Dan's nasal voice echoed in the auditorium. "I got a friend here tonight who cuts hair down in New York. She's ready to cut your hair right now."

Matt froze. Maggie watched him make himself relax, one muscle at a time, before he spoke.

"Tell her thank you," he said, "but I'm not going to cut my hair."

"Hello," Dan said. "Cody works for one of the biggest advertising firms in Manhattan. He doesn't have long hair."

"I'm sorry," Matt said, "but we're going to have to work around this. I'll tie it back and put it under my shirt. I'll wear a wig if you want me to."

Dan walked to the stage, followed by a woman in a black stretch jumpsuit. "Come on, Stone. It'll grow back. Getting your hair cut isn't going kill you. Don't make me treat you like some rude child and tie you down—"

Matt backed away. "No," he said, his voice sharp.

Dan stopped short. "Jeez, I was kidding."

Maggie quickly climbed onstage and moved to stand beside Matt. She took his hand, squeezing it, and he glanced at her.

"What's with you tonight, Stone?" Dan's eyes narrowed. "You seem a little... I don't know. Strung out?" He turned toward the rows of seats. "Hey, Dolores!"

Dolores appeared instantly, as if Dan had conjured her up. She held a plastic specimen cup in her hand.

Matt exhaled loudly. It was similar to a laugh, but it held not a drop of humor. "I just don't want to get my hair cut," he said. "That doesn't mean I'm on drugs."

"Take the cup. You know what to do."

"Are you saying that I can't disagree with you without having to take a urine test?" Matt's voice rose in volume despite his efforts to stay cool.

"This is not a disagreement," Dan said. "This is weird behavior. Go do your thing, and then get back here and get your hair cut. Dolores, go with him to the men's."

Matt didn't move. He just stared at Dan.

"What, you're not going to do it?" Dan asked. "Then get off my stage."

Matt still didn't move.

"You think you're irreplaceable? Well, you're wrong. I'll take over your part myself. No sweat. In fact, it would be a real pleasure." Dan's gaze flicked over to Maggie just long enough so Matt knew exactly what he meant.

Two little words were on his lips. Two little words that would tell Dan Fowler exactly what he should do with himself.

But Maggie was watching him, and he closed his eyes instead. He took a deep, deep breath in through his nose. He held it, and then exhaled in a large swoosh through his mouth. Eyes still closed, he drew in more air.

"What's he doing?" Dan asked.

"I think he's trying not to kill you," Dolores said drily.

Matt took three or four more deep breaths, then slowly opened his eyes. He took the specimen cup from Dolores, and even managed to give her a smile. "I'll take your drug test," he said quietly to Dan, "but you're not going to cut my hair."

DAN FOWLER'S FACE was expressionless as Maggie explained why Matt didn't want his hair cut.

But then he laughed. "You really believe this crap, don't you?"

Maggie's mouth dropped open. "Are you saying that you *don't?*"

"Yeah, I think it's fiction. Stone is what I call a pathological actor," Dan told her. "When you deal with him, it's impossible to tell where reality ends and fiction begins. I'm not sure he's able to tell the difference himself." He laughed again. "So much for you and him not being involved, huh? When did that happen?"

She didn't answer.

"I suppose that's what I get, making you guys practice all that kissing at home," he continued. "Stone's playing some kind of game with your head, Maggie. Cancer, my ass."

Maggie stood up, spitting out the very same words she knew Matt had worked so hard not to say. "You may have no trouble replacing Matt," she added, "but keep in mind that if he goes, I go, too."

"Relax," Dan said. "We'll work around the hair thing. I don't want either of you to quit, okay? I just think you shouldn't take everything Stone says as the absolute truth. Did he say which hospital he was in?"

"Yeah. The Cancer Center at the University of Southern California. Maybe you should call and check, make sure he really was there, Dan."

"Maybe I will. Oh, and in case you were wondering, his urine tests have all come up clean. So far, anyway."

"It must really suck to be you," Maggie told him.

He nodded, turning back to the papers on the table in front of him. "Yeah. Right now I wish I were Stone— imagine that." He glanced up at her. "I'll be here if you need me, you know, when you wake up from this dream you're living in."

"I won't need you," she said, seething with indignation as she walked away.

CHAPTER FOURTEEN

WHEN THE ALARM went off at eight o'clock, Maggie was already awake.

Ever since Matt had left for California two days ago, she'd been unable to eat or sleep. The only thing she could actually do was work, so she'd dug in, working late into the night on the monthly accounts, searching for some legal principle to fall back on if they couldn't increase profits.

Stevie and Matt had had their heads together for over a week now, working on something that Matt didn't want to show her until they'd done some more research.

Maggie was still trying to get her hands on that mysterious codicil—tracking it down had been much harder than she'd thought.

She got out of bed, showered quickly and was soon downstairs in the office, wishing for the nine millionth time that she'd been able to talk Matt into letting her go with him.

But he'd been adamant she remain in Connecticut. "I want to keep then and now completely separate," he'd said to her the evening before his flight. He'd smiled at her lazily as they lay in his bed. "I think of it as something out of science fiction—the time I spent there was kind of an alternate reality. If that and my present reality ever meet—boom. The whole world will explode."

Maggie had rolled her eyes. "Matt, get serious."

And he did. "I left behind an awful lot of pain and fear at the cancer center," he told her. "I know they saved my life—at least they gave me some extra time—but it's not a nice place. The tests aren't a lot of fun. And waiting for the results…"

"That's why I want to go with you," she said.

"And that's why I don't want you to come," he said. "Please. I don't want you to see me there like that."

So here she was, waiting for him.

He'd called when his flight had landed in L.A., and again several times over the past few days. He'd told her he wouldn't have any test results until Tuesday night.

It was finally Tuesday.

Maggie looked at the clock.

Eight-thirty in the morning.

It was going to be another long day.

THE TELEPHONE FINALLY rang at nine o'clock that evening.

"Hey, Mags." Matt sounded exhausted.

Maggie closed her eyes briefly, taking a deep breath. "Matt." *Tell me. Tell me, tell me, tell me.*

"Sorry I couldn't call earlier," he said. "You wouldn't believe what I had to go through to get to a phone."

If he were okay, he would have told her without any delay, wouldn't he? Maggie tried to still the fear that was rising into her throat. "Tell me," she said.

"Well, there's good news and bad news," he said. "I thought I was going to be able to catch the red-eye home tonight—"

"Oh, God," she breathed.

"No, that's the bad news," he said.

"Then tell me the good news."

"The good news is that there's no definite bad news," he said. "The test results came back...weird. They want to retest before telling me anything."

"Weird how?" she asked.

"I don't know," he said. "I just know we're back in wait mode. If you want to know the truth, I think there was some kind of error in the lab and they're just afraid to tell me. I wish they would. It's better than thinking—"

"Matt, I'm going to fly out," she said.

"No," he said. "Don't. I've been picturing you sleeping in my bed, or working downstairs and... It's been a great focus for me, Maggie. I need you there, waiting for me." Over the line, she heard a murmured voice talking to Matt. "I have to go," he said. "I'll call you as soon as I know anything. I love you."

"I'm coming out there," she told him, but the connection was already broken.

THE EARLIEST FLIGHT to LAX left Bradley Airport several hours after midnight.

Maggie bought a ticket online, and then went about the business of getting through the day.

She had to file more papers in New Haven in an effort to get a look at that damned elusive codicil to Mr. Stone's will. And there was a rehearsal starting at seven. She'd have to leave a little early to get to the airport on time.

The day passed interminably slowly. Maggie waited in line after line, dealing with uninterested, apathetic clerks as she tried to find out what had gone wrong with her petition to release that codicil.

She ate a tuna-fish sandwich standing up in a dreary deli, then went back to slug it out with more bureaucrats. At three o'clock, after demanding to speak to a supervisor, she found out that there was a form missing from the paperwork she'd submitted, and she had to get Matt's signature before anything else could be done.

She went out to join the wall of traffic on Route 95.

Back at the house, she hurried inside, only to find that she'd gone out without turning on the telephone answering machine. Matt might have called her, but she would never know. Bitterly disappointed, she sank down on the living room floor and cried.

DAN HAD TAKEN the news that Matt wasn't at rehearsal and that Maggie was going to leave early in surprisingly good form. He made arrangements for one of the men in the chorus to read and walk through the part of Cody for the evening.

They were running the second half of the second act, starting with a solo Maggie sang, alone in Lucy's bedroom. The scene immediately following the song was the same one she and Matt had auditioned with—the scene with that brain-rattling kiss.

It didn't matter how many times they practiced it, Matt still left her breathless. God, she missed him.

Rhonda, the accompanist, started to play, and Maggie tried to focus on the song. It was a plaintive ballad, in which Lucy, after becoming engaged to Cody's rival, wonders why she's feeling so miserable when she should be happy. Maggie didn't have any problem calling up feelings of misery this evening.

Please, God, let Matt and me have a happy ending.

Finally, quietly, the song ended, and Maggie closed her eyes, following Dan's blocking.

"Lucy, are you still awake?"

That voice was unmistakable, and Maggie's heart leaped as she snapped her head up.

Matt stood on the other side of the stage, wearing his familiar blue jeans and high-voltage white T-shirt. His face looked tired and maybe a little pale, but he was smiling at her.

"Matt!"

Two long strides brought him toward her, even as she launched herself at him. His arms went around her, and then she was kissing him—hungrily, breathlessly, impatiently, thankfully.

She pulled back to look up into his eyes.

He'd cut his hair. It was short—similar to the way he'd worn it in high school. She tried to swallow her fear as she wondered if he'd cut his hair because it hadn't worked as a good-luck charm.

"I'm okay," he told her. "Maggie, I'm clean. The cancer hasn't come back."

The rush of relief was so intense that she swayed. He held her tightly, kissing her again.

"Uh, people." Dan's voice penetrated Maggie's euphoria. "This little reunion is deeply moving, but it's not getting us any further along here. Do you mind sticking to what's in the book?"

Still holding Maggie close, Matt looked out at the director. "Please, can we take ten?"

"You've already taken five," Dan said grumpily. "We've got a scheduled break coming up in about twenty minutes. Let's keep it going."

"There's so much I want to say to you," Matt whispered to Maggie. He gave her one more kiss before crossing back to his mark on the other side of the stage.

They ran through their lines almost automatically as Maggie kept her eyes on Matt. She was afraid to blink, afraid he'd vanish as quickly as he'd appeared.

His hairstyle brought out the exotic planes and angles of his face. He was more handsome than ever. And as he turned his back to her slightly, she saw that he'd only cut the top and sides of his hair. The back was still long, pulled into a ponytail at his nape. He could stick it under a shirt and no one would ever know he had hair halfway down his back.

"And you're wondering what it would feel like," Matt was saying, "if you brought your lips up, like this…" He moved her face up toward him, and Maggie caught her breath at the love she saw in Matt's eyes.

He didn't say anything for several long moments. She could feel his heart beating against hers, he was holding her so tightly.

"Oh, Christ." Dan's voice echoed in the room. "Line! Somebody give him his line!"

"And if I brought my lips down, like this…" Dolores prompted from the edge of the stage.

But Matt didn't seem to hear. "Maggie," he said, his voice husky. "Will you marry me?"

She caught her breath. *Marry* him. As in forever. As in the rest of his life. As in, he now believed his life would last long enough for him to share it with her.

Joy and relief flooded through her. There was nothing Matt could have done to convince her more that he believed his cancer was truly gone.

And as for *marrying* him…

"Yes."

With a shout of laughter, Matt kissed her.

The cast broke into a round of applause.

"Oh, Lord," Dan's bored voice cut over the clapping. "I guess we'd better take a break."

CHAPTER FIFTEEN

"Stevie's late," Maggie said.

"No, he's not," Matt said calmly. "We're early."

"Aren't you even the tiniest bit nervous?" she asked him. This still seemed unreal. They'd applied for the marriage license, waited the short time it took to get it processed and now here they were, standing in a church, about to get...

Married.

Matt smiled down at her. "No."

With her hair piled up on top of her head, dressed simply in a white sundress, Maggie was the most beautiful bride he'd ever seen in his life. No, he wasn't nervous. Thankful, happy, joyous, excited— Yes, he was all those things, but not nervous.

When he'd been in the hospital, when no one would give him a good answer as to why he needed more and more extensive tests, he'd been so sure his luck had run out.

Then, finally, he'd gotten a straight answer from his puzzled doctor. He was not only clean, but a precancerous condition in his lungs had vanished. No one could figure out what had happened. And the doctors hadn't told him earlier because they hadn't wanted to get his hopes up—they'd needed to be sure that somehow the tests hadn't been botched, that the results hadn't been switched with that of another patient's.

Especially since they'd been so sure this time last year that he wasn't going to survive. Yet there he was, passing all the tests with flying colors, in apparent good health.

For now, at least.

Matt didn't know if "for now" was to last five years, ten years or one hundred years, but he did know that he wanted to spend every moment of his life with Maggie.

No, he wasn't nervous.

But Maggie was.

"Are you really sure you want to do this?" she asked. "It's so…permanent. And sudden."

"Mags, I've loved you for over a dozen years," he reminded her. "It's not sudden. But it's definitely permanent." He laced their fingers together. "You're my best friend," he told her. "And the love of my life." He had to smile at himself. "That sounds so corny, but…"

"It's not," she said. Her eyes were luminous. God, she was beautiful.

"I know," he said, and kissed her.

"Yo, aren't you supposed to wait until *after* the vows for that monkey business?" Stevie interrupted them.

"You've got to work on your timing," Matt told him with a grin.

"Oh, great elder ones," Stevie said, bowing with a flourish. "Allow me to humbly introduce my friend Danielle Trent."

This was the girl who was providing Steve with so many sleepless nights. Tall and slim with short blond curls, her face wasn't really so much pretty as it was friendly, with a smattering of freckles across her nose.

Her eyes were lovely, though—an odd shade of violet with thick, dark lashes. She underwent their scrutiny solemnly, then exchanged a look with Stevie and smiled. Her smile transformed her face, and she became suddenly, freshly beautiful. Matt found himself liking the girl instantly.

"I've heard a lot about you guys," Danielle said. "When Stevie asked me to come to your wedding, I couldn't resist. I hope it's really okay."

"Of course it is," Maggie said.

"Actually, you're a vital part of the action," Matt told her. "We can't get married without you—we need two witnesses."

"You *are* eighteen, right?" Maggie asked.

"Just," the girl said.

"Excellent," Matt said.

The pastor of the church came in through a heavy set of double doors. He shook hands with all four of them, his round face beaming. "I haven't done a small wedding like this in years," he said as he led them to the front of the church. "We'll go through the vows and exchange rings here in the sanctuary. Then you can all come back to my office and we'll do the paperwork."

"Rings," Maggie said in dismay. "I knew we forgot something!"

But Matt held out his hand and Stevie dropped a blue velvet jewelry case into his palm. "I took care of it," he told her. "The rings aren't sized or engraved, but I figured we could use them temporarily."

Maggie gazed at Matt, realizing again how much he had changed from the reckless boy she'd known in high school. He stood there, tall and strong and calmly in control, and she knew without a doubt that agreeing to marry him had been the smartest decision she'd ever made in her life.

"Ready?" the minister asked with a smile.

Maggie looked into Matt's eyes and smiled. Yes, she was ready.

Their gaze held as the man began to speak, talking of love, of commitment, of trees growing stronger with their roots entwined.

Then he turned to Matt and began the vows.

Matt didn't look away from Maggie once as he repeated the words that would bind them together. His voice rang out clear and true in the empty church, echoing among the beams and rafters of the high ceiling. There was not even the slightest trace of doubt on his face, nor the slightest glimmer of uncertainty in his voice.

Matt slipped the ring, a plain gold band, onto her finger and smiled at her, adding his own ad-lib to the well-known lines. "I promise I'll love you forever, Maggie."

Forever.

The word had special meaning to them, since they both knew well that Matt's forever might not be as long as most. Maggie felt tears spring into her eyes, but she smiled up at him.

Her own voice trembled a little as she pledged and promised herself to Matt. She pushed his ring onto his finger, then held tightly to his hand. "I promise I'll love you forever, Matt," she added, too.

"I pronounce you man and wife." The minister smiled. "You may kiss the bride."

Matt leaned down and brushed her lips with his, then wrapped his arms around her as he kissed her more thoroughly.

"You're mine now," Matt whispered to her. "*You* are *mine*."

He picked her up and twirled her around, laughing, right there in the front of the church. "All right!" his joyous shout echoed.

Stevie looked at the smiling minister, one eyebrow raised. "I dunno," he said. "I think he kind of likes her."

MAGGIE STIRRED AND slowly opened her eyes to see Matt smiling down at her.

The silvery light of dawn was streaming in the windows of the tower room. Maggie caught her breath as she saw, once again, the hundreds and hundreds of roses that sat in vases on every available surface. Those roses were the reason Stevie and Danielle had been late to the church. But they'd done a wonderful job. The flowers had given the room a fairy-tale-like quality by candlelight, a quality that survived in the pale light of the morning sun. Even after two days, the room looked gorgeous, and the scent of the roses perfumed the breeze that wafted in through the open windows.

"What time is it?" she asked Matt, lazily stretching her arms above her head.

"Almost six."

"How long have you been awake?" she asked, snuggling against him.

"A little while."

Maggie gave him a look. "What, only two hours or only four hours?"

He shrugged, smiling.

"I wouldn't mind if you got out of bed when you can't sleep."

"I know," Matt said. "But I didn't want to get up. I wanted to be here. With you."

"Do you just lie awake and think?" she asked, feeling the familiar rush of desire as her legs intertwined with his.

"Sometimes," he said. "I like to spend some time every day centering myself—you know, keeping my perspective about what's a big problem and what's a little inconvenience. Actually, much earlier this morning, I went downstairs and got my briefcase. I was reading about the great controversy between using foil bags or plastic to package the chips."

He rolled his eyes and Maggie laughed.

"After we win this inheritance thing," Matt said, pulling her closer and running his hands down her body, "let's give the plant manager a big fat raise and tell him to hold down the fort while we go on a honeymoon to some exotic, tropical paradise where we can run naked on the beach."

He kissed her, and she could feel him, heavy and hot against her.

"Or maybe Europe," he said, his voice soft, hypnotizing. "I've always wanted to go to Europe. How about you, Maggie Stone?"

Maggie *Stone*. She sighed with pleasure as he—

The telephone rang shrilly, and she jumped, then caught Matt's arm. "Don't answer it. Please? Let the answering machine pick it up."

Matt looked at her. "Who don't you want to talk to?" She kissed him, trying to distract him again, but he pulled back. "Who else would be calling at six in the morning? Angie, right?"

Maggie sighed.

Matt laughed. "Mags, there's no way Angie could have found out we got married on Friday. Steve and Danielle swore they wouldn't tell anyone and—"

"My mother thinks we've been married for almost two months now," Maggie said. "It's something she would mention if Angie called, looking for me."

"Maybe Angie knows, maybe she doesn't." Matt studied her face. "I think you should call her and tell her about us. Then you can stop feeling guilty."

"I don't feel guilty." Her voice rose with indignation.

"Yes, you do."

"No, I *don't*."

"Look at you—you've got guilt written all over your face." Matt grinned. "You can't feel guilty about going to bed with me anymore because we're married. We're supposed to be doing this."

Maggie closed her eyes with a sigh of pleasure as Matt's hands and mouth continued to roam.

"Call her, Mags," he said. "Today."

"Oh, okay."

"Promise?"

She opened her eyes, looking down at him. "No fair. I'd promise you anything right now."

He smiled and kissed her again. "Then maybe this is a good time for us to talk about that invitation we have to dinner at your parents' house this afternoon."

"Oh, no," she said faintly. "Do we have to go?"

"Yes," he said firmly. "We can use the opportunity to tell them we're married. Of course, we'll probably have to show your father our marriage certificate as proof."

"You mean the new, *unlaminated* one?" Maggie said.

Matt laughed and kissed her, and they both stopped talking, for a little while at least.

"HELLO?" ANGIE PICKED up the phone on the second ring.

"Hey, Ange." Maggie's stomach churned with dread. Whoever called this morning hadn't left a message on the machine, but deep down she knew it had been Angie. Somehow her friend had tracked her down. "It's me."

"Maggie." Angie's voice was cool, with a distance that had nothing to do with the fact that she was on the other side of the Atlantic Ocean. "'Bout time I heard from you. How's *Matt?*"

"Funny you should ask—"

"You know, I always thought you were the smartest person I knew, because out of all my friends, you were the only one who never let Matt get to you. Damn, Mags, what are you thinking? *Living* with him? You know, your mother told me you're *married,* but I knew you wouldn't be *that* stupid—"

"Angie—"

"Or even that naive to think Matt would ever commit to marriage. The man is a *snake,* Mags. He may be handsome, he might be good in bed but you cannot trust him. He'll promise you the moon, then he'll walk away and find somebody else."

"No, Angie—"

"He lies. He's a liar and a cheat— He doesn't have a soul. I swear, Maggie, get out before it's too late—"

"Stop! Angie, just *stop,*" Maggie shouted into the phone.

She could hear her friend breathing hard on the other end of the line. Her own voice shook as she started to speak, so she cleared her throat and started again. "I don't know what he did to you," she said quietly, "but he's never been anything but kind and honest to me."

"Oh, please—"

"Stop talking," Maggie said forcefully. "For once in your life, be quiet and listen to *me*."

Silence.

"I love him."

Silence.

"And two days ago, I *did* marry him."

"*What?* Oh, God, you *idiot*—"

"He's good and kind and funny and smart, and I'm crazy about him," Maggie spoke right over her.

"I thought you were in love with that jungle man from the health club."

"Matt is the jungle man. I didn't recognize him at first."

"Oh, come on! You didn't *recognize* him? God, I should have told you to marry Brock. I don't know why Matt's married you, but he must have some ulterior motive."

"Gee, thanks a million." Maggie's voice shook with indignation. "Like what? Tell me what on earth his motive for marrying me could possibly be!"

"I don't know—"

"How about because he loves me? How's *that* for an ulterior motive?"

"No," Angie said. "Matt doesn't know how to love. You're just a prize."

"What?"

"A *prize*. You're something he always wanted but couldn't have. Now he's the winner. Except now that he's married to you, every other woman on the planet is something he can't have. How long 'til he goes after some other prize? One month or two?"

"No." Maggie gripped the telephone so tightly that

her knuckles were turning white. "He loves me, Angie. He's my husband now, whether you like it or not."

"I don't like it. Damn you, Maggie—how could you do this to me?"

"To *you?* What is your problem? You sound jealous, like you're still in love with him. Is that what this is about? You're angry because I got what you couldn't have?"

"No!"

"Damn right, no! You didn't want him. You married somebody else, remember? It's not like I slept with your boyfriend—"

"Did you?" Angie asked hotly.

"What?"

"Did you sleep with him when he was my boyfriend?" Angie's voice was rough with anger. "Jesus, all this time I was trying to protect you from him, and maybe *you* were the one who started it."

"I can't believe you're accusing me of—"

"And I can't believe that you could do something like marry that lying bastard and expect us to continue to be friends as if nothing was different," Angie spat.

"I won't talk to you if you're going to call him names."

"Then obviously we have nothing more to say to each other," Angie said tightly. "Have a nice life, Mags. With luck, he'll die young and you'll still have a chance at happiness."

There was a click as Angie hung up the phone, leaving Maggie staring sightlessly at the walls.

What a horrible thing to say—even more horrible, considering the circumstances. Angie didn't know about

Matt's battle with cancer, but that was still no excuse to say such a thing.

Tears flooded Maggie's eyes and she cried.

MAGGIE STOOD IN her mother's kitchen, cutting up tomatoes for a salad when Stevie breezed in.

"Hi, y'all," he said. "Am I late?"

Maggie thrust a cucumber at him. "Wash this," she said. "And your hands."

"I know, I know." Stevie pretended to be insulted. "What kind of skeevy type do you think I am, you have to tell me to wash my hands?" He looked at her over his shoulder from the sink. "How's Matt? You bring him along, or is he locked in the office, reading financial reports from the 1960s?"

"He's in the living room, talking to Dad," Maggie said.

"You tell Mom?" Stevie asked.

"Tell me what?" Mrs. Stanton asked.

"Nothing," they both said in unison, Maggie with a dark look at her brother.

"Maggie, please go find out what Matt and your father want to drink with dinner," her mother said. "And where is Vanessa?"

"Where *is* Vanessa," Stevie echoed, with a humorous look at Maggie. "Funny how she always disappears right before dinner, when there's work to do...."

Maggie rolled her eyes as she dried her hands on a towel and went into the living room.

Her father sat along in a chair, reading the newspaper.

"Dad, beer?" Maggie asked.

He looked up at her and smiled. "Please."

"Have you seen Matt?" she asked him. "Or Van?"

"I think they're out on the deck." Her father got to his feet. "I better go see if your mother needs any help."

Maggie crossed to the sliding glass doors that led out to the sun deck. She could hear Matt talking quietly.

Looking out through the screen, she saw him sitting up on the railing. One cowboy boot was hooked around the bottom rail, the other foot swung loose.

Van was standing next to him. "...married probably next summer," she was saying. "After the divorce is finalized."

"You sure you want to jump into another marriage right away?" Matt asked her. "It seems to me you might want to take your time."

Van snorted. "You're a good one to give advice. I can't believe you and Maggie are married." She laughed, and just as Maggie was about to open the screen and join them, she said, "Do you remember that night we were up at Wildwood?"

Maggie's heart stopped. Matt and Van? At Wildwood— Eastfield's version of Lover's Lane, where kids went to party and make out?

"How could I ever forget?" Matt's voice was dry.

Maggie went back into the kitchen, feeling dizzy.

Matt had gone out with Vanessa. When? And why hadn't she known about it?

How *could* he? He'd always disliked Van. Or so he'd told Maggie...

She sat at the kitchen table, trying to calm herself. It didn't matter. It had happened ten years ago. Matt loved *her*. He'd married *her*.

OUT ON THE deck, Matt gazed at Vanessa. "You were lucky it was my car you climbed into that night. If it had been someone else's..."

She laughed. "I was so drunk." She shook her head. "I couldn't believe Bill Fitch dumped me. *He* dumped *me*. It was...mortifying." She looked at him. "I would have slept with you, you know."

He nodded. "I know."

"You were in love with Maggie, though. Even back then, weren't you?"

Matt nodded again. "Yeah."

"She is so lucky," Vanessa said. "Did I ever thank you for driving me home that night?"

He laughed. "Not exactly."

Stevie came to the door. "Dinner is served."

Van caught Matt's arm. "Thank you," she said. "Be good to my sister."

He smiled at her. "I will."

MAGGIE WAS SILENT in the car on the way home. Matt glanced at her. "That wasn't so bad, was it?"

No, it was *terrible*.

"Now that your folks know we're married, we can tell the rest of the world," Matt said. "I want to shout it from the mountaintops. Although, have you noticed that Connecticut is seriously lacking in mountaintops?"

Maggie couldn't manage more than a wan smile. Try as she might, she couldn't get the picture of Matt with Vanessa out of her head.

Had they made love in the back of Matt's car? It was ancient history and it shouldn't matter. But it did. And she had to ask him about it.

As they went into the house, Matt pulled her into his arms and kissed her. *Ask him,* she ordered herself.

"If you don't mind, I'm going to do some work," he told her. "I haven't finished reading that crap on packaging. There must be three more files I haven't even looked at yet."

"Matt." Maggie's voice sounded breathless to her own ears. "Did you ever…"

Sleep with my sister? It was what she wanted to know, but she couldn't ask. Not like that. Not point blank.

He was watching her, waiting patiently for the end of her sentence.

"Did you ever go out with Vanessa?" A better start. Much less difficult to ask. And although she already knew the answer—she'd heard him say as much—they could go from there, and—

"No," he said. He was laughing, as if he found her question amusing.

Maggie stared at him, shocked.

"I never did," he said. "I didn't think she was that attractive. I still don't. She's so desperate, you know?"

"Not even once?" she managed to say. God, was he actually lying to her?

Matt smiled, his eyes so warm and sincere. "Not even once."

Do you remember that night we were up at Wildwood? Maggie heard an echo of Van's voice. And, *How could I ever forget?* had been Matt's reply.

If he couldn't forget just a few hours ago, it wasn't likely that it had slipped his mind right now.

He was lying.

To her.

Lying.

He opened the door to the office and turned on the lights. "You coming?" he asked.

"I have to get something upstairs." Maggie fabricated an excuse as she hurried away.

"Do me a favor and bring those files on packaging down from the bedroom, will ya?" he called after her.

She didn't answer, taking the stairs two at a time, wanting to get away from him, needing to think.

She sat for a few minutes on Matt's bed, looking out the windows, at the setting sun.

Matt had lied to her.

Even more frightening was the thought that if she hadn't already known the real truth, she never would've suspected he was lying. His voice and expression had been so sincere, and his eyes...

Dan Fowler's words came back to her. *Matt is a pathological actor. Don't believe anything he tells you.*

And Angie had been adamant, calling Matt a liar again and again.

But Maggie loved him. And he loved her.

Didn't he?

She couldn't believe he would lie about something like that. He'd *married* her, for crying out loud.

She stood up, resolving to ask him again, and to tell him what she had overheard. There must be a good explanation.

Turning, she gathered up the files Matt had asked her to bring him. Three files, right? But only two were out on the bedside table.

Maggie opened his briefcase and quickly leafed through the file folders he had inside. None of them were labeled, so she opened the top one and flipped through the papers, hoping to identify its contents quickly.

She scanned an official-looking document. Then with growing shock, she read it more slowly.

It was the codicil to the will. Matt had had a copy all along. Why hadn't he given it to her?

It was a wordy and lengthy document that boiled down to one thing: if Matt were to get married before the end of the fiscal quarter, he would automatically inherit.

The bedroom, still adorned with all those roses, began to spin.

Maggie sat down. The codicil specified conditions to the marriage—the woman Matt chose had to be over twenty-five years old, with a graduate degree. She had to be an upstanding member of the community, and preferably a longtime resident of Eastfield.

Maggie was that woman. The description fit her perfectly. Too perfectly.

Angie's words of warning about Matt's ulterior motive came back with a force that nearly knocked her over. By marrying her, Matt would inherit a fortune.

He didn't love her. He'd never loved her. He had only married her because she was willing and available and met the conditions of the will.

Her mind lined up all of the facts and the implications, but still she denied it.

No.

Matt loved her. He *loved* her.

No one could lie so absolutely, so perfectly, so consistently.

Could they?

The phone on Matt's bedside table rang.

Maggie picked it up.

"Hey." She could tell from his voice that he was smiling. "You get lost up there or something? Where are my files? More importantly, where's my *wife?*"

"I'll be right down," Maggie heard herself say.

Maybe it wasn't the real codicil. Maybe the real one was different. Maybe it didn't have anything to do with marriage. Maybe...

Tomorrow the real codicil was going to be released by the court. Please, God, Maggie prayed, let it be different. Let this be one big mistake...

"TOMORROW I'LL PICK up our wedding rings at the jewelers," Matt said as they walked across the parking lot outside of the community theater. "We might as well wait to tell everyone that we're married 'til then. Is that okay with you?"

She didn't answer, and Matt laughed. "Mags, hey, where are you?"

Startled, she looked up at him, then tripped over a crack in the driveway. Matt caught her arm to keep her from falling. "You okay?" he asked.

She nodded, but he could see the strain around her eyes and tension in her mouth.

"Dinner with your parents really blew you away, didn't it?" He pushed a stray strand of hair out of her face. "I'm sorry. You didn't want to go and I talked you into it."

"Matt, do you love me?" she asked.

What? "You know that I do."

She nodded, but her smile was forced.

"You don't…" Matt cleared his throat and started again. "You don't doubt me, do you?"

"Don't be silly," she said and went inside.

TOWARD THE END of the rehearsal, when Matt was up on-stage for one of his solo numbers, Dan Fowler slipped into the seat next to Maggie.

"The Cancer Center at USC?" he said without any greeting.

Maggie felt the muscles in her face freeze. "Yes. That's where he was."

"No, he wasn't."

She looked at Dan, but he was staring up at the stage, at Matt. "All right," she said, her heart starting to pound. "What are you accusing him of now?"

Dan finally looked at her. "I'm not accusing him of anything." His voice was mild, but his eyes were flinty. "All I'm saying is that I called to verify his cancer story, and there was no record of a Matthew Stone ever having been at USC's cancer center." He shrugged and stood up. "I'll leave all the accusing to you."

CHAPTER SIXTEEN

MAGGIE'S HANDS SHOOK as she dialed the telephone. It had been torture, waiting until noon—until nine o'clock California time.

Matt and Stevie were in the kitchen, making lunch, and she was thankful for the privacy that gave her to make this call.

A call that would prove Dan Fowler wrong.

An elderly woman answered the telephone. "Cancer Center at USC. May I help you?"

"Yes." Maggie's voice shook, and she took a deep breath. "My husband was there a few weeks ago, and I need to check the exact dates of his previous stay for our insurance forms. Can you put me through to someone who can help me?"

"I should have that information on my computer," the woman answered. "What's your husband's name, dear?"

Maggie told her.

"Hmm," the woman said, and Maggie's stomach began to hurt. "*S, t, o, n, e,* right?"

"Yes."

"I don't have a Matthew Stone," she said. "Not this past month or any other time. Perhaps you're confusing us with the hospital at UCLA?"

"I'm sorry," Maggie said, hanging up the phone.

Lies. It was all lies.

"Yo, Mags." Stevie came back into the office. "Matt made you a salad. You want it out here or in the kitchen?"

Maggie just shook her head.

"Hey, ho." Her brother crossed to the door. "Mail call! Here's big Joe, the friendliest mailman in the Western Hemisphere."

He opened the office door and took a pile of mail from the dour elderly man.

"Hey, homeboy," Stevie greeted him, holding out a hand. "Gimme five."

Joe slapped a certified letter into his outstretched hand. "Sign for this one." He pointed to the form. "There and there."

At least Matt didn't have cancer. At least he wasn't going to die.

"Yo, Mags," Stevie said, closing the door behind Joe. "Looks like this is that legal thing you were waiting for."

She put her head on the desk and burst into tears.

Stevie stared. "Well, gee, I get kind of emotional when Joe leaves, too, but, he'll be back tomorrow, so—"

"How could Matt do this to me?" she said. "How could he put me through this? Pretending to go into the hospital, making me think he actually might die?"

"Is this another one of your acting things?" Stevie asked worriedly. "I hope?"

"Give me that goddamned letter." Maggie snatched the envelope from his hand. She tore it open and with shaking hands spread the document out on the table.

It was the codicil—and it was the same as the one she'd found in Matt's briefcase.

He didn't love her. He was just using her.

Correction—he *had* used her, but that was going to stop right now.

"Do you have your car?" she asked Stevie, reaching for a tissue and blowing her nose violently.

"Yeah, why?" Her brother looked very nervous. "What's going on?"

"I need a ride," she told him.

"Oh, yeah?" Matt came into the room, all smiles. "You going someplace?"

Maggie turned to look at him. How could someone who looked so beautiful do something so ugly? And how could she have been such a fool as to believe him?

His smile faded as he gazed at her. "What's the matter?" he asked.

"I know the truth," Maggie told him. She was *not* going to cry in front of him, damn it. "You son of a bitch."

Total confusion was on his face. "What?"

"God, you're good," she said. Taking a deep breath, she forced back her tears. She'd have time to face the hurt later. Right now, all she let herself feel was anger. It shot through her, icy and cold. "But you can skip the act, Matt. The codicil to the will came today. You don't have to fake it anymore. Obviously, you've won."

"Maggie, you're scaring me," he said. "What are you talking about?"

She scooped the certified letter off the desk and slammed it against his chest. "It's all right there in the codicil. But you might as well cut the crap. I know that you've already seen a copy of this."

He frowned, pretending to skim through the document.

"Or maybe you only *think* you've won," she told him,

her voice shaking. "But maybe you lose. I'm going to file for an annulment."

Stevie's mouth dropped open as he looked from Maggie to Matt and back.

"What are you talking about?" Matt said again. He looked stunned, confusion and disbelief alternately crossing his face. "Maggie, you can't be serious."

"I'm dead serious."

"What does this say?" Matt shook the document at her. "You know I can't understand this legal stuff...."

"You know damn well what it says." She headed for the door.

He lunged after her, catching her arm.

"Let go of me!" Maggie bit each word off clearly.

"Yo guys, I think I'd better go," Stevie said.

"No!" Maggie said.

"Yes," Matt countered. "Steve, go outside, all right? Give us some privacy, will you?"

"If I don't come out in fifteen minutes," Maggie told her brother, "call the police."

Matt staggered back. "Oh, my God, do you really think I'm going to *hurt* you?"

"You already have," she told him.

"How?" he asked, his eyes searching her face. "Christ, Maggie, tell me what this is about."

She went out of the office and up the stairs.

"Maggie, talk to me," he pleaded, following her to the room where she kept her clothes. "I love you, and you loved me. We're *married*—"

She spun to face him. "Not anymore."

"Why not?" he shouted, desperation in his face, the codicil to the will crushed in his fists. "Damn it, Maggie, you tell me why the hell not!"

"Okay, fine," she said. "We'll play this your way. Play the whole game out. The codicil states that you automatically inherit if you get married before the end of the fiscal quarter. But you can't marry just anyone. The conditions are listed quite clearly in the fifth paragraph."

He smoothed the crumpled paper and read. And realization crossed his face.

"Oh, bravo," Maggie applauded. "One thing I can say about you, Matt, is that you truly are a brilliant actor. But save it for the Academy Awards, because I know you've already seen this codicil. I found a copy in your briefcase."

"If it was there, I didn't know it," he protested.

She laughed. "You know, I might've believed you. But combined with the rest of it…"

"What rest of it?" He was mad as hell now, too.

"All the lies." She roughly wrestled her gym bag from the top shelf of the closet. As she spoke, she began pulling her clothes from the drawers and piling them on the bed. "All this time they were right, but I was stupid enough to believe *you*—"

"*Who* was right?"

"Angie—"

"*Damn it!* I should have known she was somewhere behind this!"

"*And* Dan Fowler."

"He's not exactly the president of my fan club, either," Matt shouted. "So come on, I'm dying to hear. What did they tell you?"

"That you're a liar," Maggie shouted back. "And they're right! You *lied* to me, you bastard. You used tricks and lies to get me to marry you!"

"God, Maggie, you don't really think that, do you? I thought you believed in me, that you trusted me...." He voice shook and he broke off. Tears glistened in his eyes. "Damn it."

The pain on his face was only an act. A tear escaped and slid down his face. It, too, was just part of his crap. "I never lied to you," he said.

"Gee, I don't know," she said as she packed as much as she could into her gym bag. "I'd call telling someone that you have cancer when you really don't more than a little white lie, wouldn't you?" She turned to face him. "I called the cancer center, Matt. They never heard of you. You were never there.

"You told me that you never went out with Van, but I heard you talking to her about going parking at Wildwood!" She stopped to take a deep breath. "You *lied* right to my face when I asked you about her!"

"No," he said, "I can't believe that's what you think—"

She plowed right over him. "But the biggest lie of all was when you married me." It was harder and harder for her to hold back her tears. "You said you loved me, but I know that's not true. I know why you married me, and it has nothing to do with love."

The look on his face would've broken her heart if she hadn't known it was all an act.

"But you know what?" she whispered. "I lied, too, when I told you I'd love you forever. Because I sure as hell don't love you anymore."

Matt turned and walked out of the room.

He came back a moment later carrying an empty suitcase. He set it down on the bed. "I'll get Stevie to help you carry your things out," he said quietly. He was almost out the door when he turned back. "I thought you believed in me, Maggie. I thought you had faith in me. But why should you be different from anyone else?"

CHAPTER SEVENTEEN

As MAGGIE WALKED into the auditorium, she saw Matt immediately, standing by the stage. He was dressed all in black, and he was surrounded by most of the female cast members. Still, he looked up at her as if he had some sort of sixth sense and could tell when she was around.

A wave of misery descended upon her, and Maggie knew in a flash that she would have to move away. She couldn't stay in town with Matt living here, too. It would be horrible to be reminded constantly of what a blind fool she'd been.

"Places!" called Dolores. "We're doing a complete run-through tonight, and we're taking it from the top."

Maggie dumped her bag into a seat and tiredly climbed the stairs to the stage.

Aware of Matt's eyes on her as he watched from the wings, she found it difficult to concentrate on the show. God, any minute he was going to come out, and she was going to have to kiss him.

She had to stay mad. If she could stay good and mad at the bastard, she'd be able to get through this.

Matt watched Maggie and felt like crying. When had it happened? When had she begun to doubt him? Or had she mistrusted him all along?

If that was the kind of person she was, then he didn't

want her. Good riddance. She'd done him a favor by leaving.

Up on the shoulders of the men's chorus, Maggie smiled dazzlingly.

Desire stirred and he closed his eyes, angry at his reaction to her. She didn't trust him—and he *still* wanted her.

And in less than a minute, he was going to have to kiss her.

Damn it. He couldn't do this.

But the stage manager gave him his cue, and he went out onto the stage. The lights hit him, and there he was. Standing right in front of Maggie. Their gazes locked. Somehow his mouth opened and the lines he'd memorized came out.

She seemed so unaffected, so calm.

But as he pulled her in for the kiss, he saw a flash of anger in her eyes. His own anger began to build, and he kissed her hard, too hard, hating himself for still wanting her, and knowing that before the night was through, he was going to go to her and beg her to come back to him.

MAGGIE SAT IN one of the dark corners backstage, praying for the fifteen-minute break between acts to end. She was using every ounce of her energy just being onstage with Matt—she didn't want to use it up confronting him offstage.

But he found her. "Maggie."

He was backlit, and his face was in the shadows. She stood up, prepared to move out into the auditorium— anywhere to get away from him.

But he caught her arm. "We have to talk."

She pulled away. "There's nothing to say."

He followed her onto the stage, out into the light. "There's a hell of a lot to say. Come on. At least give me a chance to defend myself."

"Just leave me alone."

"Maggie, God, *please*. I love you."

She looked up at him and saw his eyes filled with tears and all of her anger came roaring back.

"Good delivery. You sound *very* sincere. But the tears are a little too much, don't you think?" She pushed her hair off her face, working hard to keep her hand from shaking. "Give up, Matt. I don't believe you. Besides, you don't need me anymore. I won't file for an annulment. We'll get a divorce—after you've gotten the inheritance."

"You really think that's what this is about?" he asked. "Money?"

She didn't say a word.

He nodded. "You loved me enough to marry me," he said. "You owe me at least the chance to tell you—"

"I owe you nothing," she said.

"How can you say that?" Matt felt sick. Did she really believe that? "You should talk to your sister. If you don't believe me, you should ask her. And I'll call my doctor at the center—he'll call you. Or you can call him. I *was* there—"

"Forget it, Matt," Maggie told him. "I just don't care."

Matt stared at her. She didn't care. He was ready to beg, to plead, to *crawl,* but damn it, *she* was the one who had done him wrong. She was the one who didn't trust him. He was even ready to accept that she'd found him guilty until proved innocent if it meant he'd have her back.

But she didn't care.

The last bit of hope that he'd been carrying evaporated, and his heart broke.

CHAPTER EIGHTEEN

"WHERE THE *HELL* is he?" Dan Fowler stormed. "I knew it. I *knew* I should never have trusted that bastard with the lead to my show!"

"My brother works with Matt," Maggie told him. "I just spoke to him on the phone—he says he hasn't heard from him all day."

Outside, a storm was raging, and thunder crackled deafeningly, directly overhead.

"Beautiful, just beautiful." Dan groaned. "You guys had a fight, didn't you?"

"We split up," Maggie said, and saying the words aloud made her sick.

"And now he's gone." Dan started to pace as he swore. "The understudy is awful. We'll have to modify the dance numbers...."

"I think you should just take a deep breath," Maggie said, "because Matt wouldn't just blow off the show. He's going to be here."

Dan stopped pacing and stared at her. "You look like you've been run over by a truck. This guy does *that* to you, and still you defend him?"

"I just don't believe he would desert us one day before opening night," Maggie insisted. "He'll be here."

"Jeez, somehow I didn't expect *you* to be my champion."

Maggie whirled around to see Matt standing behind them. He looked exhausted. And he was soaking wet.

Dan swore at him, loud and long. "You're late. We're paying our orchestra by the hour, damn you. Where the hell have you been?"

Matt finally stopped looking at Maggie. "We're getting tidal flooding from this storm. I've been organizing work crews at the factory—sandbagging. I should have called, but for the past hour I've been on the verge of getting into my car and coming over here. But there was always one more person who needed to talk to me. I apologize for being late."

"Places!" Dan was already yelling. "Get Stone into costume and makeup! Now!"

AFTER THE DRESS rehearsal ended, Maggie reached over her shoulder to unzip the evening gown she wore for the show's closing number. She pulled the zipper down as far as she could, then reached around behind her, struggling to find the tiny pull.

A warm hand on her shoulder stopped her, and she felt the zipper slide all the way down.

Holding the dress to her front, she turned to face Matt.

Matt.

Tonight she'd run out of anger. All she could feel was the hurt. And boy, did it hurt bad. Because despite everything he'd done, she still loved him.

His eyes were angry, the way they'd been all night long, but his face and words were polite, cordial. "You did well tonight."

Maggie laughed humorlessly. "I know exactly how

well I did. This is an endurance test for me, Matt. I can't wait until it's over."

He nodded then, his eyes dark with misery now. "Yeah, me, too." He cleared his throat. "I just wanted you to know that I'm going to go back to California after the fiscal quarter. I've already contacted a divorce lawyer and…I want you to have the house."

She stared at him.

"There's no way I could stay in town with you living here, too," he said quietly. "I know you love it here, and…"

"That's…that's insane," she said. That house had to be worth millions.

"It's no more insane than any of the rest of this," he told her as he walked away.

MAGGIE STOOD BACKSTAGE in the dark, listening to the sounds of the people who had begun to fill the seats of the auditorium.

It was ten minutes to curtain on opening night.

Matt was in makeup, already in character, joking and laughing with everyone in sight.

She closed her eyes, wishing it could be that easy for her, too, wishing she could just snap her fingers and become someone else, if only for a little while.

But Lucy, her character, was too much like herself. It wasn't enough of an escape.

"Yo, Mags," came a whispered voice.

She turned to see Stevie. He was wearing blue jeans that were crusty with dried mud and a T-shirt that was no longer white.

"Well, gee," she said. "You got dressed up for the occasion."

He grinned. "I'm coming to the show tomorrow night. With Danny." He laughed. "We actually have a real date. Matt's even letting me borrow the Maserati."

"A date?" Maggie said. "You mean you finally—"

"Yeah, I finally took your advice," Stevie said. "See, we were out with the gang, and I just couldn't stand it another second. I said, 'Danny, I'm madly in love with you, and if you don't kiss me right this second, I'm gonna die.'"

"You did?" Maggie laughed. "Oh, my God."

"So she laughed at me," Stevie told her, "and I'm mortified, thinking, 'Wow, how totally humiliating.' But then—" he paused dramatically "—she kissed me. Boom. Right there. In front of everyone." He smiled. "She actually loves me, too."

"That's so great," Maggie said.

"So I came down here to say thank you and break a leg."

"Thanks."

"You and Matt patch it back together yet?" he asked.

She shook her head. "I don't think that's going to happen."

Stevie rolled his eyes. "You are such a fool. He loves you, Maggie."

"He married me to get his inheritance," she told him. But even as she said the words, they sounded so wrong. And Stevie was looking at her as if she were the village idiot.

"You don't *really* believe that, do you?" he said.

"I don't know," she admitted.

"Yes, you do," Stevie said. "You know him, Mags. He's a good guy. A little flaky with the weirdo diet and the strange sleep patterns, but…you *know* him."

She'd thought she did.

"He's been hanging out at the law library for very unhealthy periods of time," her brother told her. "He's working on something that would probably take you five minutes to do. He could use your help, you know. I mean, unless you don't care if he makes himself sick…."

Maggie gave him a look. "That's laying it on a little thick."

"Will you please just talk to him?" Stevie said. "If not for him, if not for you, then for *me?*"

She just shook her head.

"Places!" Dolores said.

Her brother backed away, pointing to her leg and making a breaking motion with his hands, then miming a telephone, mouthing the words, "Talk to Matt."

And tell him what?

Taking a deep breath, Maggie moved out into the center of the stage to the mark where she would be standing when the curtain opened. She closed her eyes and bent her head, forcing her body to relax.

Tonight, her character, Lucy, was going to have a happy ending.

Maggie would give anything to have one of her own.

THE CAST WENT wild behind the curtains after the final bow. The show was a huge success—the audience had laughed at all the jokes, and the applause for the musical numbers had been deafening.

Laughing, Matt picked up Maggie and swung her around and around. She was smiling up at him, her arms around his neck and, without thinking, he kissed her.

Oh, God, he was kissing her. Her mouth opened willingly beneath his and he drank her in, wishing he could slow this moment down but too afraid even to move for fear of breaking the spell. He could feel his heart pounding.

She pulled back, and he released her immediately. Their gazes locked, and Maggie cleared her throat.

"Cody and Lucy always did get a little carried away," she said.

Cody and Lucy. Not Matt and Maggie. "Sorry," he said.

"You were great tonight," she told him.

"You were, too."

The rest of the cast was making so much noise around them. Someone ran past with an open bottle of champagne.

"I don't want your house," Maggie said quietly.

"Too bad," he countered.

"Seriously, Matt," she said. "Stevie said you were working on something, but you don't have to do that. We can go into court some time in the next few weeks and show them our marriage license. You've already won."

He laughed his disgust. "You call this *winning?*" His temper flared and he walked away from her, but then walked back. Breathe. He had to breathe, but he couldn't get the air into his lungs. "I'm not just giving you the house," he told her. "I'm giving you half my share of the business, too."

She looked shocked. "Matt—"

"Hey, like you said," he told her harshly, "I won. And I wouldn't've been able to do it without your help. The house is your payoff for that. The half of the business is yours because—believe it or not—I really did think of you as my wife. But if you're more comfortable with it, you can think of it as payment for the sex."

Her eyes flared. Ooh, that had gotten her mad. Stupid, stupid, stupid. He should have just kept walking away.

In response, Maggie actually uttered words he'd never heard her say before. At least not in this decade.

But it wasn't until he was in his car and driving— too fast—out of the parking lot, that he realized he wouldn't have been able to get a rise out of her if she truly didn't care.

Maybe he was going about this all wrong. Maybe instead of trying to show her how calm and collected he was—how much he'd changed over the years—maybe he should show her...

For the first time in days, Matt actually had hope.

He headed, fast, for Sparky's—where the entire cast was meeting to toast the opening of the show. He wanted to get there first.

MAGGIE PUSHED OPEN the door to Sparky's feeling much less than enthusiastic.

But it was a tradition with the theater group to drink a toast to the show, and this year, because they'd had no volunteers willing to host a party, the party was here at the bar.

Maggie was only going to stay for the toast, and then run for home as fast as she could.

As she went inside, she saw Matt was already there— sitting at the bar. Charlene, the flirtatious soprano, was next to him. She leaned in close to tell him something. And, God, he actually had his arm around her.

Maggie looked away, but not before she'd met Matt's eyes in the mirror.

He actually had the audacity to smile at her.

She found herself staring at the old-fashioned juke-box sightlessly, blinded by tears of jealousy. No, tears of anger. She wasn't jealous, she was mad.

She couldn't believe what he'd said to her after the show. Payment for sex... And now he was here, like this, with *Charlene*....

She glanced up to see Matt standing right behind her.

Quickly, she blinked back her tears and fished in her pocket for a quarter. She pushed the coin into the slot and pretended to be absorbed in choosing her song. But he reached over her shoulder and pushed the numbers for an old Beatles song, "P.S. I Love You."

"Dance with me," he said.

Maggie gazed up at him, suddenly beyond exhausted. She'd danced with him all night long, and that hadn't solved a thing. "Why don't you dance with Charlene?"

"Look, she sat down next to me. What am I supposed to do?"

"She made you put your arm around her?" Maggie couldn't stand it anymore. "I think it's kind of obvious that it's over between us," she said forcefully. "Why don't you just relax and have a beer and a cigarette and *Charlene* while you're at it."

"Is that really what you want?" Matt said. God, she was playing right into this entire scene. It was perfect. And he was right about her still caring. Oh, man, she cared so much. He wanted to kiss her. Instead he shrugged. "Fine. You got it."

He remembered the way he used to act, back in high school, before he'd learned to control his anger. It wasn't hard to get back into character—the bad boy was a part he'd played for years. He'd already started, over at the bar with Charlene.

He spun now, nearly colliding with a waitress. He took one of the oversize mugs of beer from her tray, ignoring her protest, and crossed to a table where some of the cast members were sitting. He put down the beer, took a cigarette out of a pack on the table and, holding Maggie's gaze, he very slowly and deliberately lit it.

He picked up the beer and crossed back toward her, taking a long pull on the beer and then an equally long drag off the cigarette.

Christ! He had to work hard not to cough. God, he hated the taste of both, but he didn't let her see that.

"This is more like it." He exhaled the smoke as he gazed at her. "Isn't it? It's what you expect from me, right? God forbid I should ever actually *change*."

He took another long swig of beer as, from the corner of his eye, he saw Dan Fowler watching them with horrified fascination.

Maggie's eyes were filled with tears. "Matt, stop."

"Gee, I don't know, Mags," he said, his voice rising in volume. "I mean, you got me pegged for this role. I'm a liar and a cheat, right? At least according to Angie and Dan. A liar who smokes and drinks too much. And let's not leave out Charlene. I think she'll be glad to go home with me, don't you? Oh, but wait, maybe not after she sees *this!*"

He pretended to chug the rest of the beer, but really just poured it down his shirt. "Or this!" he shouted, and slammed the mug down with such force on top of the jukebox that the record skipped with a wild screech. The music stopped.

The noisy bar was silent.

But Matt dropped character as he stubbed his cigarette out in a nearby ashtray.

"You're ready to believe all that about me," he said softly as he looked up at Maggie, "but you won't believe that I love you. If that's really true, then go to hell, Maggie. I don't want you anymore."

He turned and walked out of the bar, knowing all too well that his words had made him exactly what she thought he was.

A liar.

MAGGIE FOLLOWED MATT out into the parking lot.

And found him on his hands and knees in the grass next to his Maserati, throwing up.

"Oh, my God," she said.

He swore. "Go away."

She dug in her purse for some tissues, crouching down next to him.

He took them from her, wiped his mouth, and sat up with his back and head against the side of his car. "Remind me never to smoke again." There was dark humor in his eyes as he looked at her. "Well, *that* sucked. So much for the tough guy act, huh?"

"Do you want me to drive you home?" she asked.

He shook his head. "No, I'm okay. It just was… I haven't had nicotine in so long, and, God, it just made my stomach…"

"That was impressive in there," she said. "Making the jukebox shut off that way…"

"Too much?"

"No," she said, starting to cry. "It was perfect."

"That's not me anymore," he told her.

Maggie nodded. "I know. I know." She couldn't bear to look at him. His words were echoing in her head. *I don't want you anymore.* "Oh, Matt, will you ever forgive me?"

"I'll think about it," he said. He pulled himself to his feet and unlocked his car door. He had a bottle of water in the cup holder and he took a swig, rinsing his mouth and spitting it out.

She wiped her face, her eyes. "Stevie told me you were working on something…?"

Matt looked at her. "Yeah. I'm not, um… I'd prefer not to use our marriage as a way to win this thing," he told her. "I mean, if it comes down to it, I will—all those jobs are at stake. But I didn't marry you because of that fricking codicil. I didn't know I had that document in my briefcase."

"I know," she said. "Oh, God, I'm so sorry."

"What'dya do, talk to Vanessa?" he asked.

"No," she said.

"You call the cancer center? I gave them permission to give you whatever information you wanted."

"No," she said.

He was surprised. "You don't want proof that—" He laughed. "Did Stevie show you the thing I'm working on?"

"Stevie doesn't know what you're working on," Maggie countered. "He told me you were doing something and you could probably use some legal help. That's all he said to me."

Matt was trying to be casual, but for someone who was such a good actor, he was doing a truly lousy job.

"So you just, like, decided that you believe me?" he said. "No proof, no…"

"It was actually something Stevie said tonight," Maggie admitted. "He reminded me that I knew *you*. That I knew you. Matt, please, *please* forgive me. All those awful things I said…"

She met his eyes, and as she looked at him, she could see tiny reflections of her face in the darkness of his pupils. She belonged there, in his eyes, and she knew she had to do whatever she could to stay right there.

But he reached for her, and as she held him, she started, again, to cry.

"God," he said, "no matter what I do, I seem to make you cry."

She looked up at him. "I'm madly in love with you, and if you don't forgive me, I'm going to die."

Fire, life and tears sprang into Matt's eyes simultaneously. He held her tightly as he laughed. "Yeah, like there's any doubt I'm going to forgive you."

"You said you needed to think about it."

"I was kidding!" He laughed. "Hey, if this failed tonight, I was going to fly my doctor out from California and pay him to follow you around until you believed me. I was going to take a lie-detector test. I was going to—"

"I love you, Matt," she said. "Do you still love me?"

"For always and forever," he promised her.

She would have kissed him, but he turned his head. "I'm not kissing you," he said. "I just barfed. But if you want to come home with me and let me run upstairs and brush my teeth, you can try that line of Stevie's again, verbatim this time, and I guarantee it'll work as well for you as it did for him."

She held him tightly. "I think I vowed to love you in sickness and in health."

Matt laughed. "Get in," he said.

Maggie got in.

And he took her home.

CHAPTER NINETEEN

MAGGIE SIGHED AS she lay with Matt in his bed. *Their* bed. It felt so good to be home.

"I was such a jerk," she said.

"Yeah," he said. "You were."

She narrowed her eyes at him. "You're not supposed to agree with me."

"I'm not going to lie," he told her as he touched her face. "Not even about something like that. I'm never going to lie to you, Mags."

"I know," she whispered.

He kissed her and she felt herself melt. And then she started to laugh.

"What?" he said.

"I'm madly in love with you," she said, "and if you don't go down on me right this second, I think I'm going to die."

He shouted with laughter. "Can't have that," he said. "God, I missed you…"

MAGGIE WOKE UP to find Matt sitting up in bed, reading the papers in a file.

The clock read 5:34.

"Hey," he said, smiling at her.

She stretched. "Did you sleep at all?"

He shook his head. "I think I was afraid if I fell

asleep I'd find out that your coming home was just a dream."

Oh, Matt... "It's not," she said.

He nodded. And handed her the file. "You awake enough to put on your lawyer hat?"

She sat up, arranging her pillow behind her. "My lawyer hat seems to have disappeared with the rest of my clothes."

He grinned at her. "I meant figuratively. And as long as we're leaning heavily toward all honesty all the time, I should probably tell you that the idea of your giving me legal advice while you're naked appeals to me in a very decadent way."

"Do I need to call you Mr. Stone?" she asked, opening the file and starting to read and...

She closed the file. And looked at Matt. "Are you serious about this?"

He nodded.

She opened it again. He'd outlined his plan for improving the company. It included on-site day care and a fitness room. It also included joint ownership in the company for every single employee from the managers to the cleaning staff.

Maggie flipped through his notes. "You're proposing to give the employees all but twenty-five percent of the company." She looked up at him. "You're just... giving it to them?"

He actually shrugged. "These people are the ones who've worked so hard to make this company successful. Can you imagine how much harder they'll work if the company actually belongs to them?"

She kept flipping through his notes. "And what's this? A grant program and..."

"Scholarships, too," he said. "Funded through the sale of some of my father's assets. I'm going to keep only two of the cars— I mean, thirteen cars? Come on. Some of those are antiques and worth a ton of money. I'm going to put it all into a trust. I've worked out the preliminary numbers—I need you to check my math. But I'm pretty sure that with the bulk of the cash inheritance included in the trust, there'll be about three million in interest each year—to give away."

"And you're going to run the grant's foundation," she saw.

"With you," he said, "if you'll take the new position."

Maggie looked up at him. "Matt, this is…"

"Crazy?" He shrugged again. "I never really wanted my father's money—I told you that from the start. I was trying to save the company. I mean, don't get me wrong—my twenty-five percent will keep me very comfortable. I'm not going to give it *all* away."

She closed the file. "Well." She frowned slightly, tapping it with her finger. "I guess my legal advice to you would be…let's try it. Let's go for it. Let's set it up and present it to the court. I can't tell you for sure if they'll accept this as the kind of improvement your father intended, but I'm willing to argue it—I think I can put up a good fight. And we do have a failsafe—our marriage certificate. I know you don't want to use it, but, like you said, you want these people to have their jobs come next Christmas."

She reached for a pen from the bedside table and started making notes right on the manila folder. Matt took both from her hands and kissed her.

"We can work out the details later," he said. "One thing I want you to do today is go through my briefcase, make sure there aren't any other unpleasant surprises hiding in there." He kissed her again. "Will you do that for me?"

"I don't need to," Maggie said.

"But I want you to," he told her as he pulled her on top of him. "Later."

"Later," she agreed.

MATT'S BRIEFCASE WAS filled with roses.

Roses and his hospital records from California.

He'd also written out an explanation of the night he'd gone up to Wildwood to a party, telling her how Vanessa had come into his car, falling-down drunk after breaking up with her boyfriend. She'd come on to him, but he'd taken her home. End of story.

There was a note from Dan Fowler, too, apologizing for giving Maggie misinformation, explaining that Matt had chosen a privacy option at the cancer center, which meant that all information about his illness—including information he himself requested—had to be obtained via mail, in writing.

And there was a copy of an email from Angie.

"Dear Mags," her friend wrote.

Matt emailed me a few days ago. I've spent some time thinking about it, and I've come to the rather earth-shattering conclusion that I was wrong.

I'm not going to tell you everything Matthew said to me (I wouldn't want it to go to your head!), but I do believe that he truly loves you. He's loved you for a long time, and I suppose I'm mostly to blame for you guys not getting together before this.

You were right—I was jealous. Even now, even

married, even completely in love with Freddy. I'm a bad person—if I couldn't have Matt, I didn't want you to have him, either. I think I knew back in high school that his feelings for you went way beyond my own relationship with him. Hell, they went beyond my relationship with you. I think I was afraid that if you and Matt got together, neither of you would have anything left to give to me.

I know now that that's not true. I love Freddy as much as Matt loves you, and love like that is like a fire. It just keeps spreading; it keeps burning brighter and bigger.

I'm sorry for the things I said to you. I hope you'll find it in your heart to forgive me.

LOL! I know you will. I know you—you've already forgiven me. You're such a pushover. You need to work on that, all right?

So stay good and mad at me another week—God, I'm such a rotten bitch—and then call me and tell me that you still love me, okay?

I love you.

Love, Angie

Maggie looked up to find Matt standing in the office door.

"I didn't need any of this," she told him. "I didn't need proof or permission from anyone to—"

"I know," he said.

She went through the pockets of the briefcase, but they were all empty.

"That's all that's in there," Matt said. He'd made sure of it.

"Are you positive?" she said.

Uh-oh. "Did I leave something out?" he asked.

She sighed. "I was sure you were going to ask me…" She stood up. "I guess I'm going to have to ask you." She took a rose from the bunch, and crossing to him, got down on one knee. "Matt, will you not unmarry me?"

He laughed.

She did, too, but back there, in her eyes, he could see that she wasn't entirely kidding.

"Oh, Mags." He got down on his knees, too, and kissed her. "Yes," he told her. But then he looked at her. "Wait, maybe I need to consult with my lawyer. The wording of that question was a little complicated. Yes, I won't unmarry you." He figured it out. "Yes. Definitely, yes."

Maggie kissed him. She kissed his face, his neck, his jaw, his cheeks, but then stopped, with only a whisper of space between her lips and his.

"I want," she said, and he could feel her warm, sweet breath against his face, "my wedding ring."

He kissed her—a long, lovely, heavenly kiss—then pulled back and reached into his pocket. He'd carried the jeweler's box with him for days now, hoping…

Opening the box, he removed the two golden bands. Hers was so small, so delicate, compared to his. But both were engraved on the inside with the same inscription. "Maggie and Matt. Forever."

Maggie looked at Matt as he took her hand. His face was serious, but his eyes were soft. She felt the world fade around her as she lost herself in his eyes.

"I promise I'll love you forever," he said softly, repeating the words he'd said at their wedding, so many long days ago. He slipped the ring on her finger.

She looked down at their hands and she knew she

was never going to doubt him again. No matter what the future brought, she would stand by Matt's side.

She held out her hand, and he placed his own ring on her palm. It was so big and solid, just like Matt himself. Yet she hesitated. "Matt," she said. "I lied to you." She forced herself to look up at him. "I lied when I told you that I didn't love you anymore. I was so angry, and I tried to stop loving you, but...I couldn't."

"We both said a lot of things in anger," he told her gently. "It's okay."

"I wanted to be sure you knew I didn't break my promise to you. I promised to love you forever, too, Matt, and it's a promise I intend to keep." She pushed the ring onto his finger and kissed the palm of his hand.

"I'm madly in love with you," Matt said, smiling at her despite the glint of emotion in his eyes, "and if you don't kiss me right this second, I'm going to die."

Maggie laughed. And then she kissed him.

And kissed him.

Forever.

* * * * *

SCENES OF PERIL

CHAPTER ONE

IT WAS THE first snow of the season.

Paige Dawson stepped closer to the front window of her mountain cabin, sipping hot cocoa from her favorite mug. Wet flurries pelted the glass and wind whistled through the tall pine trees outside, swaying the moisture-laden branches.

This storm was supposed to be a big one. Twin Lakes had seen a smattering of rain over the past few days. Now the temperature had dropped to freezing and the clouds were still full. They were in for a snow dump.

Paige had stocked up on groceries and firewood just in case. It wasn't unusual to see road closures and downed power lines in this remote corner of the California Sierras. She'd been snowed in before. Sometimes she looked forward to it. After a long week hiking and taking photographs with a wildlife research team, she should have been eager to curl up in front of the hearth with a good book.

Instead she was staring out the window, listless.

Smothering a sigh, she glanced over her shoulder at the living room couch. Her Kindle was charged and ready to go. She'd built up a cozy fire. Plush blue pillows and a soft wool blanket awaited her. Although her muscles ached with a familiar, pleasant sort of fatigue, she made no move to sit down.

When she was away from home, sleeping in a tent on the hard ground, she'd longed for her kitchen, her shower, her comfortable bed. Now that she was here, safe and sound, she felt as though something was missing.

Maybe she needed a cat.

The cabin had seemed a little empty since her brother had moved out for good. He'd been an absentee roommate anyway, staying in his college dorm during the school year and backpacking every summer. Now he was a science teacher in Southern California.

She turned back to the window, lifting the mug to her lips to drink. When a loud crack sounded in the distance, she startled, spilling cocoa from her cup. She watched a large tree branch drop from one of the towering Jeffrey pines at the end of the driveway. It landed with a terrific crash in the middle of Twin Lakes Road.

Cursing, Paige set her mug aside. Damage from downed branches and falling trees was common in the area. She could call a removal service or the sheriff's station if necessary. First she'd try to shove it aside herself. Leaving a huge obstruction in the road wasn't an option. Traffic around the lake was light in the fall, but someone could get in a serious accident. Visibility was limited and dusk was fast approaching.

She grabbed her jacket from the hook by the front door and put on her hiking boots, not bothering to lace them. Snowflakes stung her cheeks as she jogged down the gravel driveway, zipping up her jacket as she went.

As soon as she reached the fallen branch, she realized she should have brought a flashlight to signal traffic. But it seemed unlikely that anyone would be out hot rodding in a snowstorm, so she disregarded the safety measure.

The branch was large and heavy with green foliage. It lay diagonally across the double yellow line, blocking both lanes. Her side of the road was lined with sturdy pine trees. A short embankment on the opposite edge led straight down into the lake, which wasn't frozen over yet. If a driver swerved to the right, he could be in for a deadly dunk. Paige had to rectify this life-threatening situation at once.

She reached down to pick up the thick splintered end where the branch had broken away from the trunk. It was about the circumference of her thigh and wouldn't budge an inch. She'd have to try the other side. Glancing both ways, she stepped onto the asphalt and walked toward the tapered end.

Pulse racing with trepidation, she squatted like a weight lifter and grabbed hold. This end came up, with some effort. Her breath huffed out in little clouds as she began to walk the branch toward the shoulder.

That was when she heard the engine.

She froze, still in the middle of the right lane. A charcoal-colored SUV flew around the corner at a breakneck pace. There was no time to signal the driver. If she didn't drop the branch and take a dive, she was going to get hit.

Heart in her throat, she let go of the branch and prepared to jump down the embankment. But something—her bootlace, perhaps—got tangled up in the bark. She tripped and fell hard on the slippery asphalt.

The SUV barreled toward her, its front grill gleaming.

She was going to die.

Her horrified gaze locked on the driver. She saw his eyes widen. It was too late for him to slow down. To avoid her, he'd have to crash into the branch—or the lake. At the last possible second, he cranked the wheel to the left.

Saving her life. Risking his own.

She screamed and covered her head with her arms as the vehicle hit the tree branch with full force. The timber flew across the road and rocketed down the embankment. Her bootlace snapped, freeing her foot. She was lucky to keep her leg intact.

The driver slammed on his brakes and promptly lost control of the vehicle. She looked over her shoulder and watched, aghast, as the SUV went into a sickening slide. It launched off the side of the road and tumbled down the embankment, rolling end over end. The sound of scraping metal and busted glass rang in her ears.

Then—*splash*.

"Oh, my God," she whispered, clapping a hand over her mouth. He'd run over the branch *and* gone into the lake!

Paige struggled to her feet, dizzy. Her legs felt wobbly and her thoughts were scattered. She stared at the empty space where the branch had been. Pine needles and bristlecones littered the wet asphalt. Fighting nausea, she stumbled to the edge of the embankment and searched the surface of the lake.

The vehicle was nose down in the water, brake lights flashing. Its single occupant was slumped behind the wheel. The front windshield was broken, roof caved in. Her stomach clenched with anxiety as the SUV sank deeper.

Within seconds it was fully submerged.

She studied the bubbles on the surface, fisting her hands in her hair. Although her nearest neighbor was half a mile away, she screamed for help at the top of her lungs, hoping the wind would carry her voice. Her cell phone was on the kitchen counter, but calling 911 wouldn't change this man's fate.

He'd drown if she didn't take action.

She scrambled down the embankment and shrugged out of her jacket. When she reached the shore, she kicked off her boots. On a clear day, the lake was a deep, pure blue. Now, in the fading light under a snowy sky, it appeared pale gray. Red taillights were still visible beneath the silvery surface, pulsing like a beating heart.

Although Paige considered herself a brave person and a Good Samaritan, she hesitated to enter the water. Twin Lakes was fed by snowmelt, too chilly for swimming even on the hottest summer day. At this time of year, the temperature hovered around forty degrees. A quick dip could induce cardiac arrest.

While she wavered, a picture of her mother flashed before her eyes. Both of her parents had died in a car crash during the San Diego earthquake five years ago. They'd always encouraged Paige and her brother to consider the welfare of others.

The driver had chosen her life over his. It wasn't her fault he'd been driving so fast, but she felt responsible for the accident. She couldn't live with herself if she didn't at least try to rescue him.

Decision made, she waded into the lake. Her jeans soaked in the freezing water and the shock robbed her breath. She stumbled and fell to her knees. Shivering uncontrollably, she lowered herself into the water and started to swim toward the submerged vehicle. The cold invaded her body, turning her muscles to rubber. Struggling for each breath, she continued to paddle her arms and kick her legs. The short distance seemed like a mile.

Finally, her foot glanced off the roof of the SUV. She estimated the location of the front windshield and ducked under, fighting the urge to gasp as icy pinpricks assailed her face. With her arms outstretched, she searched for the driver. Her numb fingertips encountered the top of his head, covered by short hair. Jerking her hand back, she returned to the surface for air.

Her strength was already sapped, her movements sluggish. Her lungs worked furiously to expand and contract. If she didn't hurry up, they'd both die.

In a sudden burst of panic, she dove under again, finding his sweater-clad shoulders. He floated upward, unhampered by a seat belt. Fisting her hands in the fabric, she braced her feet on top of the hood and pulled him out of the cab.

Luckily, the SUV was resting on the bottom of the lake, no longer drifting downward. She pushed off the hood and broke through the surface, bringing him up with her. He didn't take a breath when she did.

Damn!

She didn't know if he could be saved, assuming she could get him to the shore. But she'd come too far to give up. Walking along the roof of the vehicle, she shoved off the end, one arm hooked under his chin. Swimming this way was a challenge, to say the least. She did a poor job of keeping his head above the surface. When she could stand, she turned around and dragged him from the lake.

Without the buoyancy of water to aid her, his weight was more than she could handle. He was a big man, long and lean. She heaved him halfway onto the shore, her frozen fingers unable to maintain a grip on his sweater. He slipped from her grasp, his upper body flopping to the ground. In a strange turn of luck, the impact seemed to rouse him.

He coughed and sputtered, expelling fluid from his lungs. Then he made an awful retching noise, so she turned him on his side, grimacing in sympathy. He'd apparently swallowed lake water, as well as breathed it.

But her heart leaped with hope because he was alive!

When the spasms calmed, he started shivering. Paige was also shaking from cold, but his condition appeared serious. He was pale, his lips blue. His dark hair was plastered to his head. There was an angry gash above his eyebrow, blood streaking down his temple. Snow continued to fall all around them, gathering on their wet clothes like ice crystals.

She put her face close to his. "I can't carry you, and I'm afraid you'll die if I leave you to get help."

He opened his eyes with a low groan. They were brown and bleary, one pupil larger than the other.

"Can you stand up?"

"Yeah," he said, his voice gravelly.

Although she doubted him, she admired his pluck. If he couldn't walk, she'd run back to the cabin, call 911 and grab some supplies. She could bring a tent and sleeping bag to him, but he might freeze to death before she returned. The nearest hospital was an hour away. What he really needed was a fire.

"Let's go," she said, pulling him to a sitting position. He squinted in concentration, perhaps seeing double. "Ready?"

With her assistance, he struggled to his feet. She

put her arm around his waist, supporting him on one side. He didn't collapse, which was good, because she wouldn't be able to drag him up the embankment by herself.

She took the first step, urging him along. Luckily, he was young and fit and strong. An extra layer of body fat would have insulated him better, but he was no beanpole. His arm felt heavy on her shoulders, his torso taut with muscle.

Maybe he was a hiker or a mountain climber. It was a little too early in the season for skiing and snowboarding.

The short haul up the embankment almost wiped them both out. She took small steps, digging her frozen, sock-covered feet into the gravel. He lumbered forward, his breathing labored and his motions clumsy. She guessed that he was suffering from moderate to severe hypothermia.

"Don't forget to feed the cat," he mumbled.

"I won't," she said.

Confusion was common at this stage, along with short-term amnesia. He'd taken a hard bump to the head and lost consciousness. She was surprised he could speak at all, let alone form complete sentences.

They reached the road and crossed it, entering her driveway. Although the distance to her front door was less than a hundred yards, they struggled. Paige had reached the summit of Mount Whitney, the highest peak in the continental United States, with greater ease. This stretch seemed impossible to traverse. He stumbled with every other step, leaning most of his weight on her. Several times she considered leaving him to get her car. She abandoned the idea because she didn't think she could move him if he passed out.

Twenty yards from the front door, he stopped shivering. A bad sign.

"Come on," she said, trying not to panic. "We're almost there."

"Sss hot," he said. "Need…rest."

He sounded drunk. She didn't think he was; his breath didn't smell like alcohol, and his stomach had been full of lake water, not booze. Disorientation and slurred speech were symptoms of hypothermia. Victims often complained of overheating and removed clothing when they were freezing.

"It's not hot," she said, her lips numb. Quite the contrary. "Keep moving."

He lurched toward the lit windows, monster-like.

"Almost there," she urged.

By the time they reached the front steps, he was beat. She attempted to help him up, but the task was beyond his current capabilities. He didn't seem to understand the concept of stairs. His motor skills had deteriorated completely.

Paige wanted to cry in frustration. They were so close! If he died on her doorstep, she'd be devastated.

She put her back to him and hooked his arms over her shoulders, letting him slump against her. Unfortunately, she couldn't bear his full weight, let alone take him up stairs. He slid off her back and landed in a crumpled heap.

Unconscious.

Skirting around him, she opened the door to the cabin and hurried inside. It was evening now, full dark.

Relieved that the power was still on, she crossed the room and picked up her cell phone, checking for service.

No bars.

With trembling hands, she reached for the cordless. Her heart sank as she heard no dial tone. The landline was out, too. Replacing the phone in the cradle, she returned to the motionless figure on her doorstep. It was up to her to save him, all by herself.

She went back outside and sat down on the top step, rolling him onto his back. With his head in her lap, she slipped her arms under his and linked her hands across the center of his chest. Flattening her feet on the lower step, she heaved with all her might, using her leg muscles to scoot backward.

"Heavy bastard," she said, teeth clenched.

After she brought him over the threshold, she straightened, dragging him across the hardwood floor. Panting from exertion, she shut the door and continued toward the fireplace. His head lolled to the side, insensible. His limp body left a damp trail along the way. She stopped at the sheepskin rug in front of the couch.

Pushing her wet hair out of her eyes, she gave him a closer study. His chest rose and fell with steady breaths. The wound on his head needed bandaging, but it was no longer bleeding. He had good features. Without the unhealthy pallor, he'd be handsome.

Moving quickly, she grabbed some blankets from her bedroom and retrieved her cold-weather sleeping bag from the closet. Tossing the pile on the couch, she pulled off her sweatshirt and jeans. His wet clothes had to go, as well.

She found a pair of scissors and knelt beside him. He was wearing a gray cable-knit sweater with a blue thermal undershirt. The garments were casual but appeared high quality, like his worn leather boots. His SUV had also been new and expensive looking. This guy was no grubby backpacker or local hunter.

Frowning, she cut through both layers, starting at the hem. When she was finished, she pulled the fabric away from his torso, revealing broad shoulders and strong arms. Her gaze trailed down his lightly furred chest and flat abdomen.

Not that she was checking out a half-dead guy, but... wow.

Mouth dry, she set the scissors aside to remove his boots and socks. He had nice feet. Kind of big and hairy but well maintained. She brought her trembling hands to his fly, unbuttoning him with cold fingers. As she stripped the wet denim down his narrow hips, his black boxer-briefs came along for the ride.

She didn't want to look. Not really. It was such an invasion of privacy, ogling a man when he was vulnerable. But his male parts were in her direct line of sight, just inches from her face, and she was only human. She looked.

Cheeks flaming, she pulled his jeans down his long legs and rolled him onto the rug by the fire. Then she covered his impressive form with the sleeping bag and blankets. She added several thick logs to the blaze and took a sip of cocoa. It had grown cold.

Although she'd planned to bandage his head, she was exhausted, and reversing the effects of hypothermia seemed more important. Shivering, she slipped out of her damp undergarments and crawled in beside him.

With the fire at his front and her body heat cuddling his back, he'd warm up in no time.

She wrapped her arms around his shoulders and snuggled close, shutting her eyes.

CHAPTER TWO

COLIN REID HAD the worst hangover ever.

His head pounded fiercely. His bladder was full, his tongue thick and his throat dry. Strangely, he had no recollection of drinking. He didn't remember much from the day before. He didn't remember night falling, period.

Something wasn't right.

The sound of fire crackling, close enough to warm his face, urged him to open his eyes. He smothered a groan as the flickering flames came into focus. His temple ached as if he'd been kicked by a horse. He lifted a hand to his head, letting out a hiss of discomfort as his fingertips encountered a tender lump.

What the hell had happened to him?

He didn't recognize the fireplace as the one in his rented cabin. The rug underneath him, also unfamiliar, tickled his bare skin.

Damn! He was buck naked.

And he wasn't alone. Colin felt a warm female form—also nude—against his back. Her breasts were touching his shoulders. One slim thigh was wedged between his legs. His morning erection rose up and said hello, responding to the stimuli.

It felt weird to become aroused over a person he hadn't seen. He didn't know who he was with or what she looked like. He didn't even know where he was. His thoughts were muddled, the previous evening a complete fog.

Was it even morning yet? The only light in the room came from the fire.

Straightening, he turned to look at the sleeping woman. Either his mind was playing tricks on him or she was smoking hot.

Her hair was a tangled mass of honey, her skin pale and fine. She had high cheekbones and a freckled nose. The sleeping bag was pushed down to her waist, revealing small breasts with soft pink nipples. Colin's pulse throbbed to look at her.

Had this beauty knocked him out and dragged him to her lair?

Eager to see more, he tugged the sleeping bag lower. She was pretty all over. Slender but not delicate. Her hips were nicely curved. She had a sweet little triangle at the apex of her thighs. He wanted to bury his face in it.

He must have made a caveman-like grunt of appreciation, because her eyes sprang open. They were blue, wide set and intelligent. They flitted down his body, settling on his erection. She grabbed the sleeping bag and jerked it back up, covering herself.

Huh. Maybe he'd gotten the wrong idea about her. If she'd had her wicked way with him, he'd like to be able to remember it.

"You're awake," she said, moistening her lips.

"Yes."

She stared at him for a few seconds. "How—how do you feel?"

"My head hurts."

"You were in an accident."

"I was?"

She nodded.

That explained the cut on his brow. He was mildly disappointed that he hadn't been kidnapped for sex. "What happened?"

"You crashed into the lake. I pulled you out."

He squinted at her, trying to evaluate her sincerity. It seemed like a wild tale. He preferred his equally far-fetched version. "How did I get here?"

"I helped you walk. You were hypothermic."

Blood started pumping away from his groin, back to his brain. No wonder they were huddled up naked together. She'd jumped in an ice-cold lake to save him, dragged his semiconscious ass to her cabin and warmed him up by her fire. "Oh," he said, embarrassed now that he'd exposed her so rudely. "I'm sorry that I, uh…" He made a vague gesture, indicating her nether regions.

Her cheeks flushed pink and her slender throat worked in agitation. He tore his gaze away from her, feeling like a perv.

"Do you remember anything before the accident?"

"No," he said, frowning. "I think it was snowing.…" As he tried to conjure up more memories, a sharp pain ricocheted inside of his skull, making him wince. "I rented a cabin near Pine Lodge. I don't know why I was out driving."

She grabbed a thin blanket and slid it under the sleeping bag. "Pine Lodge is only a few miles away," she said, her body covered as she rose.

"What time is it?"

She glanced at a clock above the fireplace. "Almost six. I'll turn on the radio and find out if the roads are closed. Do you want some water? I have painkillers, too."

He needed to use her bathroom, but he wasn't sure he could get there on his own. He also didn't want to stumble around her house naked, even though she'd already seen his full monty. "Where are my clothes?"

"They're wet," she said, clutching the blanket to her chest. "I might be able to find something of my brother's for you."

He glanced around the cabin in chagrin. Brother?

Her lips curved into a smile, as if she could read his thoughts. "He doesn't live here anymore."

He watched her walk away, bare toes padding across the hardwood floor. Even her feet were sexy. Closing his eyes, he rested his aching head on a couch pillow. The last thing he remembered was finishing his latest novel. He'd come to Twin Lakes for this purpose and to get away from it all. He'd been feeling distracted and stressed out in L.A. His Paranormal PI series, now completed, was in production with a cable-TV network. The pressure was on for him to deliver a bang-up finale.

Had he emailed the document to his editor?

Even if he hadn't, and his laptop was at the bottom of the lake, he stored his files online. A recent version of the book had been saved.

His valiant rescuer returned with a pair of gray sweatpants and a checkered flannel shirt. She set the garments on the couch and turned her back to give him privacy. Clearing his throat, he pushed back the sleeping bag and put on the sweatpants. They were a size large and fit comfortably. He preferred wearing boxers or briefs to freeballing, but she hadn't included underwear. The shirt was snug across the shoulders, so he left it unbuttoned. Grimacing, he used the couch to pull himself up to a standing position.

His headache went into overdrive and he swayed on his feet. He gripped the armrest, black spots dancing in his vision.

"Need help?" she asked when he moaned.

"I think I'm all right."

She paid no attention to his stupid male bravado. "Here," she said, putting one arm around his waist. The top of her head was at his nose level, which tempted him to smell her hair. "I don't want you to fall and knock yourself out again."

He shuffled away from the couch with her, noting that she'd also put clothes on. Black leggings with sheepskin boots and a red thermal undershirt. The shirt was snug and V-necked, with three little buttons down the front. Her breasts looked nice in it. They looked nice without it, too, but he tried not to think about that.

The cabin was cozy, with a small kitchen and living area. There appeared to be only one bedroom. The bathroom was on the left, just past the kitchen.

When they arrived at the bathroom door, he insisted on parting ways. "I can manage on my own."

Her gaze dropped to his crotch, doubtful. "Okay."

Heat crept up his neck as he closed the door. Although he didn't want her assistance with this particular task, the idea of her touching him in a different context was appealing. Maybe he'd been too buried in his work lately. Despite his head injury, his physical response to her was overpowering. He needed to get out and meet women more.

Keeping one hand braced on the sink, he managed to use the toilet without taking a dive. When he was finished, he washed up and glanced in the mirror. He'd hoped that the cut on his brow would give him a tough-guy edge. No such luck. With a lump on his forehead and one eye swollen, he looked like Quasimodo.

So much for being rugged.

He left the bathroom feeling a bit steadier. She assisted him back to the couch, her slender body warm against his side.

While he rested, she brought him some water and painkillers. He took his medicine like a good boy, watching as she added wood to the fire, folded the blankets in the living room and heated up some soup. She also turned on the TV for a weather update, although it was clear the storm was still raging outside.

Her motions were efficient and graceful. She was obviously a capable woman, but she didn't look any older than the college students in his classes. He couldn't imagine how she'd pulled him from a submerged vehicle.

"Thank you," he said.

She glanced at him, curious.

"For saving me."

"I owed you one."

"What do you mean?"

She came back to the couch, taking a seat across from him. "A tree branch had fallen into the road from my yard. I was trying to move it when you came around the corner. You swerved to avoid me."

Her account sounded so familiar—and yet when he tried to picture the scene, a sharp pain pierced his skull.

"I'm sorry," she said, as if she'd caused him distress.

"No, tell me more. Please."

She moistened her lips. "Well, you crashed into the

lake. I think you were unconscious before the vehicle sank. I waited a minute and you didn't come up. I knew you needed help, so I…I jumped in."

"Jesus," he said, studying her face. "You could have died trying to save me."

"Yes."

"Wasn't the water cold?"

"Freezing," she said.

He wasn't sure what he'd have done in the same situation. Nothing so daring and heroic, he suspected. "How did you get me out?"

"The front windshield was broken and you were only a few feet under. I didn't have to dive down far. I reached in and grabbed your sweater and you just floated up. You weren't wearing a seat belt."

He'd been driving in a snowstorm without a seat belt. "That's strange."

"Not your usual style?"

"No. I'm from L.A. We break every rule but that one."

"You were going pretty fast."

That wasn't typical for him, either. He might push the speed limit on the freeway, but he wouldn't be reckless on an unfamiliar mountain road during extreme weather conditions. "Next you'll tell me I was drunk."

"I don't think so."

"How do you know?"

"You vomited lake water. It didn't smell like booze."

He'd thrown up in front of her last night. This morning he'd exposed himself to her. "God," he muttered, dragging a hand down his face.

"Soup's ready," she said brightly. "I'll bring you some."

Although she had a round table in the kitchen with two chairs, she set up an old-fashioned TV tray for him in front of the couch. The chicken-noodle soup and saltine crackers reminded him of his childhood. It was an odd breakfast, but his stomach might not be able to handle anything more. When she grabbed a lemon-lime soft drink from the refrigerator and poured it into two cups, he felt a pang of homesickness. Perhaps the near-death experience had made him sentimental. "You must know my mother."

"Hmm?"

"This is her cold remedy."

"Chicken-noodle soup?"

"With a soda on the side."

She laughed, bringing the drinks to the couch. Not bothering with a tray for herself, she set her cup on the end table and curled up next to him with the bowl in her lap. "It's everyone's cold remedy. There's a song about it."

"I've heard it."

"Can you do the dance?"

"Maybe later," he said, smiling.

She lifted a spoonful of broth to her lips and blew. Colin dragged his gaze away from the mesmerizing sight and concentrated on his own soup. It was hot and comforting. Again he thought of his mother. She'd always taken care of him on her own. He felt a little guilty that his first concern after learning about the accident had been his computer.

"Is your phone working?"

"My cordless and cell are both out."

"Email?"

"I can check, but I usually don't have service during a storm."

He'd already known that internet access was limited in this area. It was one of the reasons he'd come, to unplug.

"Is someone waiting for you?" she asked.

"No. I was alone."

She didn't ask why, to his relief. He always found it awkward to talk about his writing. People were amazed that he'd managed to finish a book, as if this was some stellar achievement. Now that he'd found commercial success and landed a television deal, *women* were impressed. He was unsettled by the attention.

"What's your name?"

"Colin."

"I'm Paige," she said, offering her hand.

He felt a zing of electricity as his palm touched hers. "Pleased to meet you."

She drew her arm back shyly, tucking a lock of hair behind her ear. It was adorably mussed, falling in loose waves to her shoulders. "You look much better."

"I do?"

"Yes. Last night one of your pupils was this big." She made a circle with her fingers and thumb, holding it up to her eye like a telescope.

He laughed at the pirate-like expression. "I must have a concussion."

"You were talking nonsense."

"What did I say?"

"Something about feeding the cat."

He glanced around. "Do you have a cat?"

"No, but I've been thinking I should get one. The cabin has seemed a little empty since my brother left."

"Where did he go?"

"Oxnard. He moved there with his girlfriend."

"Ah. I live alone…with a cat, so I know how it is."

"Does it help, having a cat?"

"Totally. Whenever I hear a spooky noise, Ghost goes to investigate. She's much braver than I am."

She smiled, cocking her head to one side. "Why did you name her Ghost?"

"She's gray and appears out of thin air."

"I hope you didn't forget to feed her before you left."

"No, she's boarding at the cat hotel. It's very posh."

They'd both finished their soup, so she took the dishes to the sink. A local-news update indicated that portions of Twin Lakes Road and Highway 395 were impassible. Record levels of snowfall were predicted for the weekend, so the situation would get worse before it got better. Residents were advised to sit tight.

"I think we're stuck here until the storm passes," she said, turning the volume down.

"I'm sorry."

"Why?"

"You probably weren't counting on an uninvited guest."

"It's no trouble."

Although he appreciated her hospitality, he didn't want to impose. She was young and beautiful. He was a total stranger, clearly a sex maniac. Even if she forgave his earlier gaffe, she couldn't feel comfortable with this situation.

But what could he do? He wasn't strong enough to walk across the room, let alone snowshoe several miles to his cabin.

"How's your headache?" she asked.

"Not bad."

"I'll bandage that cut for you now. I meant to do it last night but I fell asleep."

When he didn't protest, she approached him with the first-aid supplies. He sucked in a sharp breath as she touched a wet cloth to his brow. "Is it tender?"

"Just cold," he lied.

She increased the pressure, scrubbing the dried blood away. He could feel fresh beads well up under her ministrations. "This might need stitches."

He winced at the thought.

"It's going to leave a scar."

"Good. I've always wanted one."

"You don't have any?"

"Not on my face."

She continued to blot his forehead with the edge of the cloth, making a sympathetic noise. Her breasts were inches from his mouth, which was disconcerting. He forced his gaze higher, only to become fixated on her smooth, pale throat. A pulse fluttered near the silky hollow. Intuition told him that the spot was extra sensitive. His mind generated an erotic picture of her underneath him, arching her neck as his lips descended.

He closed his eyes to dispel the image.

Oblivious to his lust, she applied a butterfly bandage to the wound, holding it closed. It felt better immediately. She took a bag of peas from the freezer and wrapped it in a paper towel. "This will help with the swelling."

"Thanks," he said gruffly, placing the cold lump against his forehead. Maybe he should put it in his lap.

She turned and focused her attention on the fire, stabbing at it with an iron poker. Her backside was just as luscious as her front. The snug black leggings molded to every curve. He had to close his eyes again.

After a few moments, his arousal faded. The warmth of the fire made him drowsy. Smothering a yawn, he set aside the cold peas and rested his head against a pillow. When she put a blanket on him, squeezing his shoulder gently, he was already half-asleep.

CHAPTER THREE

PAIGE WATCHED COLIN for a few minutes after he drifted off.

She supposed the concussion was making him drowsy. Although he looked much better—much, *much* better—she was concerned about his condition. Her mother had been a nurse who specialized in traumatic brain injuries.

Paige nibbled her lower lip anxiously, studying her patient. Part of her was relieved he'd gone to sleep. His presence was magnetic, unsettling. She'd met her share of handsome men, but she wasn't used to entertaining them in her cabin. Her initial estimate of his attractiveness had been way off.

He was a ten.

While unconscious, his slack features had been nice enough. He had good bone structure—strong chin, straight nose. Beard stubble shadowed his jaw. His hands were large but not heavily callused. She doubted he worked manual labor. He probably got his muscles from the gym or outdoor exercise.

Lucidity had transformed him from pleasant looking to fascinating. He had dark brows and thick stubbly lashes. The term "bedroom eyes," which she'd always disregarded as fanciful, sprang to mind. His gaze crackled with intensity. He looked like the kind of man who really…paid attention. He also had a sensual, expressive mouth. That hint of softness, paired with a strong body and angular face, appealed to her.

This morning, when she'd woken up next to him… Oh, my.

Her cheeks heated at the memory. If she hadn't been so quick to cover herself, would he have tried to touch her? He'd seemed interested, despite his headache.

She didn't flatter herself into thinking his reaction meant something. Most men responded to the sight of bare breasts. Although she hadn't intended to fall asleep naked, she couldn't blame him for noticing. She'd peeped at him first, after all.

Letting her gaze wander down the center of his chest, she took another gander. The blanket had settled around his waist, covering his splayed knees. His open shirt-front exposed a tantalizing swath of skin. He had a sexy whorl of hair on his stomach. One of his hands was draped across his lap, the other shoved beneath the blanket. She couldn't see what was going on down there, perhaps a protective cupping between his legs.

She stood and walked across the room, her heart racing. In her experience, hot guys didn't always have the best personalities. This one was clever, with a quirky sense of humor. The more he spoke, the more she liked him. She got the impression that he liked her, too. He'd definitely been checking her out.

For better or worse, they'd be spending the weekend in this confined space together. Getting to know each other. Assuming he was single and willing, he might make a pass at her. What would she do?

Her stomach fluttered with anticipation.

Casual sex wasn't a great idea. Well, it wasn't a

bad idea, either, in certain circumstances. She'd had a couple of flings with tourists. Crystal Crag attracted rock climbers in the summer, and the snow brought big crowds of sportsmen in the winter.

Paige wasn't opposed to playing the field and having fun. She hadn't invited dates back to the cabin when Paul was home because that would have been weird. Her brother's presence was no longer an issue, but the storm created its own set of difficulties. When neither party was free to leave, extreme awkwardness could ensue.

Or…feelings might develop.

She was already drawn to Colin and concerned for his welfare. Maybe saving him had forged a special bond between them. The instant connection surprised her. She didn't get attached easily and she tended to distrust charming men. After the loss of her parents and a heartbreaking betrayal at the hands of her ex, she'd learned to keep her guard up.

Crossing her arms over her chest, she stared at the frosty white blur outside her front window. The details he'd recounted from the accident were odd. He couldn't explain why he'd been driving in such a reckless, unsafe manner.

Was he hiding something from her?

With a small frown, she ventured into her bedroom for a hooded sweatshirt. Her hair was a mess, so she took a few minutes to run a comb through the tangles. Then she brushed her teeth and applied a hint of lip gloss.

Feeling better, she returned to the front room and gathered their wet clothes, taking them to the washing machine in the hallway. His pockets yielded no personal identification, just a set of keys and a money clip. His

SUV must have had a button ignition. The disc-shaped keychain said Bates Motel, Fairvale, CA.

She left the keys and cash on the dryer, guessing that Colin was a Hitchcock fan. After putting the load to wash, she wandered back to the kitchen. Although she hadn't intended to work this weekend, she was too wound up to read. Sitting down at the table, she opened up her laptop and scrolled through the photos she'd uploaded yesterday.

Of the hundreds she'd taken, about thirty were good enough to post on her website, ten were excellent and four were stunning. She'd submit those to various magazines and hope for the best. It wasn't easy to make a living as a photographer, so she'd learned to diversify. In addition to landscapes and wildlife, she covered a variety of winter sports and local events. She also did freelance page layouts for online publications. Deciding which images to use and where to place them wasn't quite as gratifying as taking the shots herself, but it was creative work and it paid well.

A few hours later, she got up to stretch. Colin was snoring softly on the couch. Her tummy rumbled as she spotted a box of blueberry-muffin mix on the shelf. The early-morning soup hadn't felt like breakfast. She'd skipped coffee, too.

After closing the file on her laptop, she puttered around the kitchen, making coffee and muffins. When the pot finished brewing, it beeped. Colin roused at the sound, lifting his head to look at her.

"Sorry," she said. "I didn't mean to wake you."

"Is that coffee?"

"Yes."

"Mmm."

"How do you feel?"

"Better," he said, throwing aside the blanket. "Hungry."

She watched him walk across the room, noting that he appeared steadier on his feet. When he tried to approach the coffeepot, she stepped in. "Sit," she said, pointing at the table. "Do you take cream and sugar?"

"If you have it."

"Actually, I don't," she admitted. "I use honey and milk."

"Sounds good."

She added a little of both to a cup and plunked it down in front of him.

"Thanks," he said, taking a sip.

"I have some muffins baking. But I can make bacon and eggs if you'd like to try something more substantial."

His eyes lit up at the word *bacon*. "I don't want to put you out."

"Not at all," she said, removing the items from the fridge. Her brother had always preferred savory breakfasts over sweet. It was kind of nice to have a man with a hearty appetite in the house again.

"Is your internet working?"

"No. I just checked."

"I like your screen saver. This is Twin Lakes?"

"With Crystal Crag in the background."

"Who took it?"

"I did."

"It's a great shot."

She glanced over her shoulder as she added bacon to the frying pan. "I'm a photographer."

"Really?"

"Yes."

"Can I see more?"

"Sure. There's a bunch of image files on the desktop. You can click on Dawson Collection for a basic mix."

He browsed the photos while she fried bacon. Although he didn't comment on every image, he seemed impressed by her skills, and he had a good eye. He questioned her about the best of each subset.

"Wow," he said, leaning closer to the screen. "Is this you in the pond?"

"It's a hot spring. But yes, it's me."

"How did you take it?"

She moved the bacon to a plate and turned down the burner. "With a timer. That was a challenging shot."

"Why?"

"Nudes are difficult, especially in color. There are so many variables to natural light and skin tone. I was also posing for myself, which is a pain. I couldn't see how it looked until I got out and dried off."

The end result was quite chaste. Her back was to the camera, one hand touching her upswept hair, the other covering her breast. The water rose to her hips and a layer of steam added a hazy border, softening the edges.

"It's beautiful," he said.

She flushed at the praise. "Thanks."

The muffins were ready, so she grabbed a mitt and opened the oven to retrieve them. As she straightened, Colin averted his gaze from her backside. She put the tin down and cracked a couple of eggs into the pan, her pulse jumping.

Although the nude photo was more revealing than her outfit, it didn't seem as personal. It had become a piece of artwork, separate from her real self. His attention felt personal, however. She got the impression that he was picturing her without clothes. He didn't have to stretch his imagination to do so.

She finished cooking and cleared the table, bringing the food to him. He picked up his fork and dug in. They ate in companionable silence. The sound of him scraping his plate was compliment enough.

"How long have you lived here?" he asked.

She drank from her coffee mug before she spoke. "Four years. The cabin's been in my family for about fifteen."

"Your parents own it?"

"No. They died in the San Diego earthquake."

His brow furrowed. "I'm sorry."

"It's okay," she said. "They were on the freeway when it collapsed."

He straightened in his chair, seeming to understand the implications. "Is that why you saved me?"

"Maybe. I thought of them in that moment."

"What were they like?"

It was a rare question. Talking about her parents' deaths usually shut down the conversation. "They were...very happy together. They argued and had normal fights, but they loved each other. And us. My little brother and I were lucky to have them."

He nodded thoughtfully.

"What about you?"

"My dad left when I was six."

Sympathy welled within her. "That's too bad."

"My mother did pretty well without him."

He'd also done well, if the expensive clothes and car were any indication. An overachiever, perhaps.

"So you and your brother inherited the cabin?"

"We inherited this and the house in Solana Beach,

where we were born. It was paid off, but neither of us wanted to live there. Paul was always traveling, and it was too big to keep up. So we sold it and kept the cabin."

"How long have you been living alone?"

"About a year. My brother invited me to move in with him and his girlfriend, but I didn't want to."

"Why not?"

"I like it here."

He glanced around, perhaps thinking she should have gone with Paul. "You definitely need a cat."

She laughed in surprise. "Where did you get yours?"

"Ghost wandered in from the street. I called her Tom for months. When I took her to the vet to get neutered, they informed me she was female."

"You couldn't tell?"

"I'd never looked."

She studied him from across the table, enjoying his sheepish grin. He'd photograph well. Sitting with his shirt hanging open, hair mussed, coffee mug in hand, he looked like a cozy housewife fantasy. Her fingertips itched to pick up her camera and snap a few candids. "I could use a cat for company."

"Why don't you have a boyfriend?"

"How do you know I don't?"

"Male intuition," he said, still smiling. "Or maybe just wishful thinking."

She glanced away, moistening her lips. "Most of the single men around here are tourists. Not long-term material."

"What about short-term?"

"I dated a snowboarder last winter."

"A snowboarder? Was he legal?"

"He was twenty-nine," she said, rolling her eyes.

"But definitely a globe-trotter. He left with the spring thaw."

His expression grew pensive. "Do you miss him?"

"A little." She'd never thought Marcus would stay, so his departure hadn't upset her. Between the two of them, he'd been more invested in the relationship. Her feelings for him had never developed beyond affection. "It wasn't serious."

Colin seemed satisfied by the answer. He leaned back in his chair, contemplating the muffin on her plate.

"Do you want a muffin?" she asked.

"I'll take that one, if you're not going to finish it."

"There's plenty more."

"I'd rather eat yours."

She gave the remaining half to him, suspecting that he meant to be suggestive. If he'd thought to amuse her with the innuendo, he underestimated his sex appeal. She melted at the thought of him devouring her.

Flustered, she rose from the table and took the plates to the sink. She was disturbed by her attraction to him and concerned about their revealing conversation. She didn't usually open up to strangers, but his questions had caught her off guard. He'd cut right to the heart of her issues. Male intuition, he'd joked. Maybe he just had good observation skills or a knack for understanding human nature.

He made her feel hot and tingly and…vulnerable. The last time she'd given herself to a man, body and soul, he'd broken her trust at the worst possible moment.

There was a reason she'd rather have a cat than a long-term boyfriend.

CHAPTER FOUR

COLIN FELT LIKE a geeky teenager with Princess Leia.

Paige sent his hormones into overdrive. He often used humor to mask his nervousness, and she had a powerful effect on him. She was beautiful, but he'd seen a lot of beautiful women. He'd even dated some. There was something else about her, a fierce independence and inner strength that appealed to him.

They just...clicked. He could feel it.

"More coffee?" she asked, lifting the carafe.

"Sure."

She refilled his cup and her own, adding a bit of milk and honey. "How long have you lived in L.A.?"

"About ten years. I was born in Colorado."

"So you know how to drive in snow."

"I'm a bit rusty, but yes. I know enough to slow down." He frowned, still unable to believe he'd been driving recklessly on a slick mountain road. He hoped there hadn't been a family emergency.

"What brought you to California?"

"A teaching job."

"Where at?"

"USC."

Her catlike gaze sharpened. "That's a tough school to get into."

"Yes," he agreed. He'd been lucky to land a part-time position. Two tenured professors had retired, and another had suffered a knee injury. The department had had a sudden opening and Colin was available on short notice.

"What subject do you teach?"

"Anthropology."

"I can't picture it."

"Why not?"

"You don't look like an anthropology professor."

"I left my tweed jacket at home."

She took a closer look at him, her lips curving into a smile. "Do your female students come to class with messages written on their eyelids? 'I love you, Dr. Jones,'" she mimicked, batting her lashes in slow motion.

He laughed, embarrassed. "Indiana Jones taught archaeology. That's not my field."

"Are you a doctor?"

"No, I'm just plain old Professor Reid. I don't steal cultural artifacts or carry a horsewhip. I am afraid of snakes, though. We have that in common."

"What about the girls?"

"What about them?"

"They don't hit on you?"

"No."

"You're being modest. Students always fantasize about cute professors."

"Maybe, but they don't act on it."

"And you're never tempted?"

"Not really. I'd get fired, and most of my students are way too young for me. I'm like a married man in the classroom. I keep my distance and don't invite personal questions. They know not to approach me with any…romantic designs."

"How old are you?"

"Thirty-two."

"That's young, for a professor."

"How old are you?"

"Twenty-seven."

Older than he'd thought. He wouldn't feel as if he was taking advantage of her if, by some miracle, she decided to heat up the furs with him, caveman style.

"Colin Reid," she said, tapping her chin. "That sounds familiar."

His muscles tensed with unease. She'd heard of him. Damn! They'd been getting along so well. He didn't want his minor fame to change the dynamic between them. She actually seemed impressed by his professor status and interested in him as a person. He was loving every second of it.

"Isn't there an author named Colin Reid?"

"Yes." Him.

"He does that Paranormal PI series," she said, rising from the table. Colin Reid was a common name, so she might not guess they were the same person. He was about to come clean when she crossed the room and picked up a reading device. "I read *Thriller* this summer. I didn't like it."

His curiosity was piqued. "Why not?"

"I'm trying to remember," she said, scrolling through the pages. The crease between her brows disappeared as she found the problem. "Oh."

"What?"

"Well…have you read it?"

"Yes." About a hundred times.

"I had an issue with one of the female characters," she said, waving a hand in the air. "It's probably nothing you'd pick up on."

"Are you kidding? I'm an anthropologist. I study people."

"You're also a man."

"So?"

She set the device aside. "Okay. The main guy, Investigator Burrows, is pretty adorable. He's sort of a bumbling James Bond, falling into bed with dangerous women and solving creepy crimes by accident."

It was a fair description of his work.

"In this one, his love interest is the mysterious hotel manager, Vanessa Black, who may or may not be a lesbian vampire."

"Right."

"There's a scene where Burrows is searching a room for clues and Vanessa comes in with her girlfriend. Of course, they have a steamy encounter while he hides behind the curtains, watching. After it's over, we discover that Vanessa knew he was there. She teases him with a kiss that tastes like her lover."

He remembered it well. Most of his readers—men and women—had enjoyed this scene. Others, not so much.

"I just thought it didn't fit in with the rest of the story. Vanessa starts off as this great character with an interesting role to play. Then she gets reduced to a sex object, flat and unrealistic. She's infatuated with Burrows, which makes no sense because she isn't into men. It was disappointing."

Colin had heard this kind of criticism before, so he wasn't fazed. His editor hadn't asked him to tone down the eroticism, and the television executives were all for it. While he tried to make thoughtful decisions, especially when it concerned violence against women or female sexuality, he didn't regret his creative choices.

With Vanessa he'd attempted to portray a character who was sort of fluid. Not a villain or a heroine, not gay or straight. But he had to admit that the sex was meant to titillate, and he wouldn't have written a man the same way.

"You're right," he said.

"About what?"

"That scene. It was objectifying."

She seemed wary of his agreement. "You found it offensive?"

"No," he said, shrugging. "I liked it."

His answer might not win him any brownie points, but at least it was the truth. He wasn't a bastion of enlightenment and his books weren't highbrow literature. He wrote them for the same reason he studied anthropology: people were fascinating.

Paige was fascinating.

He didn't mind her thoughtful commentary on his work. He admired her for caring about stereotypes, and it was kind of refreshing to hear sincere feedback face-to-face. Living in L.A. had taught him to take flattery with a grain of salt. Strangers bombarded him with effusive praise. Everyone assumed he was rich.

Colin felt a twinge of guilt for deceiving her about his author persona. He should have admitted who he was earlier. His "male intuition" told him that a woman who rescued a stranger from a submerged vehicle, brought him into her home and warmed him with her naked body wouldn't appreciate the omission. She seemed reclusive and cautious. If he confessed now, she'd feel misled.

He wanted her to keep talking. He also wanted to take her to bed. Both desires warred against his conscience, holding him silent.

She stared out the snow-speckled window, a crease between her brows. He couldn't guess what she was thinking about, his offensive scene or something else. Maybe she was sensitive to women's issues because a man had hurt her. He'd like to know why she preferred living alone and why she dated tourists who were only passing through.

"Most men don't understand how it feels to be objectified," she said.

Colin couldn't disagree there.

"But I think it can be taught."

"How?"

"I could photograph you."

The air rushed from his lungs. "That wouldn't be the same."

"Why not?"

"I wouldn't be offended if you treated me like a sex object. I'd enjoy it."

"You might," she said, smiling.

"We also live in a male-dominated society. One experience won't change the power dynamic."

"Scared?"

He realized that she was goading him into accepting the challenge—and it was working. Although he joked around a lot, he didn't want her to see him as weak or cowardly. He also made an effort to be open-minded and try new things. He wasn't an old-guard sexist, protecting the status quo. "Terrified," he said.

She laughed out loud. "But you'll do it?"

"Do what, exactly?"

"Well, let's negotiate."

"Full frontal nudity is off the table."

"Spoilsport."

"I'll show as much as you did in the hot spring."

"That photo wasn't even objectifying."

"I objectified it," he said, wagging his brows.

She gave him a scolding look. "I can work with shirt-less."

"Fine."

Giggling with glee, she went to a desk and found a sheet of paper. "You'll have to sign a release form."

"For what?"

"It protects us both. You agree to pose, and I agree not to sell or distribute the photos without your consent."

"Who will see them besides us?"

"No one, unless you want me to share."

"I don't."

"I'll write in *personal use*." She laughed again, as if imagining what kind of use she could get out of them.

Colin was already beginning to feel self-conscious. He read her form and signed it, a flush creeping up his neck. She intended to make him pose like some kind of beefcake. This was going to be majorly embarrassing.

He sat at the table while she got ready, selecting the right camera and gathering an assortment of props.

"I haven't even brushed my hair," he complained.

"I want it rumpled for a few shots."

"Should I take off the shirt?"

"Not yet."

She gave him a newspaper to read and fidgeted with

the scene, moving his coffee cup to the perfect location. Then she worked on his body positioning and the
drape of his open shirt. Satisfied, she backed up and
adjusted the lens.

Colin felt stiff and awkward. He didn't know if he
should suck in his gut or flex his muscles or what.

"Just relax," she said. "This is supposed to be a lazy
Sunday morning."

He let out a breath and loosened his grip on the newspaper.

"Try to look satisfied. Like you just got lucky."

His last relationship had ended six months ago, so it
was hard to remember what satisfaction felt like. He'd
had a falling-out with his girlfriend after she asked
him to introduce her to a television producer. He hadn't
dated since then, and a recent incident had spooked him
into virtual seclusion. Another aspiring actress, who
also claimed to be his biggest fan, had broken into his
apartment a few weeks ago.

For some reason, the memory triggered a shooting
pain inside his skull. He winced, touching the bandage
at his temple.

"What's wrong?"

"Nothing," he said.

"Headache?"

"Just a twinge."

"Do you want some more painkillers?"

"No, I'm okay."

The sensation faded and he focused on the task at
hand. Not trying to be sexy, he just started reading. She
snapped several shots.

"Good," she said. "Now lose the shirt."

He shrugged out of the too-small flannel, shivering

from the chill in the room. His nipples tightened and his chest broke out in goose bumps. She claimed that this effect ruined the mood, but it was hard for him to get comfortable again.

"Let's change locations."

"Can I comb my hair now?"

"Sure," she said.

He found a small comb and new toothbrush in the bathroom. After fixing his hair and brushing his teeth, he felt a little less scruffy. A shave wouldn't hurt, but he didn't have a razor. At least he wasn't dizzy anymore.

When he came back out, she had a ladder-back chair set up in the corner. Two girl-size pink barbells rested on the floor.

"You want me to lift those?"

"If you feel well enough."

"I can handle more weight than that."

"I don't have anything bigger."

He'd noticed a brick by the entrance, so he went to pick it up. The doorstop weighed about five pounds. "How about this?"

"Very manly," she said, humoring him.

This time she positioned him so that his bandaged eyebrow faced the camera. "Don't you want my good side again?"

"No. The injury looks kind of sporty. Just pretend I'm not here."

Following those instructions, he didn't glance her way as he did a series of repetitions using proper weight-lifting techniques. It was easier than just sitting there. He found himself enjoying the burn. "Can I switch arms?"

"Please."

While he worked his biceps and triceps, she took

photos from different angles. Although he was used to heavier barbells, the frequent reps increased his heart rate and warmed his blood. A fine sheen of sweat broke out on his upper chest.

"Nice," she said, clicking away.

Colin didn't think he was doing anything interesting or sexy, but lifting weights felt good. He always stood a little taller after a workout. Women liked physical partners. So did men. He appreciated taut curves and the sight of dewy perspiration on female skin.

"Can you do an ab workout?"

"Yeah."

She laid out a blue mat and murmured encouragement while he did crunches. Then she asked for push-ups. Then one-armed push-ups. He tried to accommodate her, but it was a difficult exercise.

"Don't hurt yourself," she said.

He lay flat, panting. "I'm fine."

"Do you feel objectified yet?"

"No."

"You're not sweaty enough."

"Sorry."

She put down her camera and came back with a spray bottle. Before she used it, her eyes lit up with invention. "I know what we need. Oil."

"Oil?"

She hurried to the kitchen and grabbed a container of cooking oil.

"Why not bacon grease?"

She paused, considering it.

"That was a joke."

"Oh." With a nervous laugh, she approached him,

pouring a small amount of oil into her cupped hand. "Let me do your back."

He turned around, nostrils flaring as she smoothed her slick palms across his shoulders, over his arms, down his spine. It didn't feel unpleasant; he enjoyed massages and soft female hands on him. But what he really responded to was the bite of fingernails in his skin as a woman came apart underneath him.

"Now the front," she said, her voice husky.

He didn't think he could endure her touch for more than a few seconds without getting excited, and he was right. His body stirred with arousal as she spread oil over his chest, stimulating his flat nipples. She moistened her lips, sliding her hands along his striated rib cage and down his clenched abdomen. By the time her fingertips slipped below his elastic waistband, he was sporting a sizable tent.

Color suffused her cheeks. She lifted her gaze to his face, but not in surprise. She already knew he wanted her. He'd greeted her with his erection this morning and had stared at her openly throughout the day. His willingness was a given, his response undeniable. Heat flared between them and his pulse throbbed with awareness. He engaged in a vivid fantasy of her oiled hand stroking his shaft.

It never materialized.

Her eyes left his and she cleared her throat, moving across the room. She added wood to the fire, as if the room had chilled. Then she went to the sink to wash her hands, drying them with a paper towel before she picked up her camera again.

"Ready?" she asked, all business.

Although her rejection was obvious, his body hadn't

quite caught up with his brain. When she glanced down, he was still half-hard. She pursed her lips, as if considering how to photograph him this way.

Colin hadn't agreed to any pornographic shots. Paige seemed trustworthy, but computers got hacked all the time. He didn't want images like that connected to his author persona. It could damage his reputation. Also, the thought of having his dick scrutinized on one of those "sexy male" sites made him cringe.

"Here," she said, tossing him a football.

"What do you want me to do with this?"

"Pose with it."

He tried out some moves, hiking and pretending to pass. Although he felt silly, his arousal faded, and he appreciated the fact that her lens wasn't focused on his male parts. "Isn't the background wrong?"

"I can change it."

She dirtied him up with ashes from the fire, smearing black under his eyes and across his triceps. Then she proceeded to direct him through a series of cheesy strongman poses—flexing this way and that, holding the ball in front of his crotch. Finally she turned him around and lowered his waistband to an indecent level.

"Now I feel objectified," he admitted.

She let out a breathy laugh. "This is nothing. For a stud calendar you'd pose naked with the ball."

"Have you done those?"

"No, but I've seen a few."

He glanced over his shoulder as she took another shot.

"Why don't you have a girlfriend?" she asked.

"Gigolos aren't allowed to have girlfriends."

"I'm serious. Look down and to the right."

"I broke up with someone a few months ago," he said, following her instructions. He hoped she noticed that he was good at taking female direction.

"How long were you together?"

"Not very long."

"Are you commitment shy?"

"No. I dated the same girl through college. Almost five years."

She stopped clicking. "What happened?"

"We just wanted different things. She was ready to have kids and settle down. I couldn't imagine doing that right after graduation. When I got the job offer at USC, she made the decision to stay in Colorado."

Paige fell silent, digesting those words. He was about to ask her the same question—was *she* commitment shy?—when she ended the shoot. "I'm done," she said, her expression closed. "You can hit the showers."

"No shower photos?"

She seemed to know he was joking, but she didn't smile. "I washed your clothes. They're on top of the dryer."

"Thanks."

"No problem."

He gave her the football, nonplussed. She placed it on her desk and attached the camera to her laptop, keeping her back to him as she uploaded the photos. He'd expected to have a laugh with her, make fun of himself, maybe flirt a little.

Instead she'd shut him out.

And even though she'd intended to treat him like a sex object, easily used and discarded, he didn't think her curt dismissal was part of the plan. Something about their conversation had bothered her. His presence bothered her.

He didn't know how to put her at ease. His skin itched with ash and oil, and a low thrum of desire still coursed through his veins. He wanted to give her pleasure, not space. But he wasn't the kind of man who forced his attentions on women.

Curling his hand into a fist, he walked away.

CHAPTER FIVE

PAIGE LET OUT a slow breath when she heard the faucet turn on.

She sank to a sitting position, knees weak. That had been one of the most challenging photo shoots of her life. Not because he wasn't a great subject. He looked very natural in front of the camera. Self-conscious at first, but once he'd warmed up…ugh. Those bedroom eyes and broad shoulders, hard stomach and sensitive lips…

Her tummy fluttered with longing and her skin flushed hot. She pushed the hair off her forehead, feeling feverish.

Maybe *she* needed a shower. A cold shower.

His physical reaction to her touch had been very exciting. She'd been tempted to slide her hand down and wrap her fingers around him, to let her eyes drift shut and her head fall back. He'd have kissed her. She knew it.

She'd stopped short of issuing such a blatant sexual invitation because…he scared her. The white-hot flare of lust threatened to incinerate them both. She also saw something more than desire in his eyes. It wasn't just animal attraction between them. They shared common experiences and connected on an intellectual level. His story of ill-fated college love had brought back memories of her own.

She hadn't felt this way about anyone since Derrick.

Colin was a tourist. Although this was her preferred type, she chose her dates with caution, always maintaining control. She couldn't do that with him. He might let her photograph him, and she suspected that he'd give her anything she asked for in bed, but he wouldn't keep an emotional distance.

He'd make eye contact as he slid into her. She could tell.

It wasn't that she avoided sensitive partners or men with good hearts. She just tended to steer clear of anyone who seemed like long-term material.

Paige had been in love once. Crazy, obsessive love. The relationship had consumed her. The breakup had just about killed her. She didn't want to go through that again, but she might be open to dating a nice local man.

Falling for a guy like Colin—no. Bad idea. Too intense.

Looking through the photos was also a bad idea. He had a mouthwatering physique. She didn't think he realized how sexy he was. Or how the soft fabric of the sweatpants outlined his masculinity, hinting at the thick fullness beneath.

She closed the picture window, her heart racing. Unfortunately, her imagination picked up where the photos left off. The sound of running water conjured a slick, soapy fantasy of lathered chest hair and hot skin.

While she sat there with a glazed-over expression, trying to gather her wits, he finished showering and came out in record time. He was wearing his jeans and the sweater she'd cut down the middle, along with a white V-neck T-shirt of hers. It was loose on her but snug on him. He looked kind of like a hipster in it. A hipster professor.

"How did they turn out?"

She glanced at the thumbnail proofs. "Good."

He came up beside her chair and braced his hand on the corner of the desk. Although he didn't crowd her, she could smell him, all clean and fresh. Swallowing hard, she clicked the slide-show option so he could study each one.

The photos, like the shoot, started off innocent and became increasingly sexualized. By the time they reached the end of the roll, he radiated embarrassment.

"Which is your favorite?" she asked, going back to the thumbnails.

His mouth twisted with distaste, as if he didn't like any. That didn't surprise her. Subjects weren't always a fair judge of their own images. "This one," he said, pointing to the least revealing kitchen shot.

Paige clicked on one from the other end of the spectrum. She'd caught him looking over his shoulder at her. The angle made his back appear broader, almost warrior-like. The oil wasn't as apparent on film. It merely helped to define his muscles and emphasize the sweaty gleam. "This is the best."

He rubbed a hand down his face, doubtful.

"What's wrong with it?"

"I look like I want to rip your clothes off."

Thrilled by this description, she examined it again. The raw sensuality in his gaze made her shiver. Portraits weren't her strong suit, so she was pleased to have taken such a compelling shot. When she photographed athletes, she usually focused on capturing the physical feat, not their facial expressions. "Hmm."

"Compare it to the one of you in the pool. Can you do that?"

With a few clicks of the mouse, she put them side by side.

"Yours is beautiful and sexy but elegant. Understated. Mine is about as subtle as that brick I was lifting."

While she agreed that the photos had different sensibilities, she liked the earthiness of his. "Maybe you're having trouble seeing yourself, or any man, as a sex object."

He mulled that over, conceding her point.

"Would you raise any protests if the photo of me was dirty and inelegant?"

"Protests? No. That's not what I'd raise."

She bit the inside of her cheek to keep from laughing. Professor or not, he reminded her of the naughty boy at the back of the class. "I'll email the proofs to you when my internet is working."

"I thought you were going to keep them for 'personal use.'"

She flushed, knowing she'd be tempted. The shots were already burning up her hard drive and giving her hot flashes. Better to get rid of them—and him—before she did something she regretted. Closing the screen abruptly, she rose from her desk. "I guess I'll take a shower, too," she said, skirting by him.

In her bedroom, she grabbed a soft blue tunic and slouchy gray sweatpants. Selecting underwear was more difficult. If she wore cute panties, she might as well throw them at him. Roomy cotton briefs would be more sensible. Feeling rebellious, she snatched up a frilly pair anyway. She wasn't so weak willed that she'd let a scrap of lace rule her libido.

Holding the clothes to her chest, she headed toward the bathroom, pausing when he approached her.

"I'm sorry," he said.

"For what?"

"Saying…inappropriate things. I joke around when I'm nervous. I didn't mean to make you uncomfortable."

His apology was sweet. And totally uncalled for. His sense of humor didn't bother her. The sexy photo shoot had been her idea. Maybe she should be apologizing. "Your jokes don't make me uncomfortable."

He frowned with confusion. "I also didn't mean to get…uh…"

"It's okay," she said, holding up a palm. "I rubbed you with oil. My bad."

"I hope you're not worried that I'm going to grab your ass or anything. I'm really not that type of guy."

"I believe you."

He fell silent, seeming unsatisfied with the exchange. If she admitted that she was rattled by the chemistry between them, not wary of him as a person, he'd feel better. But why borrow trouble? It was easier to let him think she wasn't interested.

She ducked into the bathroom, her pulse pounding. God, she was so stirred up! Her heart was racing, her body tingling. Ignoring her passion-flushed face in the mirror, she set her clothes on the edge of the sink.

His voice sounded outside the door. "You dropped something."

She opened it and found her underwear on the floor. Oops. He'd already walked away, so maybe he hadn't gotten a good look at the sheer white fabric with blue polka dots and dainty ruffled edges. Muttering "Thanks," she picked them up and shut the door. So much for not letting her panties set the mood.

The quick shower didn't relax her. As she rinsed away the soap bubbles, her nipples were still tight, her sex swollen. If she hadn't been so inhibited by his presence, she might have considered stroking herself to orgasm.

When she came out of the bathroom, well scrubbed but sexually frustrated, he was studying her DVD collection.

"You can watch one of those if you'd like," she said.

He turned to watch her walk into the kitchen. "What are you going to do?"

She had one craft activity planned for the weekend, and now seemed as good a time as any to get started. "I thought I'd make candles."

"Candles?"

"I give them away as Christmas gifts."

"Can I help?"

Nodding, she removed the necessary items from the pantry. With his help, she could knock out a double batch. She half filled two pots with water and set them on the stove. Then she put the soy wax chips in metal mixing bowls and placed them on top. "Here," she said, handing him a wooden spoon.

"What do I do?"

"Just let it melt. When it reaches the right temperature, you can stir in the coloring. I'll add scented oil and pour it into jars."

"That's it?"

"Pretty much."

"Where did you learn this?"

"From my mom. She made them every year during the first snow."

"What did she do for a living?"

"She was a nurse."

He touched the bandage at his temple, smiling a little. "I guess I'm lucky she passed some of her skills on to you."

"What about your mom?"

"She's a teacher. High school English."

The pride in his voice made her throat close up with emotion. She couldn't resist a man who loved his mother. Her brother was a teacher, too. Blinking rapidly, she busied herself by putting a set of jars on a baking sheet to warm in the oven.

"Why heat the jars?"

"Hot wax will shatter cold glass."

They made cinnamon-scented candles first. Paige added a red color chip and fragrant oil, enjoying the task. When the wax had cooled slightly, she poured it into the little jars. She let Colin mix the green wax and pine oil for the second batch. Soon the kitchen smelled like Christmas.

Some festive music would fit the ambience, but it was too early in the season. She turned up the radio anyway, listening to the latest weather report.

"Twin Lakes residents are experiencing power outages and downed tree limbs. The Jeffrey pines have been more prone to weather damage lately. Many local trees are dead or dying from poor soil conditions and an unusually dry summer."

That wasn't news to Paige. High levels of carbon dioxide had been found in the soil around the lake.

She wouldn't be surprised to find more fallen limbs on her property, maybe even entire trees, before the storm let up.

The rest of the afternoon passed quickly. She did some laundry while Colin read the newspaper she'd used as a scene prop. Before long it was time for dinner. She made grilled-cheese sandwiches and a garden salad. He insisted on helping her with the dishes when they were done.

"Have you always wanted to be a photographer?"

"No," she said, handing him a bowl to dry. "I studied a lot of different subjects in college. Art, film. I even took cultural anthropology."

"Yeah?"

"It was one of my favorite lower-division classes."

He smiled with genuine pleasure. "Where at?"

"Northridge."

"That's in L.A."

"Yes."

"So…why photography?"

She shrugged, unsure how to explain a gut feeling. "I've always enjoyed taking photos. When I started learning about the process and evaluating photographs as pieces of art, I just fell in love with it."

"Did you like L.A.?"

"Yes."

His hands paused on the last dish. "Ever thought of going back?"

Although he was probably just making small talk, his question unsettled her. "I didn't even attend my graduation ceremony," she said, shaking her head. "They mailed me the diploma. I left after my last final."

"Why?"

"My parents died that year, and I had a bad breakup with my boyfriend. I was overwhelmed."

"What happened with your boyfriend?"

She stepped away from the sink, troubled by the memory. "On the day of the earthquake, I had a morning class. My parents were scheduled to fly from San Diego to Hawaii that morning, so I knew they were near the airport. My brother called, frantic. We couldn't reach them. I went back to my apartment to watch the news."

He waited for the rest of the story, his attention rapt.

Paige was reluctant to continue. She never talked about this. The only person she'd ever told was her brother. "My boyfriend was there with another woman."

His brow furrowed with concern.

"He was a photographer, like me," she said, crossing her arms over her chest. "We met in class and shared the same passion. He was a natural behind the lens. By the end of college, he'd made a name for himself in freelance glamour."

"What does that mean?"

"Beauty and body shots. Sexy stuff for men's magazines." She paused for a moment. "You know how you said you weren't ready to settle down right after graduation?"

He nodded.

"Neither was he, I guess. We were both pretty immature. He met a lot of models and actresses, so he always had girls' phone numbers. I'd get jealous and accuse him of cheating. With success, he became distant and arrogant."

"Was he cheating?"

"Definitely. I caught them in bed together."

"What did he say?"

"That I'd pushed him away, and he thought we were separated. The second part was true. We broke up and got back together every other week. I'd stayed at a girlfriend's house the night before."

"He didn't waste any time."

She let out a shaky breath, raking a hand through her hair. "I think he regretted the way things ended, considering the circumstances. He came to the funeral and tried to apologize. My brother punched him in the face."

When he smiled in approval, she felt some of her heartache slip away. She was still pained by her parents' deaths, and she might never trust easily, but she didn't have to let an angst-filled college relationship haunt her. Everyone had a few skeletons in the closet.

She moved into the living room and added wood to the fire. The snow had picked up again, swirling outside the front window. They'd be lucky if the power stayed on. "Do you want to watch a movie?"

"Sure," he said, sounding eager.

"You're a Hitchcock fan, I take it?"

"How did you know?"

"I saw your keychain."

"Ah. That's a real movie prop. I was Norman Bates for Halloween one year."

"As Mother?"

"Of course."

She grinned, picturing him in the severe-looking wig and dress. Clean shaven, he might resemble a young Anthony Perkins. He had similar coloring and a tall, lean physique.

"You like horror?" he asked, gesturing at her collection.

"My dad was the horror buff, actually. These are all his."

"My dad, also. It's one of the few things I remember about him."

"You haven't stayed in touch?"

"No. He sent birthday cards for the first few years. Then nothing."

"What do you think happened to him?"

He shrugged. "I know he was born in L.A. and that he dreamed of being an actor. It's one of the reasons I came out here. I tried to track him down."

"No luck?"

"None."

"That's too bad."

"It's okay," he said. "I might have found him and reacted the same way your brother did at the funeral."

"With angry fists?"

"Yes." He changed the subject, removing a DVD from the shelf. "How about *The Descent?*"

"Perfect. I haven't seen that one."

Paige made hot cocoa and they settled in for a cozy evening on the couch. She tugged the sleeping bag over her lap, shivering as she watched a group of adventurous young women descend into an unexplored cave system.

It was a chilling film, relying on mood and imagination rather than special effects. When a creepy cave inhabitant appeared in the shadows, she almost jumped out of her skin. Colin laughed at her skittish reaction. She caught him watching her again after the next big scare. He'd drifted closer in case she required comforting. Suddenly her heart was racing with desire and anticipation, not fear.

Would he put his arm around her?

He found her hand under the sleeping bag and held it. She couldn't concentrate on the plot after that. His palm felt warm and broad against hers, his fingers long. She remembered the way he'd responded to her touch during the photo shoot and the way his eyes had feasted on her naked body this morning.

Maybe he was aroused right now.

Flushing at the thought, she hazarded a glance at him. He returned the perusal, his half-lidded gaze caressing her mouth. She moistened her lips on reflex as he leaned toward her. Unable to resist the magnetic pull, she moved in to meet him.

His lips felt soft on the first pass, brushing over hers to test her compliance. Her little moan must have encouraged him to go for it. He threaded his left hand in her hair and covered her mouth with his, seeking entrance. When her lips parted, he plunged inside, tasting her in silky strokes.

This was not a getting-to-know-you kiss. It was a blatant facsimile of sex. His tongue penetrated her mouth while his hand held her still. She imagined him using her body like this, thrusting deep, taking his pleasure.

She made another eager sound in the back of her throat, reveling in the possession. She wanted to suck his tongue and lick his skin. She wanted to slide her palm up his thigh and feel the exciting length of erection.

A woman screamed on film, startling a gasp from her lips.

He broke the kiss, panting. His eyes burned into hers.

She didn't have to touch him to know he was hard. This was no ordinary make-out session, stemming from an ordinary attraction. It was a full-on erotic explosion. If she didn't call a halt to the encounter, he'd be buried inside her in minutes.

"This isn't a good idea," she blurted.

"Why not?"

She picked up the remote and pressed Pause. "I don't even know you."

"I feel like I know you."

"You live in L.A."

He couldn't deny it. "I can come back."

She didn't think she was ready for a long-term relationship, let alone a long-distance one. If and when she decided to take another chance on love, it wouldn't be with a man guaranteed to break her heart.

"I've never felt this way before," he said. "I wanted you the first moment I saw you. Every time you speak or move or look at me, I want you more. I'm shaking right now, aching with the need to touch you."

"That's what scares me," she said. "It's too much."

"What do you mean?"

"If it was just sex, I might say yes."

"You're serious," he said in a flat tone. "You'd have sex with me if there were no feelings involved."

"Probably."

He let go of her hand, swearing under his breath.

"I'm sorry. I don't want to get hurt again."

It took him a minute to process her refusal. He might be a gentleman, but he was also a physical guy, primed for action. When the blood started pumping back to his brain, he relaxed. "We can do other things."

"Like what?"

"Touching and kissing?"

She smiled at his hopeful expression. "I don't think
so."

"Can we finish the movie, at least?"

"That we can do."

CHAPTER SIX

AFTER THE MOVIE, Paige went to bed.

Alone.

Colin stayed up late, his thoughts racing and his body taut with desire. He second-guessed everything he'd said and done to her. It was clear that she didn't trust him. Maybe he'd been too aggressive, too suggestive. He probably should have asked her out before he tried to put his hands on her. Keeping his author identity a secret hadn't been the best choice, either. Lust had clouded his perspective. He needed to show her that he respected her boundaries and cared about getting to know her.

They could make this work. It was a long drive from L.A., but flights were cheap and his schedule was flexible. Crazy as it sounded, he wanted to pursue a relationship with her. The more time they spent together, the more convinced he became that there was something special between them.

Meeting the woman of his dreams inspired a physical and emotional upheaval in him. He was brimming with creative energy, bouncing off the walls. He found a notebook and pen on top of her desk. For the next few hours, he alternated between fantasizing about hot sex and scribbling down ideas for a new series.

He also tried to remember what he'd been doing on Friday just before the crash. His head ached from the effort, leaving him with a vague impression of a dark-haired woman—his mother?—that faded quickly.

Around midnight the power went out. He didn't think it was cause for alarm, but he stayed alert and continued to feed the fire. The storm was really raging outside. It troubled him to imagine Paige battling the elements by herself every winter.

He finally ran out of steam and set the notebook aside. Her bedroom door was open to take advantage of the warmth from the fireplace, but he couldn't see inside. He hadn't heard any sounds from her room. No squeaky box springs or deep breathing.

He'd like to check on her. She'd be fast asleep, pretty face relaxed, soft lips parted, honey-colored hair spread across the pillow. He pictured her lying on her stomach, rolling over in those see-through panties.

Groaning, he massaged his eye sockets. She was probably all bundled up, not half-nude under the blankets. If he was going to engage in dirty thoughts, he might as well conjure an image of her buck naked, touching herself.

A terrific crash interrupted his fantasy. It felt as if the cabin had been struck by lightning or hit by a truck. Plaster rained from the ceiling and the cabin shook all the way down to its foundation.

What the hell?

He leaped off the couch and ran toward the bedroom, his pulse racing. Her muffled scream chilled him to the bone. When he reached the doorway, he froze in shock. A tree branch had smashed through the roof, creating a giant hole in the ceiling. He could see snow flurries and hear the shrieking wind.

Paige was trapped underneath the branch. Hurt badly, perhaps.

"Colin?"

The plaintive cry spurred him into action. He grabbed the end of the fallen branch and shoved it aside with all his might. Adrenaline must have assisted him, because the tree was huge. A layer of shingles and lumber had protected her from the crushing force. He ripped the broken pieces away, freeing her from the debris.

Suddenly she was in his arms and he was carrying her out the door. Her entire body trembled as he set her down on the couch. Kneeling before her, he ran his hands from her upper thighs to her stocking feet, checking for injuries. "Are you okay?"

"I think so."

Her sweatpants were torn and dirty, her shirt damp from snow. She had pine needles in her hair and a light scratch on her cheek. He rubbed his thumb over the cut, leaving a smear of blood in its wake. "No broken bones?"

"No."

He glanced toward the bedroom, amazed by the close call.

"I'd have been stuck without your help," she said.

"Good thing I was here."

Her blue eyes filled with tears.

He drew her into his arms as his throat closed up. Although he didn't believe in fate, he couldn't fathom anything less. She'd pulled him from the wreckage so he could save her from the fallen tree. This was meant to be.

After she calmed down, he released her to study the damage. Her bed was covered with snow and roofing materials. Cold air swirled in through the gaping hole in the ceiling, sucking all of the heat from the cabin.

"I'm having bad luck with tree branches this year," she said, sniffling.

"Yeah, what are the odds?"

"I should get my soil tested. There's a forest of dead trees on the other side of the lake. Carbon dioxide poisoning."

"From pollution?"

"No, I think it's a natural phenomenon. Something to do with volcanic activity on Mammoth Mountain."

"Jesus," he said, raking a hand through his hair. "Do you have any lumber? Hammer, nails, stuff like that?"

"In the garage."

She didn't want him to attempt a dangerous repair in the middle of the night during a blizzard, but he insisted. If he didn't board up the roof, the freezing air and snow would keep coming in. So he put on his boots and she let him borrow her brother's old parka. There was a pair of gloves in the pocket. She grabbed her coat and a flashlight before she followed him to the garage, where they found a large piece of plywood. First he had to clear off the roof and do something about the giant tree branch in the middle of it.

He set up a ladder and climbed it, tying a rope around the tree branch. They both moved to higher ground and pulled until the branch tumbled down the side of the house. Then Colin ascended the ladder again, shoveling away the snow and nailing a couple of two-by-fours to the top of the roof. Without those steps, he'd slide right off the icy surface.

Paige helped him lift the plywood panel. Getting the board up the ladder was a chore. His face was pelted by stinging winds and snowflakes melted in his hair, dripping chilly water on his neck. He had to take off his gloves to use the hammer. His fingertips grew numb halfway through the repair.

She stood at the top of the ladder the entire time, holding the flashlight. When the board was secure, they climbed down.

Inside the cabin, there was more work to do. Colin scooped up as much snow as he could and deposited it in the bathtub. She gathered the wet blankets into a pile and moved the debris out of the way. The hasty repair would keep the room dry, but not warm. She wouldn't be sleeping in her bed tonight.

"I'll make some more cocoa," she said, shutting the door.

He stood in front of the fire and tried to thaw his hands. She heated water over the fire, shivering. Her clothes were damp, like his. They should probably get undressed and huddle under her sleeping bag again.

He stared into the flames, reluctant to suggest it.

"Now I'm thinking I was too eager to turn my brother's room into an office," she said, handing him a mug.

"I'll take the floor. You can have the couch."

"How long were you planning to stay?"

"In your cabin?"

"In Twin Lakes."

"Another week."

"Then you have to go back to teaching?"

"No, I don't have another class until January. My schedule is flexible." After a short hesitation, he said, "Maybe we can go out to dinner when the weather clears."

Smiling, she sipped her cocoa. "You're sweet."

"I'm not that sweet."

She crawled under the sleeping bag on the couch and tugged her shirt over her head, tossing it aside. Her sweatpants followed. He knew what was left: those pretty little panties. "Well?"

His gaze rose from her bare shoulders. "Well what?"

"Are you going to stay in those wet clothes?"

He sat on the opposite end of the couch to remove his boots. His shirt and sweater were wet around the collar, his jeans soaked from the knee down. He took off everything but his boxer-briefs, which were still dry.

She scooted over to share the sleeping bag, bringing her cocoa mug. He tried to ignore the feel of her slender, mostly naked form curled up against his side. The fire blazed bright. Soon his entire body was warm.

"Who taught you how to fix things?" she asked.

"My grandpa."

"You don't have a stepdad?"

"Now I do. My mom remarried a few years ago."

"That's nice."

She set her cocoa on the end table, her breasts brushing his arm. He responded in a predictable way, already wound up from the night's adventures. Heat suffused his neck and he forced himself not to look at her.

Instead of returning her arm to her side, she placed her fingertips on his jaw and tilted his head toward her. Guarded, he studied the flare of desire in her eyes, the fluttering pulse at the base of her throat.

To his surprise, she lifted her lips to his.

PAIGE WASN'T SURE why she'd changed her mind.

Maybe because he hadn't lost interest after she'd refused him. He'd sat and enjoyed the movie like a gentleman. He actually wanted to go out on a date with her. For a professor, he was quite handy with tools.

And…he'd been there when she needed him.

She was disturbed by the thought of dying a slow death, trapped under rubble. His dangerous trek on the rooftop had rattled her further. She realized that she cared too much about Colin to let him slip away. Perhaps she'd made a mistake by shutting herself off from the rest of the world. It hadn't prevented her from developing feelings for him. Whether they slept together or not, she was already hooked.

So why deny them both the pleasure?

She knew he wouldn't make the first move again after getting shot down, so she took matters into her own hands. When her lips brushed his, he went still. He might think she was toying with him, but he didn't push her away. Instead he found a better angle to return her kiss and picked up where they left off, covering her mouth with his.

This time Paige gave as good as she got, kissing him back hotly. She moaned as their tongues met and tangled. She needed this. All of this. Every inch of him, all of his heat and taste and touch. Mouth to mouth, skin to skin, heart to heart.

But he paused, panting against her lips. "Is this gratitude?"

She twined her arms around his neck and slid her naked thigh along his. "Does it matter?"

"Well, it's not a deal breaker."

"I don't want to analyze anything," she said, kissing his clenched jaw. "I just want you to touch me."

He groaned in compliance, pressing her into the couch cushions and devouring her eager mouth. Her bare breasts brushed against his chest. Heat exploded between them and the sleeping bag fell to the floor. She clung to his shoulders, feeling the muscles bunch beneath her fingertips. He tasted hot and hungry and a little wild. She didn't know if their sexual chemistry had been amped up by her emotional breakthrough and the dangers they'd faced this evening, but it was off the charts. His raw intensity made her swoon.

With a low growl, he shifted his weight on top of her and settled between her spread legs. Hello. His erection nudged the notch of her sex, bumping a very sweet spot. She gasped into his mouth, awash with sensation. His keen observational skills translated nicely here. He lifted his head to watch her face while he repeated the action.

She bit down on her lower lip, shuddering.

"Can you come like this?"

"I usually need...direct contact."

He made a sound of approval, ready to give her exactly what she needed. His mouth trailed down the side of her neck and his thumb stroked the hollow at the base of her throat. As he flicked his tongue there, he continued the lower-body assault, stimulating her with the ridge of his erection. She arched her spine and dug her nails into his back, her breathing ragged. Her nipples were tight beads, her sex aching.

"What else do you need?"

She brought his hand to her breast.

He stared for a few seconds before he dipped his head, flicking his tongue over one ripe tip, then the other. The light rasp made her wet. She felt the cool air caress them and quivered, taut as a bowstring.

Her panties were already damp.

Impatient, she threaded her fingers through his hair and brought his mouth back to hers for a steamy kiss. Her breasts flattened against his hard, hair-roughened chest. Squirming with excitement, she reached down with her other hand. Slipping it inside his briefs, she encircled his steely erection.

"Ooh," she said. Her inner muscles clenched in response to his thickness.

He jerked in her hand, the blunt tip of his penis thrusting against the front of her panties. She knew he could feel her moisture through the sheer fabric. "Please tell me you have condoms."

She had a whole box, never opened. Giving him a push, she scrambled off the couch and padded to the bathroom to retrieve it. When she returned, he glanced at the box and set it aside, in no hurry to suit up.

"Where were we?" she asked, climbing on his lap.

While she took his face in her hands and pressed her mouth to his, he trailed his fingertips down her spine. Her tummy fluttered as he lowered the ruffled waistband of her panties. He filled his palms with the soft flesh of her buttocks and traced the sensitive cleft. She flexed her hips, rubbing herself along her length.

Faster. Harder. More.

As if sensing her urgency, he flipped her onto her back. Hands still buried in her panties, he stripped them off. She was too aroused to feel any shame about her splayed legs or the wet heat between them. He stared at her glistening center, mesmerized.

She curled her hands into fists and smothered a moan, desperate for relief. Instead of reaching for the condoms, he dropped to his knees in front of the couch. Her breath caught in her throat as he placed his hands on her inner thighs, spreading them wider. She watched his mouth close over her, vibrating with sensation. He used a light touch, a butterfly kiss. It wasn't the firm pressure she craved, but the sight was so erotic she groaned. When he introduced his tongue, penetrating her opening and tasting her slit, she couldn't take it anymore. She lifted her hips off the couch, begging him to finish her.

Smiling a little, because he knew very well what she wanted, he brought his mouth up to her clitoris. He alternated between circling the little nub with his tongue, kissing it and sucking gently. This broken rhythm kept her on the edge of orgasm—by design. He was enjoying this. Every soft cry, every strangled sob. If she let him, he might hold her captive to his delicious torture all night.

"Please," she said, twisting her hands in his hair.

He gave in easily, gliding his tongue over her until she screamed his name, bucking wildly against his mouth.

After so much buildup, her climax seemed to go on forever. When it finally ended, her skin was flushed, her heart thumping. She relaxed her grip on his hair, aware that he'd just given her the best orgasm of her life. If she hadn't already decided to take a chance on him, this would have convinced her.

"How was it?" he asked, rising to sit beside her on the couch.

"Mmm. A plus."

"That good?"

"Don't get smug, professor."

She would have gladly returned the oral-sex favor, but he tore open a condom package and donned protection. Focusing on her pleasure seemed to have caused him some discomfort. He was throbbing with arousal, wincing as he rolled on the latex.

She took pity on him. Bracing her hands on his shoulders, she straddled his lap. He let out a slow hiss of agony or ecstasy as she enveloped him. She was very wet and swollen. His jaw was clenched tight, his eyes dark with lust.

"How's this?" she asked.

He looked down at where they were joined, his fingertips digging into the soft curves of her hips. "It's good."

She brushed her lips over his, tasting herself on them. He kissed her back with fervor, spearing her with his tongue and his body. She moved up and down on him, riding him slowly, relishing the hot slide. They melded together, touching with hands and mouths and skin. She'd never felt closer or more connected to a man. He came with a muffled shout, his shoulders quaking and his fist locked in her hair. She milked him to the last shudder, drinking the passion from his lips.

After it was over, they curled up like spoons on the rug by the fire, her back to his front. He covered them with the sleeping bag, kissing her bare shoulder. She drifted off in his arms. Safe, satisfied, content.

CHAPTER SEVEN

COLIN WOKE IN the same state he had the previous morning: fully aroused with a naked woman in his arms.

This time he knew who she was.

Paige was curled up on her side in front of him, facing the fire. Memories from the night before assaulted his senses, urging him to roll her over and kiss her, to wake her with his tongue and hands. His erection nudged the soft skin of her buttocks. Smothering a groan, he eased away from her, admiring her bare bottom without disturbing her. They'd stayed up late repairing the roof, and she'd suffered a traumatic experience. He cared more about her need to sleep than his need to sleep with her.

He rose to his feet and pulled on his discarded clothes, which he'd laid out to dry in front of the fire. It was oddly quiet and bright inside the cabin. A glance through the front window revealed a winter wonderland, sparkling in the cold sunshine. The storm was over, having left a thick blanket of pristine white snow.

In the bathroom, he discovered the power was back on. Now that the sky was clear, he could probably access the internet.

To his bewilderment, he had no interest in doing so. Sure, he'd come to Twin Lakes to unplug, but he lived and died by email. He still couldn't remember if he'd sent his editor a copy of his latest manuscript. That was pretty damned important.

And yet it wasn't.

Today work could wait. Logging on would connect him to the outside world. He'd rather avoid the intrusion and stay connected with Paige. Instead of turning on her laptop, he found her phone on the kitchen counter and sent a quick text to his mother.

Hey Mom. Lost my phone. Everything ok?

She responded a moment later:

Fine honey. How's the book?

Done, he typed. Love you. Talk later.

Love you too. ☺

He set the phone down, relieved to hear all was well with her. Although the mystery of his reckless driving still remained, he wasn't ready for the weekend with Paige to end. She'd shared her body with him, and they'd had amazingly hot sex, but he wanted more. He needed to convince her that his feelings were real. He also had to tell her his author secret. They couldn't take the next step until she knew who he was. He'd have to tread lightly, considering her rocky past with that douchebag boyfriend.

From where he stood, their future looked uncertain. He'd like to be in a committed relationship with her. His deadlines weren't so tight that he couldn't visit her often. She might be open to coming out to L.A.—or she might not. His gut clenched at the thought of her shacking up with another snowboarder while he pined away.

Troubled, he put on his boots and her brother's parka to step outside. None of the trees surrounding the house appeared in danger of falling over. A snowplow was making its way down the road, clearing the street with brisk efficiency. He noticed the shovel leaning against the side of the house and picked it up, studying the long driveway.

Having grown up in Colorado, he was familiar with shoveling snow. He'd taken over the chore for his mother when he was ten. Their driveway had been much shorter. Paige must spend hours shoveling every week during the winter.

Shaking his head, he got started, clearing the sidewalk first. By the time he reached the garage, his muscles had warmed up but his hands were numb. The cold air reddened his nose and penetrated the thin work gloves.

Paige came outside with a coffee mug. She was wearing a black wraparound sweater and sheepskin boots. Her legs were exposed from upper thigh to below the knee, and her hair was adorably mussed.

She took a sip of her coffee, nodding at his work. "In a hurry to leave?"

It hadn't occurred to him that clearing the driveway would give her that impression. "No," he said, chagrined. "I wanted to do you a favor. You must spend half the winter shoveling."

"I pay for snow service, actually. They'll be here after the road opens."

He balanced his arm on the handle of the shovel, studying her amused face. She was glad he didn't want to leave. His heart thudded in his chest, thumping like the tail of an eager dog. "I guess I'm wasting my time, then."

"Well, you look great."

"Maybe I should remove my shirt."

"I'll get my camera."

He grinned at her and she grinned back, taking another sip of coffee. The moment was so sharp and bright it almost made him ache with happiness. If he wasn't careful, he'd fall in love with her.

"Why don't you come inside where it's warm?" she asked, tracing a fingertip along the plunging neckline of her sweater.

He wondered what she was wearing under it.

"I'll just finish this section," he said, dragging his gaze up to her face. He needed some time to reflect on his feelings without any distractions. Maybe he was under the influence of extreme lust.

She loosened the soft knit tie at her waist. Her sweater fell open, revealing her nudity. Bare breasts. No panties. Jesus.

Although she couldn't be seen from the road, which wasn't clear in any case, Colin glanced around the snow-covered woods to make sure they were alone. No one was walking their dog around the lake or lurking nearby.

Even so, standing naked in the cold sunshine was a damned bold move. His body heartily approved; blood rushed to his groin. Something about the sight of her in boots and a fuzzy sweater, semicovered but fully exposed, made him rock hard. Knowing she was doing this to turn him on heightened his arousal.

"Whenever you're ready," she said, going back inside.

He let the shovel drop and followed her, shrugging out of the borrowed parka and using his teeth to tear off his gloves. She met him with a kiss, her arms curled around his neck. He kicked the door shut and slipped his hands inside her sweater. Groaning, he plunged his tongue into her mouth and cupped her bare ass, lifting her against his erection. His clothed form pressed into her naked one. Her skin was so warm, her mouth so hot and delicious.

He couldn't get enough of her.

Panting, he slid his middle finger into her tempting heat, penetrating her from behind. She felt like molten honey.

"Your hands are so cold," she gasped, breaking the kiss.

He withdrew at once. "Sorry."

"I guess I'll have to do the honors." She removed a condom from the pocket of her sweater and placed it on the kitchen table. Then she brought her palm to his stiff erection, squeezing him through the denim.

He yanked his shirt over his head, eager to help.

With deliberate slowness, she released the buttons on his fly and reached inside his shorts to stroke him, rubbing her thumb over the blunt tip. When he grunted with pleasure, she sat down in a chair in front of him. His cock jerked in her hand, straining to meet her parted lips. She glanced up, watching his face as her wet, hot mouth enveloped him.

He'd been with other women this way, beautiful women, but it had never felt like this. The soft lap of her tongue undid him. She smoothed her hand down her belly, touching herself while she took him deep. He imagined her coming with her mouth stretched around him, her sweet cries muffled.

God. He was already close.

It wasn't her technique or her beauty or her lack of inhibitions that floored him. It was his emotional reaction. She was incredibly sexy, and he loved this, but he longed for a whole-body connection. He wanted to claim every part of her, to make her his.

She seemed surprised when he stopped her, lifting her up and drawing her into his arms. He kissed her parted lips, groaning with appreciation. Then he pushed her back onto the table and put on the condom.

She braced her palms on the flat surface, waiting. His gaze raked over her quivering breasts, her sleek belly and passion-flushed sex.

He entered her slowly, giving her time to adjust. She moaned and wrapped her legs around him, begging for more. When he was buried to the hilt, she crossed her booted heels behind his back. Keeping him there.

He brushed his lips over the hollow of her throat, where a rapid pulse fluttered, and brought his hands to her breasts. They were still too cool against her warm flesh. Trapping her nipples between his thumb and forefinger, he applied gentle pressure. She squirmed beneath him, digging her fingernails into his shoulders. He squeezed tighter, making her breath catch and her spine arch. She felt slick and swollen, gripping him like a silky fist. He withdrew a few inches and then surged forward again, wrenching a gasp from her lips.

He gritted his teeth as he watched himself slide back and forth, in and out. Giving her nipples another firm pinch, he lowered his hands to her hips, holding her in place for his thrusts. "Touch yourself."

Eyes half-lidded, she followed his instructions. With splayed fingers, she framed the place where their bodies were joined, feeling his shaft move within her. Then she brought those clever fingertips to her clit. Her mouth formed a sexy O as she strummed herself there.

He thrust harder, mesmerized by the sight.

She cried out, her hips bucking off the table. A coffee mug fell over the end and shattered, spilling hot liquid all over the ground.

Colin tangled his hands in her hair and surrendered to his need to dominate. He pounded into her with rough strokes, his buttocks flexing. Her breasts jiggled from the impact and the table legs scraped across the tile floor. He came with a hoarse shout, driving as deep as he could get on the last thrust.

When he drifted back down to earth, he raised his head, hoping she didn't mind his loss of control at the end.

She gave him a crooked smile, seeming unfazed. "Good morning."

"I broke your mug."

"Mmm."

He withdrew from her gently and went to the bathroom to dispose of the condom. When he returned, she'd retied the sash on her sweater and was kneeling to pick up ceramic shards. "Let me," he said, taking them from her.

She left him to it, grabbing two fresh mugs from the rack. He swept the floor and mopped it with a wet dish towel. "You're a handy guy to have around."

"Yes, I am," he said, unable to wipe the silly grin off his face. It felt damned good to make her smile, to make her cry out, to make her come. He wanted a repeat session. Perhaps a permanent loop.

But he took a cup of coffee instead, thanking her for it.

"The internet is working now, if you want to check your email."

Just like that, his elation fell flat. He didn't want to read his email or deal with the outside world. Tension vibrated through the back of his skull and settled in his gut, reminding him that he had a confession to make. "I should tell you something."

Caution flared in her eyes. "What?"

"I'm Colin Reid," he said, biting the bullet. "The author."

"The author," she repeated in a flat voice.

"I wrote the Paranormal PI series."

She set her mug on the countertop with enough force to make coffee slosh over the rim. Crossing the room, she yanked a hardback from the shelf. His first novel was there among the others. The second was on her reading device. Mouth thin, she flipped open the jacket and found his author photo.

He winced in anticipation of the book sailing at his head.

"You lied to me."

"No…"

"You said you were Professor Reid."

"I am Professor Reid. Look at my bio."

She skimmed the short paragraph, finding the section that said he taught cultural anthropology at USC. "Why didn't you tell me?"

He cleared his throat, uneasy. "Since they started making the television show, it's been kind of crazy.

People treat me differently. You seemed to like me for me, and I loved that. I was enjoying the...anonymity."

"They're making a show out of your series?"

"Yes."

She slapped the cover shut and put the book back on the shelf. "Congratulations."

"I'm sorry. I should have said something sooner."

"What do you mean, people treat you differently?"

"My last girlfriend asked me to introduce her to the producer," he admitted, raking a hand through his hair. "She was an actress."

"Did you do it?"

"No. I told her that I had no control over casting. Even if I did, I wouldn't have felt comfortable using my influence that way. Things were awkward between us after that. We broke up a week later."

"And now you think everyone is on the take?"

"Of course not."

She made a skeptical sound and crossed her arms over her chest. He walked toward her, searching for the right words and coming up empty. Being eloquent in the moment had never been easy for him. If he'd had an hour with a pen and a notebook, he'd be better prepared for this conversation.

"I can't believe you kept this from me," she said. "I opened up to you about my parents, and Derrick. I trusted you." When he tried to touch her upper arm, she jerked away. "This is why I don't jump into relationships."

"Paige, please."

"Please what?"

"Give me a chance to explain."

"What more is there to say? This *is* a deal breaker. I'd never get involved with a liar or a Hollywood big shot."

"I'm neither of those things."

"Why aren't you teaching right now?"

"I had to leave early because of a stalking incident," he said, grimacing at the sudden jolt of pain in his temple.

"Stalking incident?"

"A female fan broke into my apartment. She also trashed my office at the university."

"You told me your students don't hit on you."

"She wasn't a student."

Her blue eyes narrowed with suspicion, as if she was remembering her ex-boyfriend. He'd probably been full of lies and excuses. Colin hated the idea of her comparing him to that cheating bastard. "I think you should go."

His gut clenched with regret. He didn't want it to end like this. He wished he could confess his feelings to her and convince her that he cared, but she wasn't in the frame of mind to listen. By withholding information, he'd broken her trust. Even if she heard him out, she wouldn't believe him.

Colin didn't know what to do. He couldn't refuse to leave. This was her house and he had to respect her request.

"I'll take you to your cabin as soon as the road is clear," she said.

He nodded his acceptance, throat tight.

CHAPTER EIGHT

FOR THE NEXT two hours, they hardly spoke.

Paige just wanted to be alone. When she retreated to her room to clean up the debris from the roof, Colin followed. He helped in an unobtrusive manner, carrying the heavy pieces of lumber outside for her. She put some of the wet blankets to wash. As soon as she had phone service, she'd call a roofer.

Studying the boarded-over hole in the ceiling, she acknowledged once again that she was lucky he'd been there. She'd woken up screaming, attacked by a killer tree. Disoriented, she'd flashed back to the accident. For a second she'd thought she was trapped under the branch in the middle of the road.

She pushed aside that chilling memory and swept the floor, ignoring Colin's attempts to make eye contact. Just because he'd swerved to avoid her, saved her from being crushed and given her a couple of explosive orgasms didn't mean she was willing to overlook his deception. He'd pretended to be someone else.

If she'd known he was *that* Colin Reid, she never would have slept with him. He already reminded her of Derrick. The fact that he had crazy stalkers and Hollywood-actress girlfriends made her even more wary of him. He represented everything she hated about L.A. All of the drama, all of the hurt.

When the roads were open and her driveway was clear, they got ready to go. Paige grabbed her purse and put on her coat. She warmed up her Volvo in the dark garage, flexing her fingers around the steering wheel.

"Which cabin were you in?"

He checked his keys to make sure. "Seven."

"You still don't remember what happened before the accident?"

"I remember finishing my manuscript."

"When?"

"Friday afternoon."

The accident had occurred in the early evening, so he hadn't lost much time. A few hours at the most. She pulled out of the driveway and headed uphill toward the lodge. Before he skipped town, he'd have to talk to his insurance company and arrange for alternate transportation.

He didn't say anything until they were halfway there. "Can I call you?"

"I don't think that's a good idea."

"I'd like to see you again."

She blinked the moisture from her eyes, furious with him for putting her in this position. He'd tricked her into letting her guard down, and now she had feelings for him. Messy, painful, heartache-inducing feelings.

"This was the best weekend of my life," he said, glancing across the cab. "Not just because of the sex, although it was damned good. I liked the way you challenged me into that photo shoot. I liked making candles with you and watching movies. I love your creativity and the way you speak your mind."

The cabins near the lodge came into view. She slowed down for the turn, struggling to stay unmoved.

"I'm sorry I didn't tell you," he repeated. "I screwed up."

Paige frowned as she stopped in front of cabin seven. There was a red Mini Cooper in the covered parking area. "You said you were alone."

"I was."

"Whose car is that?"

His face went pale. "I don't know."

An ugly suspicion gripped her and refused to let go. That was a young woman's car. "Maybe you went out and celebrated after finishing your book. There are plenty of ski bunnies at the lodge."

He touched his temple, not denying the possibility.

"Do you have a girlfriend?"

"No," he said, appearing flummoxed. "I would have told you that."

"Like you told me everything else?"

"That's not fair, Paige."

"Isn't it?"

"I'm not him," he ground out. "I'm not your ex."

She stared stonily ahead, her throat raw with emotion. Damn him anyway. And damn her for falling for him.

"I'll return the jacket."

"Don't bother."

He got out and slammed the door, cursing under his breath. She shifted into Reverse and sped away before he could see her tears. Although she wanted to drive fast and reckless to match the awful tumult inside, she kept a steady pace. Her shoulders shook from the effort to control her feelings. A sob escaped her lips as she parked in the garage and hurried into the house, throwing herself on the couch.

Where they'd made love.

Images of their bodies entwined, undulating in front of the fire, bombarded her. If she buried her face in the pillows, she'd be able to smell him. Disturbed by the thought, she scrambled to her feet. The kitchen wasn't safe, either. It reminded her of the magnificent pounding he'd treated her to.

She took his book off the shelf and hurled it at the table in a futile attempt to dispel the erotic memories.

Chest constricted, she sat down at her computer desk. A simple search of his name led to dozens of author photos and articles. He was a member of some kind of literary rat pack, hanging with a group of handsome, artistic-looking men and fashionable women. Tears blurred her vision as she clicked away.

She found a recent news story about the stalking incident. Kathy King, his "biggest fan," had broken into his apartment when he wasn't home and fallen asleep in his bed. Since her arrest, she'd been released from jail and was awaiting sentencing. The photo accompanying the story showed a pretty, dark-haired young woman standing by a red car. She held an autographed copy of one of Colin's novels.

Paige studied the screen, troubled. What if he wasn't lying?

"Oh, my God," she said, clapping a hand over her mouth. The red car in the photograph was a Mini Cooper—the same one at the cabin. Kathy King must have tracked Colin down on Friday afternoon. He'd risked the snowstorm in his haste to escape.

It all made sense.

Stomach twisted with tension, she drove back to Colin's cabin. She considered calling 911 on her cell phone but she wasn't sure what she'd say. There might be trouble at cabin seven? Serial napper strikes again?

She parked her Volvo and grabbed the only weapon she could find, a heavy-duty ice scraper. Holding it in one hand and her cell phone in the other, she ran toward the front door. It was ajar.

"Colin?"

Eerie silence greeted her.

Paige dialed 911 from the threshold, trying not to panic. "Colin, are you there?"

Before the operator answered her call, a woman rushed through the doorway, wielding a small black object. Paige stumbled backward and tried to block the attack with her ice scraper, but it was too late. She was struck by a searing jolt of electricity. Her legs gave out and she collapsed on the snow-covered sidewalk.

COLIN REMEMBERED WHAT had happened Friday night.

A stress headache had formed while he was arguing with Paige. He'd been anxious and annoyed with her for making false accusations, frustrated by his inability to defend himself. Had he hooked up with a ski bunny? It wasn't something he would normally do, like driving fast in a snowstorm without a seat belt.

He'd watched Paige's car disappear, his fists clenched and his mood dark. Then, as he'd turned to approach the front door, a memory had hit him.

Kathy. She'd been here on Friday.

He remembered walking outside just as the snow started to fall. He'd been trying to call his mother, searching for an area with better cell phone reception.

Kathy's little red car had been parked down the street. She'd gotten out and approached him, smiling. They'd met several times at public events, so he'd recognized her. She was pretty and petite, dark haired. While he'd stood there, unsure what to do, she'd run to the open door of his cabin and dodged inside.

It was bizarre behavior, to say the least. He'd never been in a physical altercation with her before. When she'd broken into his home in L.A., he'd noticed the busted locks and called the police. After her release, he'd been awarded a restraining order. She wasn't supposed to come within a hundred yards of him.

At that point, Colin should have climbed into his SUV and driven away. He didn't for a very stupid reason: his laptop. He hadn't wanted to leave his laptop in her possession, considering her penchant for smashing his stuff.

He'd gone inside, thinking he could handle a small, slightly unhinged young lady. He hadn't expected an ambush with a stun gun. Maybe she'd miscalculated the voltage, because the jolt hadn't incapacitated him. When she'd tried to tie him up, he had knocked her hands away and lumbered to his feet, crashing out the door.

His brain had felt sluggish, his muscles weak as he'd climbed behind the wheel. He'd glanced into the rearview mirror, worried that she would try to follow him. He'd seen Paige in the road and swerved. Everything after that was black. He still had no recollection of the crash or near drowning.

The pain in his head faded as he weighed his options. He wouldn't underestimate Kathy again. She was still inside, ready to electrocute him. He didn't know if she wanted to cut off his balls or play house.

Several of the nearby cabins appeared occupied, but he decided to walk to the lodge, which was about a mile uphill. Phone lines might still be out. He could wait in the lobby without disturbing anyone.

He was almost there when the hairs on the nape of his neck stood up in awareness. Glancing over his shoulder, he saw Paige's car coming from the opposite direction. She was heading toward his cabin.

"No," he shouted, waving his hands in the air. She didn't see him.

Damn!

Abandoning the idea to find help in the lodge, he broke into a run, determined to reach Paige before she got attacked by Kathy. He'd been able to shake off the jolt of electricity, but she might not fare so well. Her body weight and muscle mass were much lower than his. He slipped in the snow and almost fell, cursing. His heart pounded with adrenaline and a cold sweat trickled down his spine. He'd never been so scared in his life.

When he reached his cabin, he saw Paige sprawled outside the front door. She was alive and conscious. Kathy stood over her with the stun gun in one hand.

Colin halted in his tracks.

This was like a scene from one of his novels, only he was no hero. Neither was Investigator Burrows, but he always managed to have a stick of dynamite or some other handy item in his pocket.

Kathy crouched down to pet Paige's mussed hair. "Is this your girlfriend?"

His voice shook with fear. "No."

"Don't lie to me!"

"I'm not."

"Why'd you run away from me?"

"You shocked me," he said. "I was…confused."

Kathy swept Paige's hair aside and pressed the weapon against her pale throat. "Do you love her?"

He took a deep breath, praying they'd get out of this unharmed. "No," he said, too loudly. Unconvincingly, to his ears. "I love you."

"Really?"

"Yes," he said, holding her hopeful gaze. "Leave her alone and come with me."

She moistened her lips, deliberating.

"We can run away together."

Kathy removed the stun gun from Paige's throat. Tears of relief filled Paige's eyes, spilling down her cheeks. When he offered his hand to Kathy, she took it with a shy smile. He forced himself not to look back at Paige again.

He was reluctant to climb in the Mini Cooper, but he didn't know what else to do. The idea of tackling Kathy to the ground or striking her made him queasy. She still had the stun gun. If they tussled, she might use it on him and go after Paige again. He wanted to get Kathy as far away from Paige as possible.

She put the Mini in Reverse and backed up too fast, narrowly missing Paige's Volvo. "Oops," she said with a nervous giggle.

He massaged his temple, racked by uncertainty. Kathy didn't look like a dangerous psychopath. She was young and cute, with chic clothes and expertly tousled brown hair. If she hadn't been a fan, he might have asked for her number.

Before he met Paige, that is.

She veered left toward Twin Lakes. Her driving was probably not erratic enough to attract the attention of law enforcement. Colin studied the door handle, wondering if he should try to take a dive.

"Where are we going?" he asked.

"Not far."

After they passed Paige's cabin, she accelerated steadily, her tires slipping and sliding across the icy roads. Maybe she suspected he was considering an escape attempt. "I know you don't really love me."

He made a strangled noise, unable to form a response.

"But this way we can be together."

With a sinking heart, he realized what she planned to do. The next curve in the road skirted the edge of the lake. It was only a few hundred yards from the spot where his SUV had submerged.

"No," he said, bracing himself for the impact. "Don't do this."

She drove faster.

"Please!"

The car sailed off the edge of the road, hitting the surface of the lake with a terrific splash. Her air bag deployed in a burst. Colin had neither seat belt nor air bag, so he was treated to a hard slam against the dash.

Within seconds the cab started to fill with icy water.

He shook his head to clear it, fumbling for his door handle. There was an ominous click as she pressed a master button to lock the doors and windows.

Trapping them inside.

Her air bag deflated quickly, leaving white powder on her face. Even that looked cute, as if she'd just powdered her nose.

"Unlock the door," he growled.

She shrank away from him, holding the stun gun in her clenched fist. "No."

He gritted his teeth as the water poured in the engine compartment, swirling around his ankles. The car continued to sink downward. Colin searched for an object to break the window and came up empty. He shoved a hand into his jeans pocket, finding his set of keys... and a single nail, left over from last night's emergency roof repair.

The Mini Cooper was a convertible with a sturdy canvas top. Ripping through it with his bare hands would be about as easy as kicking out the window with booted feet. But maybe he could tear a hole with the nail.

Gripping the blunt end of the nail in his fist, sharp end sticking up, he punched at the canvas, ripping a tiny slit.

Kathy squealed a protest and tried to stun him.

"Goddamn it," he muttered, blocking her attack with his left arm. He grasped her slender wrist and twisted her hand around, turning the weapon back on her. He worried that the water would disperse the electroshock, but it didn't.

She convulsed like an epileptic and slumped over the steering wheel.

Tossing aside the stun gun, he went back to work on the top. After several more blows, he'd created a large enough hole to fit his hands through. The freezing water was above his waist now, robbing the strength from his muscles and impeding his ability to breathe. Holding the nail in his teeth, he gripped the edges of the canvas and tore it apart.

Before he left the vehicle, he glanced at Kathy. She

was still groggy. Even if she wanted to get out, he didn't think she could manage without him. Leaving her here meant letting her die. Precious seconds ticked by as the water crept up to his chin.

Attempting to save her life might endanger his own, but screw it. Colin pulled her toward him and shoved her through the narrow opening in the roof. The vehicle was almost completely submerged. Once she was outside, he followed. It was a tighter squeeze for his broad shoulders. Just when he thought he wasn't going to make it, the canvas ripped wider.

He broke through as the car shifted, plummeting toward the bottom of the lake. Kathy almost slipped beneath the surface. He shoved his forearm under her chin and started swimming. It was less than twenty feet to the shore.

The distance stretched into infinity.

By the time he arrived, his body was shaking uncontrollably. He felt as if his heart might seize from the cold. They could both go into cardiac arrest. Panting and shivering, he dragged Kathy out of the water and rested her on the snowy bank.

Her skin was pale, her lips blue. "Why did you help me?"

Colin didn't have an answer for her. Two squad cars approached from the opposite side of the lake, lights flashing.

Thank God.

CHAPTER NINE

IT TOOK PAIGE several minutes to climb behind the wheel of her car.

The aftereffects of the electroshock made her clumsy. She picked up her phone and dropped it twice. Cursing, she tried again, redialing 911.

"I need help," she told the operator.

"We traced your previous call, miss. An officer is on the way."

Paige reported the incident, along with a description of the assailant's car, as she left the scene. Her heart raced with anxiety as she drove down Twin Lakes Road. She spotted the crash site and pulled over, sobbing with relief when she saw Colin on the snowy embankment.

The rest of the day passed in a blur. Kathy and Colin were treated for mild hypothermia at the local hospital. Before her release, Kathy was arrested for violating the restraining order. She offered a tearful apology, admitting that she suffered from a chemical imbalance and hadn't been taking her medication.

The arresting officer took her away in handcuffs. He predicted that she'd serve time in a criminal facility or mental institution.

Paige and Colin were interviewed by the police department. Crime-scene investigators searched his cabin and took photos of the contents before they returned his belongings. Kathy had ransacked the place, but she hadn't destroyed his clothes or laptop. Both vehicles were dredged from the lake that afternoon.

Colin opted to stay at the lodge for the remainder of the week. He also made arrangements to rent a car. It was almost sunset by the time they left the station.

"Why don't I buy you dinner?" he asked, leaning against his rental. He was wearing jeans and a brown wool pullover. His hooded jacket looked insufficient for the cold. Typical Southern Californian style.

"I should buy you dinner."

"We'll flip for it."

After promising to meet him at the lodge, she went home to change. She selected a pair of faux-suede leggings and a soft cowl-neck sweater with tall leather boots. After applying light makeup, she left the cabin.

They shared a surprisingly relaxed evening, considering the circumstances. He didn't bring up their earlier argument. She got the impression that he just wanted to be with her. Nothing else was important.

Although she felt the same way, she knew they had to talk. She couldn't move forward without acknowledging her mistakes.

"I'm sorry about Kathy," he said, beating her to the punch.

"It wasn't your fault."

"I feel responsible. She attacked you because of me."

She sipped her hot cider, contemplative.

"If I'd been up-front with you from the beginning, we wouldn't have argued. I might have remembered what happened sooner."

"You weren't responsible, Colin. *I'm* sorry for not believing you."

He seemed to understand why she'd overreacted. Why she was slow to trust and wary of relationships. "It's okay."

"You're nothing like him."

"Your ex?"

She nodded. "I think success changed him, but we were both so young. He craved the limelight and basked in attention from women. He wouldn't have thought twice about introducing a pretty actress to a producer."

His mouth quirked into a smile. "I'd rather avoid the limelight, especially after today."

She smiled back at him, her stomach fluttering. Her former boyfriend had been wildly passionate. So was Colin, but his intensity translated into deep caring for others, whereas Derrick had wallowed in self-absorption. Paige was still uneasy about their whirlwind romance, despite Colin's good-guy credentials. Her feelings for him scared her. She didn't want to be consumed by desire, subsumed by love.

"My parents had a very emotional relationship," she said. "They weren't settled, if that makes sense. They didn't get too comfortable and take each other for granted. My mom got mad and tossed my dad's cell phone into the lake one year. I think they argued because they loved each other so much."

He reached across the table to hold her hand.

She took a ragged breath. "I've always wanted a love like they had, but I've been afraid of getting hurt again. It broke my heart to lose them."

Colin didn't downplay her fears or tell her she should change. He simply accepted them and accepted her for who she was. "I'm surprised to hear you're afraid of anything. You're the bravest person I've ever met."

Sniffling, she wiped her cheeks with her fingertips. "You're pretty brave yourself. Rescuing a woman who tried to kill you."

"Why did you come back to my cabin?"

"I found an online article about the stalking incident and a picture of Kathy beside her red car. I realized that I was wrong about you. When you said you loved her, I knew you'd been telling me the truth."

"How?"

"You're a terrible liar."

He laughed, squeezing her hand. His claim that he wasn't in love with Paige had also sounded false. Although she didn't mention it, and neither did he, an undercurrent of emotion surged between them.

"We don't have to rush anything," he said. "I have this week off, and most of next month. I can write anywhere."

"Maybe I could visit you in L.A."

"Really?"

After a short hesitation, she nodded. "I can work anywhere, too." Nature photography was her main interest, but the shoot with Colin had encouraged her to branch out. She might have been avoiding portraits and weddings because they were so emotive.

"I'd love that," he said, excited. "I'll introduce you to Ghost and show you around my neighborhood. There's a movie theater a few blocks away that plays old horror films every weekend."

She pulled her hand away, stirring her cider with a red cinnamon candy stick. "Meeting your cat is an important step."

"Let's just take it one day at a time," he said, his eyes twinkling.

"What about tonight?"

"Tonight?"

"Do you have plans?" She brought the swirled candy stick to her lips and sucked on it teasingly.

"I'm hoping to get you up to my room in the next five minutes. What happens after that is more of a fantasy than a plan."

She let him pay the check, and they went upstairs. As soon as they were inside his room, he covered her mouth with his, kicking the door shut with his foot. She twined her arms around his neck and gave him a cinnamon-flavored kiss, overflowing with happiness, determined to make his fantasy a reality.

* * * * *

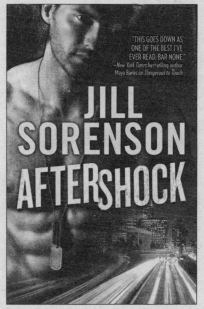

JILL SORENSON

He's her only hope...

Park ranger Hope Banning's plans for a little R & R are put on hold when a plane crashes at the top of a remote mountain. Hope will have to climb the summit and assess the situation. And the only climbing partner available is Sam Rutherford—the enigmatic man she spent a night with six months ago.

Ever since Sam lost his girlfriend in a falling accident, he insists on climbing solo. But Hope and any potential survivors need his help. As Sam and Hope set out on an emergency search-and-rescue mission, he realizes the sparks still sizzle between them. And when they learn a killer is among the survivors, they must place their trust in each other for a chance at happiness.

Available wherever books are sold!

Be sure to connect with us at:
Harlequin.com/Newsletters
Facebook.com/HarlequinBooks
Twitter.com/HarlequinBooks

TM www.Harlequin.com

REQUEST YOUR
FREE BOOKS!

2 FREE NOVELS
FROM THE SUSPENSE COLLECTION
PLUS 2 FREE GIFTS!

YES! Please send me 2 FREE novels from the Suspense Collection and my 2 FREE gifts (gifts are worth about $10). After receiving them, if I don't wish to receive any more books, I can return the shipping statement marked "cancel." If I don't cancel, I will receive 4 brand-new novels every month and be billed just $6.24 per book in the U.S. or $6.74 per book in Canada. That's a savings of at least 22% off the cover price. It's quite a bargain! Shipping and handling is just 50¢ per book in the U.S. and 75¢ per book in Canada.* I understand that accepting the 2 free books and gifts places me under no obligation to buy anything. I can always return a shipment and cancel at any time. Even if I never buy another book, the two free books and gifts are mine to keep forever.

191/391 MDN F4XN

Name _____ (PLEASE PRINT) _____

Address _____ Apt. # _____

City _____ State/Prov. _____ Zip/Postal Code _____

Signature (if under 18, a parent or guardian must sign)

Mail to the **Harlequin® Reader Service:**
IN U.S.A.: P.O. Box 1867, Buffalo, NY 14240-1867
IN CANADA: P.O. Box 609, Fort Erie, Ontario L2A 5X3

Want to try two free books from another line?
Call 1-800-873-8635 or visit www.ReaderService.com.

* Terms and prices subject to change without notice. Prices do not include applicable taxes. Sales tax applicable in N.Y. Canadian residents will be charged applicable taxes. Offer not valid in Quebec. This offer is limited to one order per household. Not valid for current subscribers to the Suspense Collection or the Romance/Suspense Collection. All orders subject to credit approval. Credit or debit balances in a customer's account(s) may be offset by any other outstanding balance owed by or to the customer. Please allow 4 to 6 weeks for delivery. Offer available while quantities last.

Your Privacy—The Harlequin® Reader Service is committed to protecting your privacy. Our Privacy Policy is available online at www.ReaderService.com or upon request from the Harlequin Reader Service.

We make a portion of our mailing list available to reputable third parties that offer products we believe may interest you. If you prefer that we not exchange your name with third parties, or if you wish to clarify or modify your communication preferences, please visit us at www.ReaderService.com/consumerschoice or write to us at Harlequin Reader Service Preference Service, P.O. Box 9062, Buffalo, NY 14269. Include your complete name and address.

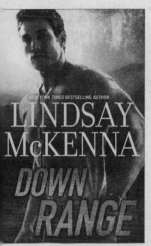

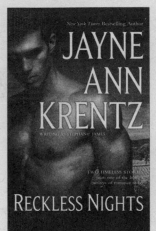